Sam didn't really want to raise his children alone.

And T.J., he knew, had their best interests at heart. His little Jenny was definitely getting attached to her. And young Jason had opened up to her far more than he had to any other woman.

Still, his kids needed more than for T.J. to be there for them as a neighbor, a friend, a baby-sitter. They needed a mom.

Unfortunately, T.J. just wasn't someone Sam could look to for a relationship. He doubted she'd ever let a man get that close again. He figured the only reason she hadn't backed away from him by now was because of their kids.

As much as he found himself thinking of her... wanting her...Sam had the feeling that if he made a move, T.J. would freeze up like a shallow pond in winter.

Dear Reader,

A rewarding part of any woman's life is talking with friends about important issues. Because of this, we've developed the Readers' Ring, a book club that facilitates discussions of love, life and family. Of course, you'll find all of these topics wrapped up in each Silhouette Special Edition novel! Our featured author for this month's Readers' Ring is newcomer Elissa Ambrose. *Journey of the Heart* (#1506) is a poignant story of true love and survival when the odds are against you. This is a five-tissue story you won't be able to put down!

Susan Mallery delights us with another tale from her HOMETOWN HEARTBREAKERS series. *Good Husband Material* (#1501) begins with two star-crossed lovers and an ill-fated wedding. Years later, they realize their love is as strong as ever! Don't wait to pick up *Cattleman's Honor* (#1502), the second book in Pamela Toth's WINCHESTER BRIDES series. In this book, a divorced single mom comes to Colorado to start a new life—and winds up falling into the arms of a rugged rancher. What a way to go!

Victoria Pade begins her new series, BABY TIMES THREE, with a heartfelt look at unexpected romance, in *Her Baby Secret* (#1503)—in which an independent woman wants to have a child, and after a night of wicked passion with a handsome businessman, her wish comes true! You'll see that there's more than one way to start a family in Christine Flynn's *Suddenly Family* (#1504), in which two single parents who are wary of love find it—with each other! And you'll want to learn the facts in *What a Woman Wants* (#1505), by Tori Carrington. In this tantalizing tale, a beautiful widow discovers she's pregnant with her late husband's best friend's baby!

As you can see, we have nights of passion, reunion romances, babies and heart-thumping emotion packed into each of these special stories from Silhouette Special Edition.

Happy reading!

Karen Taylor Richman
Senior Editor

Please address questions and book requests to:
Silhouette Reader Service
U.S.: 3010 Walden Ave., P.O. Box 1325, Buffalo, NY 14269
Canadian: P.O. Box 609, Fort Erie, Ont. L2A 5X3

Suddenly Family

CHRISTINE FLYNN

SPECIAL EDITION™

Published by Silhouette Books

America's Publisher of Contemporary Romance

To Evelyn Pillinger,
a true friend in every sense of the word.

 SILHOUETTE BOOKS

ISBN 0-373-24504-1

SUDDENLY FAMILY

Copyright © 2002 by Christine Flynn

CHRISTINE FLYNN

admits to being interested in just about everything, which is why she considers herself fortunate to have turned her interest in writing into a career. She feels that a writer gets to explore it all and, to her, exploring relationships—especially the intense, bittersweet or even lighthearted relationships between men and women—is fascinating.

CLASSIFIEDS

Second Week of August

WANTED: Live-in housekeeper/cook/nanny for single father and 2 children, ages 4 & 6. Harbor Island. Excellent salary. Ask for Sam. 360-555-1212.

Third Week of August

WANTED: Live-in housekeeper/cook/nanny for single father and 2 children, ages 4 & 6. Nice location on Harbor Island. Own room and private bath. Excellent salary. Ask for Sam. 360-555-1212.

Last Sunday

WANTED: Live-in housekeeper/cook/nanny for single father and 2 children, ages 4 & 6. Children well mannered. Father tries to be. Beautiful location on Harbor Island. Own room and private bath. Free air transportation to and from interview. Excellent salary plus bonus. Ask for Sam. 360-555-1212.

Chapter One

Something about her seemed familiar.

The thought distracted Sam Edwards from his phone call as the slender, almost waif-like woman in baggy bib overalls walked through the flight office door. Maybe it was the hair, he thought. A riot of deep-auburn curls tumbled down her back, practically begging to be free of their restraining clip. Or maybe it was the delicate line of her profile.

Definitely familiar, he thought, giving her a nod to let her know he'd be right with her. He just didn't have time to figure out where he'd seen her before with his mother's voice buzzing in his ear.

"You don't need another housekeeper," Beth Edwards informed him over 130 miles of telephone line. "You need a mother for these babies. If you won't move back to Seattle so your father and I can help you, then at least think about finding a nice young lady to marry and help you raise them.''

His hand tightened on the phone. Turning his back to the woman who was glancing from her watch to the large aerial map on the wall, he kept his voice calm. ''I don't want another wife. I just need another baby-sitter. Preferably one who can clean house and cook.''

''Children need stability, Sam.''

''That's what I'm trying to give them.''

''Well, I don't see how hiring another stranger to take care of them is going to do that,'' she returned with a sigh. ''Jason is far too quiet for a six-year-old. I don't think he's said more than a dozen words to me and your dad since you dropped him and Jenny off here last night. And Jenny,'' she continued, speaking of her four-year-old granddaughter, ''that precious child is going to need braces if she doesn't stop sucking her thumb. She should have been broken of that habit long before now.''

Sam didn't for a moment doubt his mom's concern or her caring. He knew she meant well. He knew she had only her grandchildren's best interests at heart. But the last thing he needed from her or anyone else was to be told what his kids' problems were. There wasn't a soul on the planet more aware of those problems than he was.

He also knew that in another ten seconds his mom would launch into her lecture about how he spent too many hours away from his children, especially in the summer when the demands of the air charter business he and his partner owned claimed so much of his time.

He was doing the best he could. His best was all he could do.

Swallowing his frustration with life in general and his mother in particular, he lowered his voice another notch.

"I can't talk about this right now." He wasn't about to respond to her suggestions with a stranger pacing the polish off the floor behind him. "I have four fishermen outside waiting for me to fly them to Ketchikan and someone else just came in.

"No, I'm not avoiding the subject," he insisted, forcing calm. "I'm just going to do what I said I'd do and find another housekeeper. Give the kids a hug for me, okay? I'll call them when I get back tonight."

He swore he could feel his mother's displeasure vibrate through the line when she said she'd be glad to give the kids a hug and reluctantly said goodbye. Trying to get Beth Edwards to let go of an idea was like trying to part a rat terrier from a fresh bone. She simply refused to let go. Especially when she thought she knew what was best for those she cared about. His mom had been at him to move back to Seattle since his wife died three years ago. The suggestion that he marry again, however, was one she hadn't sprung on him before.

The thought of moving his kids from the only home they'd ever known put a knot the size of a fist in his gut. As for finding another wife, the idea was incomprehensible. He couldn't imagine ever again having what he and Tina had shared.

He dropped the receiver in its cradle. Masking a wealth of frustration, he glanced at the woman studying the huge map of the northwestern U.S. and Canada covering the wall. Her anxious glance focused on the red *You Are Here* arrow in the middle of Puget Sound.

"Can I help you, ma'am?"

T. J. Walker took another cautious glance at the gaping expanses of water between the dots of land on the map and stepped closer to the long counter that bisected the small, utilitarian room. Mail and packages formed small towers inside the open door to the airplane hangar. The scent of industrial-strength coffee mingled with a hint of aviation fuel and the fresh sea air that filtered in from outside.

Her attention narrowed on the man behind the long expanse of gray Formica.

Sam Edwards was tall, remarkably built and undeniably impressive—in a rugged, commanding sort of way. His hair was short and dark, a color the same rich shade as that of the sables that had terrorized her baby deer until she'd trapped and moved them to the other end of the island. But it was the eyes beneath the dark slash of brow that caused her a split second of hesitation. They were a sharp, biting blue, as intense and clear as an Arctic summer sky.

From what she had heard, she was probably the only single female on Harbor Island who hadn't shown up at his door at one time or another with a casserole and an invitation to call her sometime. Not that she would ever do such a thing. Even if she were in the market for a man—which she definitely was not—she'd been brushed aside too many times in her life to willingly seek rejection.

"I think so," she finally replied. "Hope so," she was quick to amend.

"I know you." Those incredible eyes narrowed on her face. "You're from around here."

"From down the road a couple of miles, actually." Anxious to get to the reason she was there, she offered a quick, easy smile. "I ship my pottery from here, and we've seen each other at the preschool. My son is the same age as yours. Andy Walker?'' she prompted. ''And I work part-time at Bert and Libby Bender's bookstore.''

Everyone knew the elderly Bert and Libby Bender. Everyone but this guy, it seemed. The nod he gave her was vague, more expected response than actual recognition.

It was apparently her pottery that nudged his memory. ''I didn't recognize you without your packages. So,'' he prompted, his smile polite, his manner all business, ''what do you need?''

''Flying lessons,'' she replied, voicing the idea that had occurred to her less than an hour ago. ''Actually, I need to know what you charge for them, first. And how long they take. If I can't learn in a few weeks, or if they're too expensive, my idea won't work.''

The lady had a plan. One that had her looking both uncertain and more than a little animated. Still trying to shift gears between the call from his mom and needing to hurry because he had paying passengers outside, Sam didn't bother to ask what that plan was. It was none of his business, anyway.

''Sorry,'' he murmured, prioritizing. He needed his flight log, flight map and his sunglasses. He figured he should grab the bag of chips off the desk, too. He hadn't had time for lunch. ''We don't give flying lessons here. To learn to fly you have to take ground school first.''

''Ground school?''

''Classroom instruction,'' he clarified, rolling his flight map and stuffing it into a tube. ''There isn't a ground school on Harbor, but you might try the community college in Bellingham. I can look up the number for you, but that's the best I can do to help.''

The man's expression was one of total preoccupation. His tone remained polite but utterly final.

Undaunted by the fact that she barely had his attention, T.J. snagged the cap of his tube from the near end of the counter.

"I don't want to take ground school. Not yet, anyway. All I want is to see if I can get a plane off the ground, fly it around and land it. There's no sense wasting time taking ground school if I can't do that, is there?"

Her odd logic had him looking up from his search. Taking advantage of his silence, she held out the cap. "Your sister said you're a very patient man. That's what I need. Someone with patience who can help me figure out if what I want is even possible."

Sam's forehead lowered, his eyebrows forming a single slash. The mention of his sister immediately canceled his concern about waiting passengers. "You know Lauren?"

"Sure. I run into her at my mom's shop at least once a week."

"Your mom's shop?"

"The Herb Shoppe and Video Store," she clarified. "My mom is Crystal Walker. She owns it."

He knew the place. He and his kids were in there at least twice a week. "And she told you I was patient?"

"No. Lauren did."

"That's what I meant," he muttered.

"Aren't you?"

Patient? he thought. Once, maybe. Anymore, he wasn't so sure. "What I mean," he said, forcing the patience he was beginning to doubt, "is why would Lauren tell you something like that?"

"Because I called her as soon as I left Doc Jackson's

office to see if her husband could help me with the flying thing. She said Zach is really strapped for time right now because they've started Lamaze classes, but I should talk to you. She thought you'd make a better instructor, anyway, because you're so…patient.''

Sam purposefully ignored what he considered extraneous information—the woman's references to Doc Jackson, the local vet, and Zach McKendrick, his business partner and brother-in-law—and focused on the uncomfortable sensation brewing in his gut. For the past year, his little sister had been after him to get involved in something other than his children and his work. With the conversation with his mother still fresh in his mind, he had the sudden and uneasy feeling that his female relatives might have begun a campaign to find him a mate.

The thought had him taking a closer look at the woman he now recalled having seen at the preschool with her small son.

Her long, wildly curling hair was the color of mahogany licked by firelight. Hints of ruby and topaz shimmered in its depths. The green of her eyes was more a smoky moss than emerald. She wore no makeup on her flawless skin, and there was a willowy look about her slenderness that struck him as rather graceful in a coltish sort of way.

Yet there was nothing immediately striking about her—not with her natural and well-scrubbed looks. And definitely not dressed as she was in the loose overalls that hid nearly every potential curve. She downplayed every asset she had. But he didn't doubt for a moment that any number of men would find her attractive. Beautiful, he supposed, his glance slipping over the ripe curve of her unadorned mouth. She just wasn't the sort of petite blonde he'd always been attracted to himself. The delicate type his wife had been.

Not that he was looking for a woman, he reminded himself. Blond or otherwise.

"I'm sorry. I can't help you."

"I'll pay you double."

"Money isn't the issue. I'm really not the man you're looking for."

Desperate for something to bargain with, she looked toward the telephone. "I'll baby-sit your children."

He opened his mouth, automatically prepared to decline. What came out was a disbelieving huff of air and a flat "You're kidding."

"No. No, I'm not," she insisted, utterly determined to get him to agree. "I couldn't help overhearing your conversation when I first came in. I wasn't trying to listen," she explained, looking as if she felt guilty, anyway. "But I heard you say you need to get another housekeeper. And I know how hard it's been for you to keep help."

"It hasn't been *that* hard," he muttered. Having gone through five housekeepers in the past three years might sound as if the problem rested with him, but that wasn't the case at all. "There were reasons those women didn't work out."

"Oh, I know," she assured him easily. "Your first one moved to be near her children, and I think you fired one because the kids didn't like her. Two quit because your house is so remote, and they didn't like being isolated all week. And I heard that the last one left because you weren't interested in having her warm your bed. You wouldn't have to worry about any of that with me," she assured him, her beguiling eyes utterly sincere and steady on his. "Especially the sex part. I'm not going to bed with you."

Sam wasn't sure which threw him more. The way his stomach tightened as their eyes remained locked, the blunt way she'd just told him she wasn't going to get naked with him or the casual way she proceeded to lay down her rules before he could even tell her he wasn't interested.

"I know you're looking for a live-in," she told him, pushing her hands into the deep pockets of her pants. The tank top she wore was the same brown as the buttons on the sides of her overalls. It exposed the delicate line of her collarbone, the elegant line of taut, smoothly muscled arms. "I wouldn't be able stay at your place, though. Or do your housework. I have other obligations during the day," she explained, apparently referring to her son and her job at the bookstore. "But you can drop the children off at my house in the morning and they can come to mine after school until you find someone else."

She tipped her head, a lock of her impossibly curly hair falling over her shoulder and curving against her small firm breast. "When are they coming back from your parents' house?"

It wasn't like Sam to be caught so completely off guard. As with any parent of two small children, his days inevitably unfolded around the unexpected. Then there was his job. Flying cargo and passengers in the unpredictable weather and rough geography of the San Juan Islands and the Alaskan panhandle pretty much demanded that he immediately adapt to the unforeseen. He was usually pretty good at it, too. The juggling aspects of it, anyway.

"Next week. The day after Labor Day," he expanded,

mentally shaking his head at both her proposal and her persistence.

"That's when school starts."

"Right. Look," he muttered, needing to get a grip on the situation. "Thanks for your offer, but I really need a live-in. And I need her now. There are times when I'm late or when I can't get back because of the weather. I never know when that might be."

"It's not an offer. It's a proposition. Child care for flying lessons."

Sam blinked at her undaunted expression. The woman was as tenacious as the barnacles clinging to the pilings of the float plane pier. "I said I don't give them."

"You could always make an exception," she suggested ever so reasonably. "Besides, you don't need to make up your mind right now. I'm sure you'll want to check me out since you don't really know me. I know your children, though. Your wife used to bring them to the bookstore. Your sister still does. Jason has always liked stories about anything with big teeth and claws. Jenny adores any cover with glitter on it, but *The Little Mermaid* is her favorite."

Sam thought of the book atop the stack on his little girl's nightstand. His sister had bought that very book for Jenny months ago and several other books since. But the story of the mermaid was what Jenny insisted he read to her nearly every night.

This woman knew his kids. She even remembered what they liked.

The breath he drew was long, low and vaguely reluctant. He wasn't at all prepared to accept her impulsive proposal. He was, however, a practical, logical man who was somewhat desperately in need of child care.

Conceding that he might have been a little hasty in his dismissal, he made a mental note to ask around about her, stuffed his map tube under his arm and slipped his sunglasses in his pocket. "Let me think about it."

Having everything but his lunch, he glanced at her across the counter. As dogged as she'd been, he expected her to be pleased. What he didn't expect was the impact of her bright, easy smile.

"That's fair enough," she said and held out her hand across the beige Formica.

He automatically took it.

Her skin was soft, her nails short and unpolished. In his big hand hers looked as small and feminine as his daughter's. But what struck him most was the warmth of her flesh against his as the pressure of their fingers increased in the businesslike handshake and the faintly erotic scent of wildflowers that lingered in the air when she turned a moment later and walked away.

With his focus on the baggy denim covering her hips, he heard the jingle of the bell and watched her slip out the door. Through the multipaned window, he saw her climb into the battered olive-green Jeep parked just outside.

Sam's glance jerked to the black-rimmed clock above the water cooler. Realizing that he was now even later than he'd been five minutes ago, he headed for the door himself. He had no idea what to make of T. J. Walker's energy, her off-the-wall proposition or the jolt of sensual heat he'd just felt. It had been over three years since he'd known the comfort of a woman's body. He missed the softness. The feminine scents. He missed the feel of gentle curves and silken hair.

He didn't at all appreciate T. J. Walker reminding him

of that. The last thing he needed was to add that particular brand of frustration to all the rest.

Ruthlessly shoving aside the thought, he grabbed the mail sack and the bag of chips and strode toward the gleaming white Cessna parked near the hangar. Spotting their pilot, four fishermen rose from their coolers and hauled up their heavy backpacks.

He had a flight to concentrate on. He had people to tend to who were relying on him to get them safely to their destination. He wasn't about to jeopardize anyone's safety by being preoccupied.

Chapter Two

Two days, Sam thought. His kids had only been gone for two days, and he was already going stir-crazy in the too-quiet house.

Plowing his fingers through his hair, he turned his back on the fading view of the ocean and massive boulders beyond his lawn and leaned against the railing of the long redwood porch. He'd once loved this time of day, the peaceful moments between dusk and nightfall when people and creatures started settling down, settling in. Now he faced his evenings trying not to think too much about the night ahead and occupied himself with his children's routine and whatever chore or task demanded to be done.

The problem tonight was that without the kids there had been no routine. There had been no coloring with Jenny, or roughhousing with Jason or cuddling with both of them on the couch while they watched the Disney

Channel or some animated video for the hundredth time. There had been no cajoling to get them to brush their teeth. No bedtime stories. There had been nothing to claim his attention or to take the emptiness out of the rambling log home he'd had built for Tina and their family.

He needed his children back. He knew they were perfectly safe with his parents. They were undoubtedly being spoiled rotten at that very moment, too. But they belonged here. On Harbor. With him.

He just needed someone responsible to be with them while he worked.

He also had no idea who that someone could be.

He couldn't ask his sister for help. Lauren had enough on her plate being pregnant and still putting in fifty hours a week managing a department store in Bellingham. Taking them to the day-care center in town wasn't a viable option because his hours often extended beyond theirs. If the week before Labor Day hadn't been one of the busiest times of the year for his business, he might have been able to cut back on his flight time and stayed with them himself until he found another housekeeper. But he and his partner were shorthanded even with the other two pilots in their hire.

It wasn't helping matters that he hadn't had a single useful response to any of the ads he'd placed under Domestic Help Wanted in either the local or the mainland newspapers.

The haunting hoot of an owl filtered toward him from the forest of pine trees behind the house. Crickets chirped from the bushes in response.

Preferring to drown out the melancholy sounds, he picked up the hammer he'd used to repair a loose board and tossed it with a clank into his toolbox. With the thud of his boots on now-sturdy planks, he headed for the door before he could think too much more about why he'd put off going inside.

It took him all of a minute to return the toolbox to its place under the workbench in the basement. Less than that to climb back up the stairs, head through the big country kitchen and find himself back in his living room.

The spacious area was bright with the glow from the massive brass lamps on the pine end tables. Noisy audio from the big-screen TV filled the room with canned laughter. But the vitality in the comfortable, once-inviting space was only an illusion.

No matter how bright the lights, how loud the television, radio or CD player, there was still something—someone—missing. He noticed her absence even when the children were there.

Hating the emptiness, wondering if it would ever go away, he picked up the portable telephone from the table by the butterscotch-colored leather sofa. He needed to call his kids and say good-night. But he had another call to make first.

He'd paced two laps around the braided burgundy throw rug when his sister answered on the third ring.

"Hey, sis."

"Sam." Lauren Edwards McKendrick sounded as if she were smiling. "We were just talking about you."

"You and Zach?"

"Me and Mom. We just hung up a couple of minutes ago."

Two women discussing a man was seldom good news for the latter. Especially when they were all related.

"Are the kids okay?" he asked, not about to ask for

details of that conversation. Picking up a red thread from the rug, he balled it between his fingers. "I tried to call them about an hour ago, but there was no answer."

"They went out for pizza. And she said the kids are fine. I'm sure Jason will tell you, but he has a loose tooth. He wants a dollar for it. Mom says the Tooth Fairy won't go past a quarter."

He frowned, wondering which tooth it was. "She needs to account for inflation. She's still thinking of when we were kids."

"Probably. So," Lauren said, her tone softening, "how are you doing over there?"

The piece of lint went sailing into the dark fireplace. Lousy, he thought. "Fine," he replied. "I just need some background on someone. Do you know T. J. Walker?"

"T.J.? Sure. Everybody does."

"I mean really know her. I've seen her before myself when she's brought packages in to ship, but I need something more than nodding acquaintance information. She offered to watch the kids for me until I can find a live-in."

Puzzlement entered his sister's voice. "I thought she was going to talk to you about flying lessons."

"She did. The other just sort of came up."

"How do you get from flying lessons to baby-sitting?"

"Does it matter?"

"No, but it does sound a little odd."

He couldn't tell if it was a smile or curiosity in his sister's tone. Either way, he wasn't interested in explaining how T.J.'s proposition had come about. He wasn't completely sure himself, other than that the woman had simply refused to take no for an answer.

"It probably does," he agreed, letting it go at that. "So is she someone I can trust with my kids?"

"I don't know why you couldn't," came her thoughtful reply. "From what I understand, she's lived most of her life on the island, and you know everyone around here knows, or knows of, everyone else. You even know her mother," she reminded him. "I'll admit Crystal is a little…different," she said, diplomatically describing T.J.'s mom, "but I've never heard anything negative about either her or her daughter. If there were reasons not to trust T.J., someone would have mentioned them by now."

Sam continued pacing as he weighed his sister's logic. In summer, tourists and summer residents overran the island, and most of the faces were unfamiliar. The permanent population of Harbor was just over 1,200 and spread out at that. But the locals did tend to keep track of those who truly belonged there.

Thinking about it, even he knew people who knew T.J. His sister, for one. And, as his sister had just mentioned, T.J.'s mother. But, then, there wasn't anyone on Harbor who owned a VCR who didn't know the outgoing, middle-aged hippie who still wore love beads and tie-dye with her flowing gauze skirts. Her store was probably the only one in the San Juans where a person could get a free astrological reading along with the latest video release and an herbal cure for whatever ailed him.

"Oh, and I saw T.J. once myself with children during story hour at the bookstore," Lauren continued helpfully. "She seemed great with them. Nurturing, I guess you'd say. Anyway, the place I usually run into her is at her mom's shop. All we've ever really talked about is books, videos and herbs. But as far as I'm concerned, she's one of the nicest people in town. Very sweet. Very generous." She paused. "I heard she does something with animals, too."

The wary feeling Sam had experienced when his sister's name had first come up with T.J. slithered up his back again. His sibling's description of the woman was beginning to sound like a sales pitch.

"Sam? Are you still there? You're not saying anything."

He paced to a stop in the middle of the deserted room. "You're not trying to set me up with her, are you?"

A choke of disbelief filtered across the line. "You asked what I know about her. All I did was tell you what I'd heard and give you my impressions."

"Yeah, but you were the one who suggested she talk to me about flying lessons. And Mom's latest solution to my life is for me to find myself someone to marry so I'll have help raising the kids."

"Oh, good grief," Lauren muttered. "I suggested you because I think you'd be a good teacher. And our mother is making you paranoid. I know as well as you do that you don't just go out and find someone to spend the rest of your life with. Besides," she continued, ever so reasonably, "if I were to set you up with someone, it wouldn't be T.J. From what I've heard from Maddy, she's far too independent for marriage. Maddy should know, too. She told me she's tried to fix T.J. up for years. She even tried to get her and Zach together before I met him." A shrug entered her voice. "T.J.'s not interested in a relationship."

For a moment Sam said nothing. Maddy O'Toole owned the Road's End Café, which happened to be *the* place for gossip on Harbor Island. Sam didn't frequent the establishment himself. Between his work and his children, he took little time for socializing, and any meals out were usually at Hamburger Heaven, Jason's favorite. He remembered his wife talking about Maddy, though. And he knew from Zach that anything that happened on Harbor usually filtered through the Road's End. Word was that gossip obtained from Maddy was pretty much gospel.

"You know, brother dear," his sister gently chided, "you would know these things if you'd get out and get a little more involved in what's going on around you. All you do is work. You're not doing yourself any favors turning into a recluse."

Sam pinched the bridge of his nose. He dearly loved Lauren. There had even been a time after his wife's death when he hadn't known how he would have survived without his sister. But the last thing he wanted was for her to get started on her favorite theme. He wasn't being reclusive. He just didn't have the time or the inclination to add anything—or anyone—else to his life.

"I'm involved with you and Zach and my kids," he defended, forcing a smile into his voice. "That keeps me crazy enough."

Taking the hint, Lauren chuckled. "We keep you sane. It's Mom who makes you crazy. Just remember that she means well. And that she loves you. And, Sam," she concluded, "T.J. is probably just the person you need. From what I've heard, she can deal with practically anything."

T.J. wasn't dealing well at all with what she'd just heard.

"Brad was here?" Her voice dropped to a disbelieving whisper. "On Harbor?"

Maddy O'Toole stood next to her in the cramped bookstore aisle between self-help and romance and lowered her voice another notch.

"I thought for sure he had come by to see you," the forty-something redhead quietly declared. The *he* she referred to was Brad Colwood, the man who had fathered T.J.'s six-year-old son, then disappeared like smoke in a stiff breeze. "I mean, he was asking everyone around here about you. Edna at the ferry office. Linc over at the aquarium. Me and Mary and Alice," she enumerated, adding herself and her waitresses to the list.

"I was here all day, Maddy. Libby didn't work yesterday because Bert's arthritis was acting up. I couldn't even leave for lunch."

"Your mom didn't hear about him being here?"

"I didn't see her yesterday. But she would have called if she had." Crystal had about as much use for Brad as she did another bunion. "I'm sure she would have."

"Well, I don't have a clue what to make of his coming here, then. Actually, I wasn't even sure what to make of him," the puzzled woman confided. "I barely recognized him when he came into the café. His ponytail was gone, and the clothes he was wearing were straight out of *GQ*. I swear the watch he wore cost as much as Alice's divorce. And his car—"

Canceling any further inventory, Maddy shook her head to get herself back on track.

"Anyway," she murmured, "he spent a good twenty minutes working his way through his chowder and asking about everybody else he'd known here before he finally got around to asking about you. He said he'd heard you'd had a child and started asking questions about Andy.''

''He knew his name?''

Maddy hesitated. ''I can't remember if he mentioned it first. Or if someone else did.''

A sense of unease had hit T.J. in the stomach the moment Maddy said she'd seen Andy's father. Now it balled into a knot of pure apprehension.

Grabbing Maddy by the wide pocket of her green Road's End apron, T.J. tugged her friend farther down the aisle. Two teenage girls were giggling over a hottie on the cover of *People* magazine. Wanting to get out of earshot, T.J. came to a halt by a postcard carousel and cast a furtive glance toward the service counter angled against the back wall. Her son had flopped on the floor behind the counter and was coloring in his coloring book next to his pet *de jour*.

''What kind of questions did he ask?'' she insisted.

''Mostly he wanted to know what kind of child Andy is. If he's bright. What he's interested in. That sort of thing. And he wanted to know if you'd ever married.''

''What did you tell him?''

''That you worked here at the bookstore and that he should ask those questions of you.'' Maddy's protective concern turned to compassion. ''He really sounded interested, T.J. When I told him to come see you, he said he wouldn't know what to say. It was almost like he was trying to get the courage to see you again. Maybe he didn't come here because he never got that courage,'' she suggested. ''It could be that he heard how well you were doing without him and he decided he didn't have the nerve to face you after all.''

At Maddy's hypothetical conclusion, T.J. shot another quick glance toward her son. "Is he still on the island?"

The café owner quickly shook her head. "He left yesterday afternoon. I saw him drive his red Jaguar onto the ferry myself. Hard to miss that car," she explained, impressed despite herself. It wasn't often that a luxury car showed up on the island with its gravel roads and rugged terrain. Even the newly monied who'd built million-dollar summer homes in the more remote areas drove modest SUVs or trucks. On Harbor it was considered bad form to be too ostentatious. "The 3:10 ferry," she added, wanting to be as accurate in her account as possible.

Brad was no longer on the island. He'd come. Asked his questions. And gone.

T.J. should have felt relief knowing he was no longer there. And she supposed she did. She just didn't feel enough to relieve the uneasiness still knotting her stomach.

"Take it from me," Maddy said, all friendship and sympathy. "It's never easy when your past turns up. Especially in the form of a man. The good news is that once they've satisfied their curiosity about whatever brought them back, they're usually gone."

T.J. forced a faint smile, as much for Maddy's benefit as her own. "Do you think that's it? That he was just curious about us?"

"It makes perfect sense that he would be. Any man with a soul doesn't forget that he ran out on a woman who was going to have his child. Maybe something happened to make him turn philosophical, and he's looking at where he messed up his life. Maybe he's just come out of a relationship and wants to go back to something familiar. Or," she suggested, brightening, "it could be that he finally smartened up, realized what a jerk he'd been and he's finally wanting to make things right.''

It was clear enough to T.J. that Maddy, the ever-hopeful romantic, was seeing a hint of potential in the man. T.J. could practically hear the local matchmaker's mental wheels grinding out her argument now. She would insist that Brad needed to do his share of groveling to properly prove how sorry he was. But, like the prodigal son, if he was sorry enough, he could be welcomed back into the fold. After all, he was the child's father. And T.J. really had cared a great deal about him.

The thought that Brad Colwood might want to make up for abandoning her and her son would never have occurred to T.J. on her own. In all her twenty-seven years, she had never once known any man who returned to repair the damage he'd left behind. If a man came back at all, it was only to collect something he had forgotten, then move on again leaving a little more pain in his wake.

Reminding herself of that hard-learned bit of reality, hating the sense of foreboding it gave her, T.J. did her best to mask her growing trepidation. There was something Maddy didn't know. Something T.J. had mentioned to no one.

Brad's appearance yesterday wasn't his first attempt to get information about her and her son. He had written to her three months ago asking how she was doing and if she would please tell him about their child. He'd wanted a picture.

That letter had been the first communication she'd received from him since he'd bailed out on her after learning she was pregnant. She'd ignored it, along with the sense of unease it gave her. Just as she had ignored a second letter that had come two weeks ago.

As far as she was concerned, Andy was hers and no one else's. Brad had no right to information about him. Not now. Not after so long. She didn't care if he had faced some sort of epiphany about himself or if his heart had been broken and he was seeking solace in an old relationship. She especially didn't care if he was simply curious. She wanted nothing to do with the man who had refused to acknowledge his child and left her to have her baby alone.

"He can't make things right," she finally replied to Maddy. "Things are right just the way they are. I'm just going to hope he's dropped off the planet again."

The middle-aged Irish woman opened her mouth, undoubtedly to ask T.J. what she would do if he came back, but the bell over the door gave a melodic tinkle. Two ladies in cargo shorts and tank tops strolled in, their pale skin pink from a morning in the sun.

The women gave the bestseller display a desultory once-over. Seeing nothing they were interested in, the blonde in the black baseball cap turned to the brunette in the red one and they left to join the stream of summer people clogging Harbor's main street. The door had yet to swing closed when three more potential patrons wandered in.

The long, low moan of a ferry whistle filtered inside.

"This obviously isn't a good time to talk. Look," Maddy continued, her voice low as she backed up the aisle with T.J., "I didn't mean to hit you with this out of the blue. I really thought you'd seen him. I just wondered what had happened."

T.J.'s smile was soft, forgiving. She liked Maddy, but

she wouldn't have told the woman what had happened even if Brad had shown up. There wasn't a malicious bone in the older woman's body, but Maddy was notorious for trying to fix peoples lives. She also never failed to solicit everyone else's opinion about how that could be accomplished—which meant anything she said to Maddy would be all over town in under an hour.

"Don't worry about it, okay?" she asked, truly hoping she wasn't about to become a staple on the local grapevine. "I'm glad you let me know he was here."

"Miss?" An elderly woman in an orange T-shirt and pea-green sun visor had stopped near the wildlife section. She waved to T.J. over the shoulder-high bookshelves. The older gentleman in baggy safari shorts, dark dress socks and sandals had to be her companion. He wore orange and pea green, too. "Can you help us?"

Eyeing the couple as she and T.J. returned to the counter, Maddy whispered, "If anyone asks, the pies today are apple and fresh blueberry."

"What about your cobblers?"

"Peach and cherry."

"Chowder of the day?"

"Fresh corn."

"Got it."

The bell over the door sounded again, the call of seagulls drifting inside along with the fresh salt air and an eclectic blend of buyers and lookers. T.J. loved the hustle of summer and the variety of people who visited the friendly little shop. Just as she loved the quiet solitude of the island when fall and winter came and the residents could reclaim their turf from those who had come to watch the whales, kayak in the coves and hike the lush forest. She liked belonging here.

At the moment, she was simply thankful she was busy. Busy was good. Busy meant she didn't have time to obsess over what Brad's reappearance might mean.

She soon discovered that she didn't have to be consciously thinking about it for the development to affect her. What Maddy had told her silently preyed on her nerves as she went about her chores, helping customers, answering their inevitable questions about the history of the island, the best places to spot dolphins, where they could find rest rooms. The distractions helped. But she couldn't shake the agitation that put her senses on alert and had her darting furtive glances toward the door every time it opened.

The sight of any tall blond male with angular features caused her stomach to drop.

She was overreacting. She knew she was. Maddy had said she'd seen Brad leave on the ferry, and as sure as rain in the northwest Maddy would let her know if he was back. Still, T.J. couldn't help the prickling sensation at the back of her neck when, just before noon, the tinkle of the bell caught her kneeling behind the counter. Before she could rise from where she was restocking bags beneath it, her heart jumped when something heavy hit the long, gray surface above her head.

Still on her knees, she glanced up to see a large dog-eared volume in the space between the cash register and a display of novelty note cards. The book definitely wasn't from the store's stock. Not tattered as it was. The thought was lost, however, as her wary glance shot past the front of worn jeans to the tall, broad-shouldered male in a chambray work shirt.

Sam Edwards' impossibly blue eyes met hers.

"Hi," she said, unbelievably relieved to see that it was him.

A faint frown furrowed his brow as she rose and pushed back her hair.

"Hi," he echoed, staring at her hand.

Realizing her hand was shaking, she shoved it into the pocket of the teal work apron she wore over her T-shirt and long khaki skirt. *Benders' Books* arched across the bib in pale-yellow embroidery.

"I wondered if I would hear from you," she admitted, forcing a smile. She glanced at the book. From upside down, she read *Principles of Flight*. "I take it you've reconsidered your stance on the lessons?"

Watching her curiously, Sam nudged the volume forward. The vitality that had so impressed him the other day was missing. So was the ease and brightness of her smile. Her lips were curved in greeting. But the light he'd noticed before in her eyes was nowhere in evidence.

"What can I say? I recognize a deal when I see one," he admitted with a casual shrug. "That's why I came by. To tell you I'll take you up on your offer...if it still stands," he qualified. "And to bring you this, if it does."

Her glance fell back to the book.

"I thought it would help us both if you're familiar with the instruments and parts of the plane we'll be flying." Aware of a teenage boy in black spandex shorts, a racing shirt and a crash helmet browsing the magazine racks a few yards away, he consciously lowered his voice. "Unless you've changed your mind," he said, looking as if he thought she would be more enthused about his acceptance of her proposal.

"No. No," she quickly repeated. "I haven't changed my mind."

She really hadn't. Not about her part of the proposition, anyway. She was just feeling so uneasy about Brad
at the moment that she wasn't sure about going through
with the rest of it. She couldn't tell Sam that, though.
Not without him asking questions she'd rather not answer—especially with a customer less than ten feet away
and her very bright little boy playing underfoot.

"Flying lessons for child care," he said, sounding as
if he wanted to be sure they were actually on the same
track.

"Flying lessons for child care," she echoed and
watched his eyes narrow on her face. His glance was
thorough and assessing as it moved over the faint strain
in her features.

Had any other man studied her so openly, she would
have immediately drawn back. The mechanism was
purely protective, an instinct that snapped into place
when any male over the age of consent paid more than
passing attention to her. But she knew for a fact that this
big, attractive pilot was there only because of his children. Since she'd practically badgered him into cooper-
ating with her, she didn't doubt that his only interest was
in trying to figure out why she didn't seem more pleased.

"I really do appreciate you bringing the book," she
insisted over a faint churring near her feet.

He still looked skeptical. "Then give me a call after
you've read the chapters I've marked. We'll set something up."

"How about I call you at the airport tomorrow?"

Skepticism turned to curiosity when the soft sound
continued. His glance shifted to the space beside her. "If
you think you can get through the material that fast,
that'll be fine."

The churring turned to a squeak. The moment it did, his brow snapped low.

It was such a relief to have his scrutiny off her that some of the strain slipped from her smile. "That's our newest guest," she told him, wondering at the faint flutter he'd left in her stomach. "I think he's hungry again."

Sam watched her disappear beneath the counter, then rise a moment later holding a small wire animal carrier. As she set it on the yard-wide surface, a chestnut-haired little boy the same age as his Jason rose from the floor.

Crossing his arms on the counter, the slightly built child plopped his chin on his narrow wrists and smiled up at Sam.

"Hi," the boy said easily.

A dimple winked by his perfect little mouth. His eyes were the same gray green as the woman's beside him.

"Hi, yourself," Sam replied, recognizing him instantly as her son.

"Winona Sykes brought him to me a few days ago," T.J. continued, smiling at the tiny ball of fur in the cage. Reaching through the wires, she gently stroked one tiny hand-like paw. "He's only a few weeks old and needs to be fed every couple of hours. That's why we bring him to work with us."

Sam recognized Winona as the mayor's wife. He recognized the critter in the cage as a baby raccoon. The thing was so small its mask had barely begun to show. "Why did she bring it to you?"

"People often bring me wounded or orphaned animals." She spoke with a shrug in her voice, as if there was nothing at all unusual about the occurrence. "Or I rescue them myself if I hear of one that needs help. We have about a dozen animals living at our place right now.'' Softness entered her voice as she glanced at her son. ''Isn't that right, Andy?''

The child's nose wrinkled as he cranked his neck back. ''I forgot. How many is a dozen?''

''Twelve.''

The wrinkles remained long enough for him to equate the number with the word. Comprehension dawning, he gave his mom a nod. ''Yeah. A dozen. 'Cept this makes thirteen.''

''The animals are why I wanted to see if I can fly,'' she explained to Sam as she reached beneath the counter. ''Doc Jackson has to move to the mainland because his heart is getting bad and there's no one to take his place.''

With a metallic clink against the counter, she set a can of kitten formula on it, popped the top and poured an ounce into a medicine cup. After drawing some of the liquid into an eyedropper, she touched the end of the dropper to the tiny animal's seeking mouth.

''Can I do it, Mom?''

Smiling at her son's request, she handed over the dropper. ''Just remember to keep him on his stomach. That's the way these guys eat best.

''I suppose I can learn to do rabies checks and that sort of thing myself,'' she continued to Sam while she watched her son dispense several drops into the hungry orphan's waiting mouth. ''I won't risk having an infected animal around Andy or the other animals,'' she explained. ''But without a vet, I won't be able to take care of the sicker or more severely injured ones.

''Unless,'' she added, suddenly meeting his eyes across the cage and the counter, ''you would be willing to fly them to the vet over on Orcas Island or to Bellingham yourself?''

For the first time since he'd walked in, Sam saw a flicker of spirit in her delicate features. That look was nothing less than pure hope.

He immediately felt himself take a mental step back. Despite the odd strain he'd sensed in her, there was an artlessness about this woman that tended to pull a person in, to put him at ease. He freely admitted he was drawn by the gentle way she soothed the little animal, by her concern for it, by her willingness to take it in. But her innocent request for his involvement clearly threatened the boundaries he'd drawn around his life.

He hadn't realized how protective his instincts had become until he felt them kick into place.

"Sorry," he muttered, refusing to consider why those instincts were there. He thought only of the hours involved transporting her and heaven-only-knew what sort of critters around the San Juans. "I'm not in a position to help you. I already spend too much time away from my kids."

"Of course." Hope died as quickly as it had arisen. "I didn't really think you'd be interested."

"It's not that," he insisted, feeling lousy for turning her down. Feeling a little defensive, too, for being put in that position. "I really can't take more time from them than I do. How were you planning to get them to Orcas or Bellingham yourself, anyway? Do you have access to a plane?"

"I hadn't thought that far ahead," she admitted with an amazing lack of concern. "I only found out that Doc Jackson was leaving an hour or so before I talked to you about lessons. I figured I'd get through those, then worry about what I'd fly."

He didn't know which surprised him more, her candor

or the quickness of her decision to approach him. "Had you ever thought about flying before?"

"Not really." She hesitated. "Never, actually," she admitted and edged down the counter to intercept the man approaching the cash register with a magazine and a handful of postcards.

The two-tone melody of the door's bell announced more shoppers. Asking her son to set the cage on the floor and finish feeding the raccoon there, she stepped over his coloring book and took the copy of *Cycling World* the guy in the spandex handed her.

One of the women who'd just come in had two cranky toddlers in tow. She asked for children's books.

A woman in a huge straw hat wanted to know if the store had free maps.

Since they really had nothing else to discuss, Sam gave the manual a pat and said, "Call me."

She promised that she would, but Sam could swear the odd strain had slipped back into her smile.

Telling himself it was none of his business why that faint tension was there, he stepped out into the crowd of visitors eating ice-cream cones, window shopping and queuing up at the expedition office across the street for whale excursions.

He'd already completed two flights that morning. He had three more that afternoon. Two were short hauls of supplies to sportsmen's camps on a couple of the more isolated islands. One was a passenger and mail pickup in Seattle. When he returned, there would be the usual maintenance on the planes, logs to fill in, manifests to file, tomorrow's cargo to sort.

He headed around the corner and climbed into the midnight-blue pickup truck with E & M Air Carrier Service emblazoned on its door panels. As long as he was going to be on the mainland, he should be thinking about picking up office supplies and ordering a new seat bracket to replace the one he'd found cracked yesterday on their oldest Cessna. Instead, his thoughts crowded around a woman who made no sense to him at all.

He couldn't believe she'd never given any thought to flying until an hour before she'd shown up at the airstrip.

She already had him wondering why she'd seemed so subdued compared to the other day. Now she had him flat-out baffled by her apparent tendency to leap first, then look. Considering that she'd decided to take flying lessons in less time than it took most women to pick out a dress—and that she'd come up with the offer to watch his children in mere seconds—it seemed that T. J. Walker simply took on whatever came her way and battled the consequences and details as she went along.

He didn't know what to make of her. As a pilot he knew what it was to go with his gut, to rely on training and instinct to make split-second decisions. But he could back up those decisions with years of experience and advance preparation.

He had no idea what she based her decisions on.

The warm sea breeze blew through the truck's open windows as he drove past the pier and the ferry dock and skirted the fourteen square blocks of businesses and weather-grayed buildings that comprised the town of Harbor. He would have thought that a woman who tended a small zoo of high-maintenance animals in addition to working part-time and raising a child on her own would need to be organized to survive. An organized person would think twice before committing herself to something that would eat up a hefty chunk of her time. But the more he thought about it, the more it seemed to him that her idea of preplanning was simply to take a deep breath before she plunged in.

His scowl of incomprehension was threatening to become permanent by the time he swung onto the long open road that edged the ocean and led to the airport. Logic told him he didn't need to understand her. All he had to do was trust her. And there, he supposed, he really had no problem.

Her little boy had appeared well cared for. He'd been clean and healthy and had obviously been raised to be friendly and caring. Just meeting the child spoke well of his mother. Aside from that, anyone who rescued and cared for injured animals would have to have a very soft heart.

The arrangement was only temporary, anyway. Hopefully, it wouldn't have to last more than a few weeks. Just that morning he'd received a promising response to one of his ads. He had an interview for a week from Saturday with a woman from Bellingham who was leaving her position as nanny. She'd be available as soon as the family moved east at the end of the month.

In the meantime, it seemed he was going to teach a woman with a soft heart and no apparent sense of logic how to fly.

Chapter Three

T.J. was intimately familiar with nearly every square mile of Harbor Island. She knew the lush mountainous forest that filled its interior and the hiking trails, caves and clear creeks meandering through it. She knew its coves and tide pools and had introduced her son to all manner of seals, urchins and starfish. She knew who lived in the secluded cabins, houses, shacks and the occasional mansion tucked into the trees or overlooking the shore.

She disturbed little of it. Not the wildlife and not her neighbors. She regarded herself and her son simply as part of the ecology, custodians of their own small space in the woods and observers of all the rest.

She felt safe on Harbor now. Secure in a way that had eluded her all the years she'd been growing up. That was why she'd come back after only a year away at college. It was why she wanted to raise her child in Harbor. But that hard-won sense of security felt threatened at the moment. It had ever since Maddy had told her about Brad.

Try as she might, T.J. simply couldn't shake the feeling that she hadn't heard the last of him.

She wasn't sure if she was simply being cautious or actually getting paranoid, but she checked her rearview mirror twice before she pulled her ancient Jeep off the shore road and headed for the blinding-white hangar at the edge of the airstrip. She had no idea what she expected Brad to do. Or if he would do anything at all. As she glanced at the child craning his neck from the seat beside her, she just knew she didn't want Andy to know she was concerned.

Not that he was paying any attention to her. His focus was glued to the half dozen private airplanes parked away from E & M Air Carrier's huge hangar.

He practically vibrated with excitement as he grappled with the latch on his seat belt. "Can I go look at a plane? I won't get too close. I promise."

"Jason's dad is expecting us in the office, honey."

"Is Jason here?"

"He's visiting his grandma in Seattle right now."

Seat belt unfastened, he reached for the rusting handle on the door. "Can I see a plane after, then?"

"If it's not too dark."

Her son grinned. "'Kay," he murmured, not bothering to press.

He was such a good little boy. Affectionate. Obedient. He never demanded anything the way she often heard children do in the bookstore when they would beg, cajole or cry for just one more toy or treat. He simply accepted what she said and moved on to whatever next claimed his interest.

Tugging her heavy denim bag over her shoulder, she

climbed out of the battered, but blessedly reliable, old vehicle and automatically took Andy's hand. She didn't know why he was always so agreeable. It could have been because he knew there wasn't money for extras. Or because he instinctively understood that she already gave him everything she could and that it all came from her heart. Maybe it was because, even with Crystal living nearby, he knew it was really just the two of them and that they had to take care of each other because there wasn't anyone else who would.

Whatever it was, she told herself, pushing open the door next to the black letters indicating Office, she was simply grateful he was hers.

Andy looked up at her, confused. "There's nobody here."

"I see that."

The small waiting room with its huge map on the wall was empty. So was the space across the long counter where filing cabinets and two gray metal desks—one cluttered, one painfully neat—occupied the area.

Sam had said he would be available that evening. He'd told her that yesterday when he'd brought her the book weighing down her bag. Though she hadn't talked to him since then, she had left a message with one of his employees that she would be by after she got off work at eight and asked that he call if the time wasn't convenient. Since she hadn't heard from him, she'd assumed the timing was fine.

Still clutching Andy's hand, she moved to the end of the counter to peek through the open door behind it. The door opened directly into the hangar. Wondering if the guy named Chuck who had taken her message had forgotten to pass it on, she glanced into the cavernous space.

A white aircraft far larger than the tiny two- and four-passenger planes outside occupied the middle of the huge hangar. The cargo pods on its underbelly hung open.

While her son whispered a reverent "Wow," T.J.'s attention settled on the big man in a khaki shirt and jeans.

Sam was shifting boxes from the underbelly of the plane to a low flat dolly—large boxes that he handled two at a time and that were heavy enough to make the dolly buck when he hefted them onto it.

He didn't seem to notice her and Andy when they moved to stand in the doorway. Not sure if they should enter, she simply watched, unwillingly fascinated by his strength. She was intrigued, too, by the concentration etched in his features. No one could deny the sense of capability surrounding him, or the masculine beauty in his sculpted profile.

Sam Edwards was an incredibly virile and handsome man. T.J. had always thought him so—much as she had always thought redwoods mighty and the ocean vast. It was simply a fact of nature, and she appreciated beauty in nature wherever she found it. She had just never before considered exactly how broad his shoulders were. Or how strong the muscles in his back and thighs had to be to raise him up so easily as he hefted the heavy loads. His arms had to feel as solid as stone.

She imagined his arms felt rather empty, too.

Her grip tightened slightly on her son's little hand. She couldn't imagine how difficult it must have been for him to be left alone to raise his children, or how hard it had to be for his children to have lost their loving mother. She had known Tina. T.J. had even helped her out on occasion at the preschool where Tina had worked by bringing animals for the children to learn about and helping when the aide wasn't available. She had been on school field trips with Tina, too, where they had talked about measles and how to get their offspring to eat vegetables. When Tina had brought Jason and Jenny into the bookstore, they had talked about children's books.

The beautiful, bubbly ex-cheerleader had doted on her children and adored her husband. They had clearly cared for her, too. The few times T.J. had seen Sam with them at community functions, it had been clear that their family had been as happy as any around.

Watching him now, when she was so aware of his physical strength, she couldn't help but wonder at the fortitude and tenacity he had to possess. Rumor had it that he seemed to be doing well now, though he stuck close to work and his family. But she remembered hearing early on that he'd taken his wife's death as hard as any man could.

As if he had finally become aware of how intently he was being watched, Sam's motions began to slow. With his last box unloaded, he straightened like a pinnacle rising from the sea, plowed his fingers through his hair and turned toward the doorway.

The bright fluorescent lights illuminated the sculpted lines of his face when his glance jerked from them to his watch. "I didn't realize how late it was," he called to her. "How long have you been standing there?"

Longer than I probably should have, she thought. "Only a couple of minutes," she called back. "I hope you don't mind us coming through the office."

"Not a problem. Come on over."

Since he stayed where he was, near the plane, she gently tugged Andy forward. She was halfway across the gray concrete floor when she noticed the lines of fatigue fanning from the corners of Sam's eyes. Deep creases bracketed his mouth. She'd noticed the lines before, but thought only that they added interest to a face that would have been too perfect otherwise.

With his loss fresh on her mind, she realized now that what had carved the furrows so deeply could very well have been grief—and a kind of weariness that ran soul deep.

She stopped a couple of yards away. "I didn't know if you got my message."

Looking very competent, very capable and very...big, he ran an impersonal glance from her short T-shirt to the hem of her baggy linen pants, then smiled at the child clinging to her hand.

"I got it about an hour ago." Turning, he reached inside the open door of the plane's cabin and pulled a clipboard from the pilot's seat. "I just wanted to get the cargo unloaded before we got started. We can talk while I work on the plane."

Concentration sharpened his features as he dropped the clipboard atop the stacked boxes and made a note on an attached form. His manner was as brisk and businesslike as his tone. She had no idea what time he'd started work that morning or how many places he'd flown over the course of the day. But from the fatigue he dutifully ignored, she had the impression of a man running on nothing but reserves.

Still, he offered another easy smile to the little boy who peered past him to the plane. Andy hadn't budged from beside her. Sheer awe rooted him to the concrete.

Sam's preoccupation lifted when he noticed where her son was staring. "Have you ever seen a plane up close before?" he asked the silent child.

Solemnly, Andy shook his head to indicate that he hadn't.

"Then, you've never been inside a plane before, either?"

Without a blink, the little boy shook his head once more.

"Do you want to sit inside this one?"

The awe in Andy's expression moved into his voice. "Inside it? Can I? Really?"

"Promise not to touch anything?"

Andy nodded so fast that his bangs bobbed.

"Wait a minute." T.J.'s wary glance darted past the open cockpit door to the complex array of gauges and gadgets on the control panel. "Is it safe for him to be in there?"

Looking intimately familiar with the workings of a worried mother's mind, Sam paused. "I wouldn't have suggested it if it weren't," he replied, reasonably. "Would you rather he didn't?"

Andy's eyes beseeched her. Eyes of startling blue met hers with calm patience.

"If you're sure he'll be okay..."

"I'm sure." He arched one eyebrow. "Do you want to let go of his hand?"

Andy nodded, his expression still pleading. "You can come, too, Mom."

At her son's encouragement, she finally let go. She always kept a close eye on her son. Especially in unfamiliar places. That was why she was right behind them when Sam swung her child up in one arm, carried him to the plane and plopped him onto the pilot's seat.

"Here you go," he said to Andy. "You can sit in here while your mom and I talk. That's the throttle and this is what steers the plane. And this," he said, digging something out from the utility box by the seat, "is a Game Boy. Do you know how to work it?"

"Uh-huh."

"Good. Then you can play with that. Hands off everything else. Okay?"

"'Kay," Andy murmured, obligingly. His nose wrinkled. "What's a throttle?"

"It's like the gas pedal in a car," T.J. replied from behind Sam's broad back.

"Oh."

"Look," she murmured, touching Sam's arm to get his attention. The muscle beneath the soft khaki felt every bit as hard as she'd imagined. "You're sure he's okay in there?" she asked, feeling that heat move into her palm.

He turned, causing her hand to fall, then forced her to back up as he stepped toward her. "I'm positive. Even if he does touch something, it might mess up an instrument, but it won't hurt him." His big body towered over hers as he nodded toward the exposed engine. Its cowling lay on the ground. "You don't have to worry about him starting it up, either," he murmured, sounding as if he knew she was thinking just that. "I have the key, and the fuel line is disconnected."

He was crowding her, though she didn't think he was doing it on purpose. There was just nowhere else for him to go with the door open, the plane at his back and her blocking his path from the front.

Jerking her focus from his firm mouth to his wide chest, she curled her fingers over the odd heat lingering in her hand and backed to the middle of the long high wing.

"You've been reading." He offered the observation as he followed her, obviously referring to her response about the throttle. "Did you get the chapters finished?"

Nothing about him made her think he was at all affected by her proximity. Uneasily aware that she was not unaffected by his, she thought about the book she carried and willed herself to relax.

"Some of them. Most of them," she corrected, her glance automatically seeking her son.

She had been more anxious than usual about her little boy over the past couple of days. Every time she lost sight of him, which was never for more than a few moments, a bubble of panic rose in her chest, pumping adrenaline into her veins, making her heart lurch. But she could easily see Andy holding the Game Boy in a death grip as he stared, enthralled, at the complex instruments.

He was fine. Sam had even assured her that he was safe.

For the moment, with Sam there, she realized that Andy truly was.

The knot that had formed in her stomach yesterday morning actually began to loosen. Grateful for the respite, only now realizing how tense she had been, she pulled the book from her big denim bag and held it out with both hands. "I'm afraid I won't be needing lessons, though. Thank you, anyway."

The weathered creases in his forehead deepened as he reached for the bulky volume. Confusion colored his tone. "What changed your mind?"

"That book, for one thing. I had no idea until I started reading it how complicated it all would be. Even if you could teach me how to get a plane off the ground, I can't afford the money or the time it would it take for real lessons and to get a license. Doc Jackson will be leaving in a couple of weeks. It would be a couple of years before I could fly a plane on my own."

"It wouldn't take *that* long."

"It would for me. I wouldn't want to leave Andy all those hours, either." She didn't want to leave him at all. "It's like you with your children," she explained, because there was no need to tell him why she didn't want her child out of her sight. "You said you hated leaving them any more than you already have to. I feel the same way about Andy.

"I'll still watch Jason and Jenny," she hurried to assure him, "but I'll have to find some other way to get veterinary care."

Ratchets and wrenches rattled as Sam set the book atop the chest-high portable toolbox under the tip of the wing. The entire time she'd been backing down from flying lessons, he'd been waiting for her to back down from watching his kids. He'd felt it coming as surely as sunset over the Pacific. Since she had just unexpectedly eliminated that worry, he now was simply feeling mystified.

He had already told himself he didn't have to understand this woman to work with her. He'd even expected her to throw him off guard. After all, it wasn't every day a man encountered a woman who informed him out of the blue that she wasn't going to sleep with him. Or who practically begged him to teach her to fly so she could rescue the local wildlife.

He'd been unwillingly impressed by that desire, too. Though he'd never considered himself particularly jaded, he had to admit there really wasn't much that did impress him anymore.

He also had to admit that the idea of sex with her had crept into his thoughts with disquieting regularity.

The phenomenon was nothing more than a power-of-suggestion thing. He wouldn't have thought of it if she hadn't put the idea in his head. He felt certain of that.

But thoughts of how soft her skin would feel, of burying his fingers in the wild tangle of her hair, of how shapely she was beneath the baggy clothes she wore, had crept into his mind, his sleep. The unwanted mental images had to be why his body had tightened when she'd touched him. And why the fresh wildflower scent of her had him feeling as taut as a trip wire every time he breathed it in.

"Do you mind if I ask you something personal?"

"That depends." With his glance on her mouth, hesitation slipped over her face. "What do you want to know?"

"Why are these animals so important to you?"

The nature of his interest made her lips curve. "For some of the same reasons children are important. They need protection and care," she explained. "Because I care, I do what I can for them."

She looked as she sounded, as if she were certain he would understand something so basic.

He didn't understand at all.

Not sure why it mattered, he ran a skeptical glance from the curls disappearing behind her back, over her clear, unembellished skin and paused at the hand-strung brown beads skimming her collarbone. His assessing glance narrowed on her shoulders.

He was unable to detect so much as a hint of a bra strap or cup beneath the soft fabric of her shirt, nothing to support or mold the high, gentle swells of her breasts. Making himself ignore the thought of how perfectly she would fit in his palms, he forced his glance to the loose linen drawstring pants riding her slender hips.

There was nothing artificial about the woman. Nothing made up, made over, restrained, restricted or enhanced.

She was completely, unabashedly natural. He'd even bet her underwear was 100 percent pure cotton.

Not that he was ever going to find out. Since he was no more interested in a relationship than he'd heard she was, his thoughts were actually leaning more toward her beliefs than her bedroom. He now had the nagging feeling she was one of the vegan ilk who had refused to baby-sit at his house because he had leather furniture. "You're a vegetarian."

At the flat conclusion in his voice, T.J.'s expression mirrored his own.

"So?" she prompted.

"So are you into some esoteric philosophy that regards animals as gods or something?"

She had already struck him as being a little unconventional, which made her fit in perfectly on Harbor where eccentricities were the norm. The island was populated with a curious blend of kiwi farmers, entrepreneurs, loners and dot-com millionaires, each perfectly content to march to his own drummer. Considering who her mother was, he figured T.J.'s philosophies could be light-years away from his more traditional leanings.

"Do you mean, do I worship cows and that sort of thing?"

"Well…yeah," he rather unintelligently concluded.

Her smile emerged, as warm as sunshine and faintly chiding. "My burgers are made of tofu," she admitted, "but I've never confused something on four legs with anything other than what it is. I just happened to grow up with animals. They were always around the communes we stayed in when I was a child."

One slender shoulder raised in a faint shrug. "They were my friends," she explained, her voice softening as she thought of how much company and comfort those animals had given her. "It's only natural that I should provide a safe environment for those who need it now."

For a moment, Sam said nothing. He simply watched her study the wrenches on the cart before she glanced around the cavernous space. She seemed infinitely more at ease than she'd been when he'd first seen her standing in the office doorway, and terribly curious about what surrounded her.

He was feeling more than a little curious himself. Her comments about being raised in a commune had just summoned images of tie-dye and love beads.

He'd certainly heard of the communes of the sixties and seventies and their free-living lifestyle. He even knew several aging hippies himself, a few of whom ran the Mother Earth Spa on the north end of the island and whose faithful clientele flew in regularly on his airline. Then there was her mother.

"The animals lived in the commune with you?"

"I don't remember any living with us. Except for this mangy yellow dog someone had. But he didn't stay very long. The guy or the dog," she mused. Having perused the wrenches on the cart, she looked back at him. "Metric, right?"

He nodded at her query and watched her glance swing to a spare propeller blade hanging above the long, brightly lit workbench. "For as far back as I can remember," she continued, crossing her arms as if to keep from touching anything, "if I wanted company I headed for the woods."

"How many people did you live with?"

"Anywhere from half a dozen to twenty or so."

"Weren't there any other children?"

"Sometimes. That depended on where we were. And on the weather. Winter tended to weed out the wannabes.'' Tipping her head back, she studied the structure of the wing flap above her. ''Even when there were other kids, they didn't stay long enough to really get to know.'' No one stayed long. Ever. Transience had always been part of the life. ''But there were always animals. I'd find their dens and play with the babies.''

''You're kidding.''

Her attention remained on the wing as she shook her head, her smile rueful. ''I know. I'm lucky I didn't lose a limb.''

''Or your life.''

''That, too,'' she easily agreed. ''Some babies' mothers can be very protective. I think bears are the most aggressive,'' she mused, still checking out the hardware. ''But I ran into a beaver once that was a close second. She wasn't happy at all about me playing with her kits.''

Without thinking about what he was doing, Sam let his glance slide over the long line of her throat as she followed the flap to the light on the wing tip. His first inclination was to ask where her mother had been while she had wandered the woods in search of playmates. He wasn't sure he wanted to know, though. Wasn't sure he wanted it to matter.

What she'd just so artlessly told him conjured the uncomfortable image of a very isolated child.

''It sounds lonely.''

Her inspection of his plane came to an abrupt halt. Meeting his eyes, she tipped her head to study his.

''It was,'' she admitted with compelling candor. Sympathy unexpectedly moved into her soft expression. Her voice, already quiet, quieted further as she searched his face. ''It's hard, isn't it? Feeling alone like that, I mean.''

She had caught him off guard before. She'd just never caught him as unprepared as he felt at that moment. As it had the other day at the bookstore, her candid manner had pulled him past the protective wall he'd built around himself, caused him to be curious and left him without the distance he tended to keep between himself and nearly everyone else.

He had no idea what he'd done to give himself away, but she had somehow recognized the emptiness living inside him. As ruthlessly as he battled that feeling, as diligently as he tried to avoid thinking about why it was there, the last thing he wanted was to talk about it now.

He dealt with the feeling enough when he was alone.

Feeling exposed, hating it, he took a step back and nodded toward the plane. "I think I'd better check on your son."

The understanding in her eyes flickered out like a candle in a draft. He could even feel her draw back from him as he moved past her, tension radiating from him in waves.

"Hey, buddy," he called, forcing that tension down for the child's sake. "How's it going in there?"

"Do I hafta get out now?" came the little boy's reply.

T.J. blinked at Sam's back and tried to focus on what he was saying to Andy. Something about rudder flaps, she thought, but little registered. The way he'd so abruptly changed the subject made it feel as if he'd just slammed a door in her face.

Not at all sure what she had done, she was trying to figure it out when the distant drone of an airplane filtered in with the breeze. In a matter of seconds the sound intensified, reverberating through the building, then faded off as the plane passed, banked and set itself down on the runway.

"That's Zach," Sam said, appearing to note the tail numbers of the E & M craft taxiing off the runway.

Wanting to see what was going on, Andy crawled to his knees on the seat. "I was sure Chuck would get here before him."

Sam seemed to be talking more to himself than to the child who now asked if another plane was coming soon.

All T.J. cared about was getting out of there before they were joined by anyone else. Feeling awkward and uneasy, she moved to where Sam shadowed the cockpit door.

"Come on, Andy," she murmured, edging in front of Sam's solid-looking chest. "It's time for us to go. Mr. Edwards has things he needs to do, and we don't need to be in the way."

Andy clearly didn't want to leave. There were too many new things here for him to see. Though disappointment made him hesitate, he dutifully put the Game Boy back from where he'd seen Sam take it and held his arms out so she could lift him to the ground.

Andy's tennies hit the concrete with a faint squeak. Turning, she automatically took her little boy's hand before glancing up at the man towering over her. Something like caution shadowed his features, along with a fair amount of the reserve she was feeling herself.

"It's Sam," he corrected, frowning at her turn toward formality.

"Then thank Sam for letting you sit in the plane, Andy."

"Thank you," came the child's sweet reply. He smiled then, the dimple in his cheek as deep as a cherry pit. "It was way cool."

A smile involuntarily twitched at the corner of Sam's mouth. "Way cool, huh?"

The child's head bobbed, but Andy's attention was already being diverted to the plane that had taxied to a stop near the hangar. The circular gray blur of the propellers slowed to reveal three still blades.

"Well, we'd better get going," T.J. said quietly, heading around Sam with her son in tow. "I've kept you long enough."

A muscle in Sam's jaw jerked. "You haven't kept me from anything."

She shrugged, offering a smile that looked uncomfortable at best. "Your partner is here, and we need to get home and feed the animals." With the graceful sweep of her hand, she motioned toward the open end of the hangar. Dusk had already robbed the sky of its color. "It will be dark soon."

Sam's only response was a nod. He hadn't meant to be rude when he'd walked away from her moments ago. He knew he had been, though. He also knew he had offended her in the process, but he'd had no idea how else to handle her question. He had no intention of opening a vein for this woman. Or anyone else, for that matter. And that's what it felt like he would be doing if he were to acknowledge to anyone else the void inside him. So he let her go with a wave to her kid and swore silently to himself as he watched them walk away. From her polite reserve after he'd killed the light in her eyes, it was as clear as rainwater that she'd crawled inside a shell.

He'd liked her a whole lot better when she was being feisty and straightforward. She seemed far less vulnerable that way.

The knowledge that he'd been the one who'd caused her to withdraw kicked him square in the conscience as his partner walked inside. All she had done was let him know she understood how lost and alone a person could sometimes feel. Just because he didn't care to share that understanding didn't mean he couldn't have handled the situation with a little more finesse. After all, he still needed her to watch his kids.

"Hey, Sam. That was T.J. wasn't it?"

"Yeah. It was."

"That must have been one tough first lesson."

His partner of thirteen years strode past the loaded cargo dolly with his log book in one hand and pure speculation carved in his face. Zach McKendrick was a regular guy. The best, as far as Sam was concerned. He was also an excellent business partner and one of the best bush pilots in the entire northwest. The strapping, ex-jet-jockey didn't make a bad brother-in-law, either.

"What makes you think the lesson was tough?"

Scratching his jaw, Zach shrugged. "It's not like her to ignore a person. I know she saw me, but she kept going anyway. She usually asks about Lauren. Makes small talk, you know?" His shrewd eyes narrowed. "She seemed awfully anxious to get out of here."

"She has animals she needs to feed." Later he might consider that he'd truly screwed up his best prospect for temporary child care. Now he just wanted to do something…physical. "Do you have anything to unload?"

"The mail from the outer islands. Are you changing the subject?"

"Yeah," he muttered and grabbed an empty dolly. "I am."

Curiosity arched Zach's eyebrows. "Why don't you want to talk about T.J.?"

"Because she's not taking the lessons." That was part of it, anyway.

"Does that mean she won't be watching Jas and Jenny?"

That was another part of it. "I don't know yet. I

haven't had time to come up with anything else to barter with.''

Considering the way she'd withdrawn from him, the bigger problem was whether she'd be willing to barter at all.

Chapter Four

She had no one to blame but herself. She'd dropped her guard. Forgotten to be wary.

T.J. dumped a scoop of sweet oats into a dented metal pie pan and set it inside one of the large wire enclosures she'd built into her woods. It had been more than twenty-four hours since she'd walked away from Sam Edwards, yet she simply couldn't shake the sting she'd felt when he'd so abruptly rejected her understanding.

It didn't help matters that she'd run into his sister a while ago, and now felt embarrassed on top of everything else.

The scent of damp pine and sea air filled her lungs as she pulled a deep breath. She needed to let it go, at least for now, so she could focus on her chores before the last of the day's light faded. She and Andy had returned from a birthday party for one of his friends less than twenty minutes ago and the pale twilight wouldn't last much longer. She had already helped her tired little boy through a modified version of his nighttime routine and tucked him into bed. Now she needed to get the animals fed so they could bed down, too.

Calmed by her own rituals—at least, telling herself she was, she grabbed the hose and the handles of her loaded wheelbarrow and headed into the woods. The narrow path led to the big enclosures she'd built near the creek at the back of her house. Inside the farthest one, two orphaned fox pups stopped chasing and tumbling with each other long enough to check out the food she spooned into their dishes. Heading back up the path after she'd secured the door, she slipped fish into a cage for the seagull someone had shot in the wing and left to die and veggies into the enclosure for a wild hare that had tangled with something with claws, murmuring to them all along the way.

Even as occupied as she was, she couldn't shake the feelings still nagging at her.

Those feelings were mercilessly easy to identify. She felt regret because she had clearly stepped into Sam's personal space and stepped over a line he didn't want crossed. And stung because she'd reached out only to have him pull back like a snapped spring and slam an invisible door. The embarrassment was there because, thanks to Lauren, she now realized he probably thought she'd been coming on to him.

The embarrassment she could live with.

It was the rejection she hadn't been prepared for.

She'd left herself wide open for it, too, which wasn't like her at all. Over the years, she'd honed her reserve with men, developed a finely tuned sense of caution with any human possessing a Y chromosome. She trusted only

children, animals and books and neither expected nor
wanted anything from any male other than her son.

That reserve had failed her, however, with Sam Edwards. Until the moment he'd walked away from her in
the hangar, her usual reticence simply hadn't existed.

The front wheel of the wheelbarrow squeaked as she
moved her supplies toward the next enclosure and the
hole of twilight at the beginning of the path. It had taken
her only minutes of the drive home last night to figure
out why that caution hadn't been there.

The sympathy she'd felt for him having lost his wife
and being left to raise his children on his own had prevented it. Even the way he kept to himself, his work and
his little family had served to sabotage her usual defenses. It was almost as if she'd sensed a kindred sprit
in him, as if they'd had so much in common that there
had been no need for protection. Only, there hadn't been
a connection at all. She just hadn't been able to avoid
responding to him any more than she could avoid responding to any wounded animal.

Water trickled from the end of the long garden hose
as she hauled it back up the path. She was almost finished
with her chores, but she wasn't finished lecturing herself
just yet. After all, no one knew better than she did that
wounded animals needed to be approached with caution.
She'd learned that lesson when she was eleven years old
and tried to play nurse to a cougar. The beautiful sleek
animal had been hit by a car and left for dead by the side
of the road. The big cat had turned on her when it had
come out of its stupor and missed slicing her face with
its claws by scant millimeters before bolting into the
woods to heal or die on its own.

A person would be a fool to forget a lesson like that.

Two adolescent raccoons chittered as she left a plate

of cat food in their enclosure and added more water to the plastic bowl they'd dumped. In the larger enclosure at the edge of the trees by her lawn, a lame doe made her way to the sweet oats T.J. had left her a while ago. Mindful of the doe's daughter following her as she fed the last of her charges, she smiled at her little shadow.

"This isn't for you," she murmured to the tiny fawn and dipped into the sack of oats once more. "It's another serving for your mama. You need to talk to her about your meal."

The fawn's back barely reached T.J.'s knees. With the metal scoop in one hand, she bent to smooth her other hand over the white spots scattered over the animal's lovely rust-colored coat.

She'd barely touched the soft hide when she suddenly went still.

So did the fawn. Her little head jerked toward the narrow gravel road beyond the house as the sound of crunching rock and a vehicle engine grew louder. Seconds later, the animal's whole body on alert, they both stood frozen in the headlights of a large dark truck.

Sam barely noticed the charming little weather-grayed house, tucked back as it was in the trees with moss covering its wood-shingled roof. With dusk settling in and the thick canopy of leaves and fir boughs filtering the light in this secluded place, he wouldn't have noticed T.J. at all had he not just caught her in his headlights.

She stood beyond the house at the edge of a clearing where lawn met woods. A snug T-shirt skimmed over a fluid skirt that ended just above her ankles. There was a definite wariness about her as she straightened and watched him climb from his truck, but at least she didn't bolt for the thick cover of the trees the way the fawn did at his approach.

Taking that as a good sign, he stuffed his hands into the pockets of his khakis as he crossed toward her, his stride casual, his attention on her surroundings. Beside her, an old red and rusting wheelbarrow held a burlap bag of feed and what looked to be empty cans of pet food. A few feet away a long garden hose snaked across the lawn from the spigot at the side of her house.

It was difficult to see into the trees with all the shadows, but he caught the dull glint of chicken wire wrapped around trees and secured with stakes. He could barely make out the frame of an open wire-mesh door. Near a low bush inside the enclosure stood a small deer with a bandaged foreleg. The fawn he'd spooked concealed most of itself behind her.

T.J. waited until he stopped a few feet away.

"Hi," she finally said, looking oddly relieved and definitely uncertain.

"Evening," he murmured. In the pale-gray light, her flawless skin looked as smooth as marble. "I know you haven't been home long," he told her, "but I was on my way home myself and wanted to catch you before you went to bed. Did I come at a bad time?"

"I'm just finishing." She tipped her head, curiosity joining wariness. "How did you know I just got here?"

"Lauren said she stopped at Pelican Pizza to pick up their dinner and ran into you and about a hundred kids."

An unwilling smile curved the corner of her mouth as she turned to the wheelbarrow. "There were only twenty-six. It was Timmy Lawson's birthday party." Timmy, the birthday boy, had just turned six, and his mom had invited the entire preschool. Recognizing frazzled when she saw it, T.J. had stayed to help her out.

"I had a nice visit with your sister," she said, reaching for a bottle of pills between the cat food cans and the feed sack. "She said she thinks you're missing your kids. I told her I imagined you were."

She couldn't tell if it was displeasure or discomfort he felt at having been the topic of conversation. Either way, he frowned.

"She also said you asked her if she was trying to set us up."

The frown moved into his voice, but she couldn't hear what he muttered. His terse tone was too low.

Not about to ask him to repeat whatever it was, wanting only to set the record straight, she kept her attention on the tiny pill she stuffed into a berry. "She doesn't think you believed her when she denied it."

"I never said I didn't believe her."

"You probably didn't have to," she told him, a shrug in her voice. "You're actually very good with silence." With the pill buried, she slipped it into the squirrel hutch a few feet away. "You didn't have to say a word for me to get the message yesterday."

Intensely aware of Sam's scowl at her back, she watched the ball of gray fur with stitches in its hind leg sniff and scarf down its antibiotic. The moment the medication was gone, she turned to meet that scowl head-on.

"At least now I understand why you couldn't wait to get away from me when I asked if you agreed that it was hard being lonely."

For a moment he looked as if he were about to deny that he'd been in any sort of a rush at all. Instead a certain wariness entered his eyes. "You do?"

"I do."

"So why is that?" he asked.

"Because it's a subject that's hard for you to discuss.

I'm sorry I trespassed," she murmured, apology mirrored in her eyes. "You probably thought I was coming on to you like all those women who bring you casseroles when you're between housekeepers. That I was trying to get close to you, you know?"

Inside, Sam felt himself shift uncomfortably. Outwardly he didn't so much as blink. She'd nailed him cold. But *all those women,* she'd said, as if he were some sort of…what did his sister call it? Chick magnet?

"There haven't been that many women," he concluded, definitely uncomfortable with the term.

"That's not what I've heard."

"Well, there haven't," he insisted, not totally sure why he was defending himself.

"It must be relative."

"Excuse me?"

"Comparative," she clarified, thinking he looked a little lost. "Like to you, there haven't been that many women compared to what you consider a large number. I know of at least a half dozen, and that seems like a lot to me."

"There haven't been that many," he repeated, unable to imagine where she was coming up with the number.

Over the past three years, there had been a few women who'd shown up bearing food. Everything from baked lasagna to chocolate chip cookies. But a half dozen?

A couple of them had been Tina's single friends.

One had run a lodge on another island.

Another had worked the front desk for the kids' pediatrician and had been old enough to be his mother.

"Sure there have," T.J. countered, her tone utterly matter-of-fact. "There was Sunshine from the spa and that woman who bought the gift shop by the aquarium and sold it last year. And Doreen from the preschool,"

T.J. continued, thinking back. "Then, there was Maddy's sister last summer and the baby-sitter you had to let go because you found her waiting for you in your bed—"

He'd forgotten about most of those others. "She was barely eighteen," he pointed out. "Practically jailbait."

"She still counts," she reminded him ever so reasonably. "We're talking numbers here. And for what it's worth," she concluded before he could debate the issue any further, "I wasn't."

"Wasn't…?"

"Trying to get close."

In the pale-gray light, he watched her slowly rub her hands over her bare arms. The warmth of the day had dissipated, and the moisture of the damp earth cooled the air considerably. Yet it didn't seem to be a chill that had her hugging herself as she was. Despite her unnerving candor, she seemed a little embarrassed—and rather protective of herself as she sought to set the record straight.

"For what it's worth," he began, deliberately echoing her, "I didn't think you were."

It was her turn to be skeptical. "You didn't?"

"No."

"Oh. Well…that's—" even worse, she thought, because she hadn't had to bring it up at all "—good, then," she concluded.

He watched her hug herself tighter and give him an awkward smile. He supposed he could explain why he'd never considered her to be anything like those other women. Or how he'd found nothing even remotely calculated or predatory about her. But silence on the subject seemed safer. She'd claimed he was good at it, anyway.

"Look. I'm at a disadvantage here," he confessed, not at all comfortable with how much she seemed to know about him. How well she actually seemed to know him, for that matter. "How do you know about those ladies? And my housekeepers? You even knew why they all left," he recalled, frowning when he remembered how she'd enumerated the reasons for their various departures the other day. "Did you get all that from my sister?"

"Your sister has hardly told me anything about you at all."

His tone said he clearly begged to differ. "She just told you I thought she was setting us up."

"Only because she asked when we were going to do the trial flight thing. When I told her we weren't doing it, she thought you were the one who'd called it off."

"Why would she think that?"

"Because she didn't think you believed her when she said she wasn't trying to get us together. Apparently, you're not ready for another relationship. That was my conclusion," she offered, in case he was thinking his sister had spilled that, too. "Not hers."

Sam ran his hand over his face. He wasn't going to touch that one, either. "You haven't answered my question. If not from my sister—"

"People just say things in passing." Her shoulders lifted in a shrug. "And you know Maddy and my mom," she reminded him, sounding as if that should explain everything. "As small as the core of this community is, it's hard not to know something about everybody."

He'd been hearing that a lot lately. And he supposed she had a point, for most everyone else. The flaw in that argument for him was that he had never paid much attention to what didn't directly affect his family or his business, so he'd pretty much ignored the grapevine.

Maybe if he hadn't, or if he would get out more, as his sister kept prodding him to do, he might not feel as disadvantaged as he did at the moment. He wasn't going to worry about that now, though. All he cared about was that he was at a definite handicap where this woman was concerned. She was a complete mystery to him. And becoming more so by the minute.

As she stood with the gentle breeze nudging the soft curls from her delicate features and the wild fawn edging closer to peek from behind her skirt, she reminded him of the ethereal wood sprites and fairies in his daughter's storybooks. Something utterly feminine, gentle, serene. But there was also a sense of capability about her, along with a veiled reticence that made her seem anything but fanciful.

"I guess you can pick up things about people in a place like this," he finally admitted, more intrigued than he wanted to be by her contrasts. "I just haven't picked up that much about you. That's why I came here," he told her. "I want to know what kind of rescue shelter you're running and find out how often it is that you need a vet."

Caution entered her eyes, making her look faintly skeptical at his interest.

"It's not a formal shelter," she told him. "I just care for animals I've found. Or who have found me," she amended, thinking of the beautiful doe with the broken leg who'd wandered onto her lawn from the road a quarter of a mile away. "As to my need for a vet, I tend the minor things like cuts and simple gunshot wounds in limbs, but not internal injuries or bad breaks. In winter, I need the vet about once a month or so. During tourist season it can be a couple of times a week."

That was when there were so many off-islanders around, tourists who failed to watch out for the animals crossing the road early in the morning or evening to get to their watering holes. She didn't explain that, though.

It wasn't that sort of curiosity she sensed in him. "Why do you want to know?"

Because he didn't share her tendency to leap before he looked, he thought. He needed information before he committed to anything.

The information he needed at the moment was whether or not he had any bargaining power with her and how safe his kids would be if he could talk her back into watching them.

"These animals," he continued, ignoring her curiosity to satisfy his own. "Do you keep anything…big?"

"Big as in…?"

"With large teeth. Claws. That kind of thing."

"Someone brought me a young bear once," she admitted, "but I won't keep anything that can escape and hurt Andy or the other animals. I called the Fish and Game Department, and they took him right away."

She eyed him evenly. "Are you going to tell me why you're asking?"

"Because I want to know if you'd be interested in trading child care for free flights, since the flying lessons fell through." An offer of money she could easily refuse. An offer to help her animals was something he knew she would have to at least consider. "For every day you watch my kids, I'll make sure you get a free flight to a vet after Doc Jackson leaves."

"I already told you that I'd watch your children. Just because my needs changed didn't mean your children's did."

Disbelief made him hesitate. Her matter-of-fact tone made it sound as if she hadn't considered backing out at all. "I thought you might have changed your mind."

"Why would I? They still need care, don't they?"

From the way she'd withdrawn from him yesterday,

Sam would have bet his best fishing rod that all bets were off.

He was not, however, about to press that particular point.

"I hardly expect you to do it for nothing."

If need be, T.J. would have done just that. She had wondered off and on all day if he would still bring his children to her. For their sake she had almost called him to ask. She could still remember the awful insecurity of being a child and never knowing who would be there for her. Of never knowing routine or stability or all the things she tried so hard to provide for her own little boy. It was an awful way for a child to grow up.

She had the feeling Sam struggled hard to provide routine and stability for his children, too.

She was not letting empathy for him influence her, she hurried to assure herself. She just happened to understand his need to reciprocate.

"Then, I'll accept your deal," she assured him. "I wouldn't trust anyone who offered something for nothing, either." Her eyes narrowed. "You're still looking for full-time help, aren't you?"

"Absolutely. We're probably only talking about a couple of weeks at the most. I have an interview with a woman who can start before the end of the month, if everything works out."

"Okay, then."

Okay, then? he mentally echoed. Just like that?

"Good. Great," he amended, unable to believe how easily the negotiations had gone. He'd fully expected that he would have to do some apologizing, begging maybe. Whenever he'd messed up with a female, it seemed there'd always been some groveling in order. "How about I call you tomorrow about times and all that?"

"When are you bringing them home?"

"On Labor Day."

That was only two days away. "School starts the day after. Why don't you just drop them off that morning on your way to work?"

He didn't realize how relieved he was until he felt himself smile. "That would be great. Thanks."

Crickets joined the rustle of animals settling in for the night as she offered a faint smile in return. "You're welcome," she murmured and reached for the handles of her wheelbarrow.

"There's just one more thing," he said, not quite ready to go. There was something else he needed to know—the very *least* of what he should know of the woman to whom he was entrusting his children. "What does T.J. stand for, anyway?"

With her hands gripping the wheelbarrow's handles, she glanced at him across the feed sack and empty tins.

"Tierra Jade," she replied, her voice as soft as the sounds surrounding her. "It's supposed to mean precious green stone of planet earth or something like that."

The green stone he could understand. The color of her eyes was too subtle to be emerald. But jade described them perfectly.

"Planet earth?"

"What can I say?" she murmured, suddenly, beautifully self-conscious. "My mother was a flower child."

"I think Sam is a Scorpio. I should do a chart."

"You don't need to do a chart," T.J. insisted, over the strains of a sitar coming from The Herb Shoppe and Video Store's tape deck. "I'm just going to watch his children for a few days."

Over the coral rims of her half glasses, Crystal Walker

tolerantly eyed the sedate young woman she still couldn't believe she'd raised.

"The two of you have lived on this island for years and been nothing more than nodding acquaintances. There's a reason you've come into each other's lives right now." Looking every inch as convinced as she sounded, she struck a match and touched it to a thick sage-green candle on the handmade soaps and candles display. Green tea and lime was her latest creation in her aromatherapy line. "Ask him for his birth date and exact time of birth."

"We haven't come into each others lives," T.J. countered, watching the woman, who looked nothing like her, move to another candle. Crystal's long brown hair was generously threaded with gray. Parted in the middle, it hung in two enviably straight and swaying slashes over her shoulders. "We're only on the periphery. As for why that's happened, I'm pretty sure it's because he needs a baby-sitter. And no," she murmured, "I'm not going to ask him when he was born. You know I don't believe in that stuff."

"Fine. Then, I'll ask Willow from the herb farm to do a tarot reading. She's subbing for Doe at yoga class over at the spa right now, but she'll be in this afternoon."

"Mom," T.J. muttered, making two syllables out of the word the way Andy sometimes did.

Utter innocence danced over Crystal's rounded features. "What? There's something going on with you right now, honey. A planetary convergence, maybe. Or maybe your aura is fractured. First that Bradley pops up out of the blue," she muttered, pronouncing his name like an oath, "now you're involved with Sam."

"I'm not *involved* with him. And I don't want a chart or a reading." She especially didn't want to start thinking about Brad. It had been four days since Maddy had seen him. Crystal hadn't said much about him. She never had. But T.J. knew his reappearance troubled her. "I just want to return these."

T.J. set two children's videos on the long purple counter and gave the woman behind it an affectionate smile. Crystal was in a summer phase at the moment. Shades of poppy, rose and coral swirled over the caftan that covered her from neck to clogs. She would soon move into autumn and, until the blue phase of winter, be dressed in shades of rust and brown from head to toe.

Crystal had always believed in being one with the seasons.

She had also preached constantly that a person had to be true to herself. Apparently remembering that, she gave a martyred sigh. "If you won't get his birth date so I can do a chart, then at least wear this. I should have given it to you after Maddy told me what's-his-name had been here, anyway."

Silver rings flashed from every finger but the third one on her left hand as she searched a counter display of energy bracelets, mood rings and necklaces. Lifting a silver chain from which was suspended a stone of lime green, she motioned T.J. closer and slipped it over her untamable auburn curls.

"Peridot is perfect for you. It will lend you inner strength."

"Do you think Sam's children are going to be that much of a challenge?"

Her mom eyed her evenly. "It's not his children I'm concerned with. It's you I'm worried about. All anyone has to do is suggest pairing you with a man and you pull into that shell of yours faster than an Alaskan crab. I wasn't suggesting anything romantic between you and

Sam,'' she defended, sounding as if the idea was ludicrous. ''I just wanted to do a chart to see why your paths are intersecting now. And don't take off that stone.''

Satisfied that the peridot would do its thing, she swiped back her hair and picked up the videos. ''They can be very powerful. And they're highly sexed, you know.''

''Peridots?''

''Oh, please, T.J. Not the rock. Scorpios.''

T.J. refrained from rolling her eyes. The woman was as transparent as the thumb-size crystal hanging around her neck. She and Maddy had been trying for years to find her a mate, something T.J. found rather contradictory on Crystal's part, considering that the woman had never settled down with a man herself. ''I'm going to try not to think about that.''

''Andy?'' she called past the walls of videos lining half of the small, colorful store. Herbs and just about anything that could be made from them lined the shelves at the other end. ''Come say goodbye to Grandma. We have to go open the bookstore.''

Long strings of purple and turquoise beads formed a curtain in the doorway behind the counter. That portal led to the small living quarters where T.J. had lived for a few years herself, until she'd left for college.

Knowing that Crystal always kept her cookie jar filled with cookies for him, Andy had headed straight for the tiny kitchen the moment they'd walked in the door. Now, though T.J. had fed him breakfast less than an hour ago, he came back out with crumbs and a grin on his face.

His grandma wrapped him in a big hug.

Moments later T.J. dropped a kiss herself on Crystal's cheek and ducked out before the woman who was more like a New Age godmother than a parental figure could plant anything else in her head that she didn't want to think about.

She didn't want to worry about Brad.

She didn't want to think about Sam.

Highly sexed indeed.

Oddly it was that thought of Sam that caused her to reach for the stone Crystal had given her. She was already aware of Sam's strength and virility. She would even admit, to herself, anyway, that she'd wondered how it would feel to be held in his arms, sheltered, protected. But the thought of him in need of a woman put images in her head that had nothing to do with protection and elicited a few buried needs of her own.

Crystal had said the stone was for inner strength. As T.J. busily buried those needs, she considered that what she might really need was a stone for immunity.

Chapter Five

"I don't get it. He was fine with the idea of coming to see you and Andy. Then, I told him you were going to watch him and his sister for a few days and he went into a full pout."

Sam stood by the driver's door of his big blue truck. From beside him, T.J., in baggy denim overalls and a dirt-brown tank top, watched his frown land on the towheaded boy ignoring them across the long bench seat.

When Sam looked back to her, his low voice took another dive. "I was under the impression that you two got along."

Totally confused by the behavior of the quiet but usually amiable little boy, T.J. could only shake her head. "We do."

The doubtful look on Sam's rugged features clearly questioned her claim.

Ignoring his silent disbelief, she snagged back a handful of her hair, stepped past his big frame and leaned through the open window.

When he and his children had arrived minutes ago, four-year-old Jenny had hopped out right behind her dad, grinned at T.J. and promptly run off with Andy and the seven pounds of striped gray cat that had become his favorite pet. Jason had refused to budge.

"Don't you want to come say hi to Andy?" she asked, noting a definite stubbornness in the child's profile. "Since you've never been to our house before, I know he'd like to show you around."

Despite her friendly tone, the response from inside the truck's cab was total and complete silence. The blond little boy in the new Seattle Sonics T-shirt simply continued staring out the side window.

"Jason?" she asked, her tone encouraging.

The child didn't so much as blink.

At a loss, she pulled back—and felt his father's broad shoulder bump hers as Sam leaned into the window himself. Displeasure creased his profile.

"Hey, buddy. What's the problem in here? T.J. asked you a question. Answer her."

Nothing.

"Jason," he prodded, his tone growing insistent.

"Please, don't." T.J. touched his shoulder, urging him back. "If he doesn't want to come out, he doesn't have to."

Beneath the soft chambray of Sam's shirt, his muscles felt as solid as concrete posts. As hard and honed as they already were, they actually knotted tighter at her touch.

Aware that she'd caused him to stiffen, disconcerted by the response, she pulled back and reached for the crystal hanging between her breasts. She'd barely clasped it in her fist when Sam backed his dark head from the window and straightened to face her.

With his impossibly blue eyes steady on hers, the nerves in her stomach jumped.

Preferring to ignore how his tension affected her, she calmly nodded toward her tiny house with its willow rocker on the porch and geraniums spilling from its window boxes. "Let's go over there. We shouldn't talk in front of him."

In the dappled shade beyond the porch, Andy sat on the lawn with Jenny, playing with his kitten. The cat was using the pink ribbon that had fallen from the girl's curly blond ponytail for batting practice.

"He's never been that way with me before." With that muttered claim, Sam stopped by the redwood picnic table T.J. had sanded and restained herself. "I can't believe he's clammed up like that."

"He's never struck me as a very talkative child," she offered.

"Yeah? Well, that's not shyness over there. He's being flat-out defiant. I've never seen him act like this."

T.J. had never seen Sam this way before, either. Tension vibrated from him like sound waves from a tuning fork as he jammed his hands into the front pockets of his khakis.

"Why don't we sit down?"

"No, thanks." His restless glance moved from his daughter to his son. "We won't be staying that long."

He had already told her that. It was Labor Day and he had two more flights between now and nightfall, campers he needed to pick up from more remote islands, he'd said. Because his sister had the day off, Lauren was doing a hot-dog thing for the kids and would keep them until he returned. He'd only come by now so the children could see where they'd be coming in the mornings and after school for a while.

As tightly scheduled as he was, T.J. couldn't help being impressed by his obvious consideration for their comfort with their caregiver—even if his little boy was proving rather unappreciative.

"He's had a long day," she finally said, thinking she preferred to stand herself. The agitated way Sam fiddled with the change in his pocket was making her edgy. When she was edgy, sitting was impossible. "Maybe he's just tired."

Her suggestion met with tolerance. "That's not it. I told him on the way back from Seattle that we were coming here to see you and Andy before I took them to Lauren's. He was actually excited about it."

"Excited...until you mentioned that I'd be baby-sitting him?"

"Until then," he confirmed. "The minute I said it, he got quiet."

There was no doubt in T.J.'s mind that Sam was more concerned than he was annoyed with his son's attitude. She didn't doubt, either, that his need to get back to work added a dose of impatience to the mix. He'd told her that his present schedule kept him running fourteen hours a day. But, rushed or not, he suddenly didn't appear interested in going anywhere until he'd figured out his son's unexpected problem with her.

Through the faint patterns of leaves reflecting off the front window of the big vehicle, she could see the top of Jason's head. The defiance in the usually agreeable child had been apparent. It had been in his silence and in the angle of the small jaw that threatened to be as stubborn as his father's in another ten years. What wasn't so obvious was the reason that stubbornness might be there.

"What did you tell him about staying here?" she asked, curious about that problem herself.

With his arms crossed over his massive chest, Sam looked as big and unyielding as the ancient evergreens beyond him. "That I'd be bringing him and his sister here for a few days," he replied, repeating what he'd said before.

"Until…?" she prompted.

"Until I hired someone else to stay with them at home." A considering frown lowered his brow. "Maybe that's it."

"What is?"

"They're not used to being taken care of at someone else's place. They've always had someone at their house."

T.J. already knew that he didn't want to disrupt his children's lives any more than he had to. His determination that they have a live-in had made that clear enough. But something about Jason made her feel his behavior had to do with more than being cared for on unfamiliar ground. It hadn't been fear or displeasure she'd sensed in him. It seemed more like withdrawal.

"That could be," she murmured, shoving aside the suspicion taking root in her mind. She had unwittingly trespassed into forbidden territory with Sam before. She wasn't about to do it again. Aside from her own need for self-preservation, Sam was Jason's father. The man lived with him, loved him. If he thought he understood his son's attitude, he probably did. "No one knows him better than you do."

There had been no mistaking her hesitation. Sam saw

it as clearly as he saw her cautious glance toward his son. "But you think it's something else."

"I didn't say that."

"You didn't have to. I can see it in your face. Hey," he murmured, catching her arm when she stepped back. "If you have an idea about what's going on here, tell me." His tone softened. "Please."

There was no mistaking his concern. She could see it carved in his face, hear it in the depths of his voice. This was his child they were talking about, and he wanted whatever help he could get to understand him.

The thought that Sam truly might not understand his own child hadn't even occurred to her until that moment. But it was that kind of strain she saw etched around his mouth, that kind of worry putting the plea in his eyes.

The realization effectively annihilated the defenses that had risen even before he'd touched her. The disquiet this big, capable man felt because of his son seemed to override everything else for him at that moment. He didn't even notice that his fingers were still curled around her arm.

At least, he didn't seem to notice until she released the breath she'd held and glanced toward his hand. Looking as if he'd just become aware of the suppleness of her muscles, the smoothness of her skin, he drew a deep breath and lowered his hand to his side.

"It's just a possibility," she murmured, covering the spot where his heat lingered when she crossed her arms, "but maybe he's feeling insecure because he's facing another change. He's always been okay with me as Andy's mom. Or as the lady at the bookstore. I've just never been the person who takes care of him before. Now that I am, that puts me in a different context entirely."

His puzzled glance moved from where her fingers

curled over her bicep. "Why would you taking care of him change anything?"

"I'm just one more," she said, bracing herself for his rejection of her theory. "Nearly every woman he has trusted to be there for him has left him. One way or another," she expanded carefully. "This could just be his way of protecting himself."

The caution he heard in her tone was mirrored in her expression. Hearing her theory, Sam felt a stiff dose of caution himself.

His son had lost his mother first. Then their first housekeeper, a wonderful Mrs. Claus-type his little boy had come to adore, had moved away. But Jason had seemed okay with the rest of the women who had cared for him over the past few years—except for the one he'd actually told Sam he didn't like because she was always yelling at him and his sister to be quiet while she was on the phone, which apparently had been most of the time.

Sam hadn't liked that one, either, and had let the woman go the moment he'd found a replacement.

A replacement, he thought.

A substitute.

The words echoed uneasily in his head as he watched T.J. warily watch him. She almost looked as if she expected him to turn and walk away.

When he didn't, her grip on herself seemed to relax.

"Whatever his reasons," she said, "please don't be upset with him for not answering me just now. And don't worry about him staying here. I'll ask him to think of the time he spends here as playtime with Andy and suggest that he just think of me as Andy's mom. That's something that's not going to change for him," she added with a soft smile. "He's known me as Andy's mom for a long time."

For a moment Sam said nothing. Everything she had said made far more sense than he wanted it to. It also caused him to feel a heavy sense of guilt. He hated that he couldn't find some nice grandmotherly type to permanently be there for his children. Someone whose first priority was the care of his offspring. That's all he wanted. It's what he was trying desperately to get.

All he could do now, though, was play the hand he'd been dealt—and consider how disturbed he was by this intriguing woman's insight.

He considered, too, how very disturbed he was by her.

He wasn't sure what it was about her. The uncanny way she had of targeting the very things he wanted least to consider. The odd wariness he'd sensed in her the last couple of times they'd met. Or simply the way her fresh scent taunted certain of his nerves. He just knew that there wasn't much of anything about her that didn't give him pause.

"I'm not upset with him," he assured her, pointedly overlooking the direction of his last thoughts. His needs came last. "I just want to make sure both of my kids are okay when I'm not with them."

"Would you feel better if we asked Jason if he'd rather stay home than come here? In case that is the problem? It would work best for me if you'd drop them off here in the morning, but I could stay with them after school at your place after I get my chores finished here."

His eyes narrowed. "You insisted that going to my place wouldn't be a possibility."

"That was before," she replied with an amazingly easy shrug. "And if we do go, Andy and I would come home after you got off work. It's not for that long, anyway."

Not waiting for a response, she crossed the lawn to his

truck. Hands in his pockets, he stayed a few steps behind her, shaking his head at the chameleon-like qualities she possessed. At the moment, it actually didn't bother him that she'd so quickly changed her mind. Her concern was for his son. That was all that mattered.

He had worried about Jason long before the child had gone brooding on him a while ago. In the years since his son had lost his mom, he'd gone from a rambunctious and precocious three-year-old to a reticent child of six. Sam's own mother had even expressed concern over how quiet Jason was with her and his granddad. It seemed that with the exception of children at school, his little boy really didn't get involved with much of anyone.

Unable to imagine that T.J. would have any better luck with Jason than she'd had a while ago, he watched her rest her elbows on the driver's side window frame and lean in to talk to Jason. He was sure she was asking him where he wanted to stay and doing what she'd said she'd do by telling him to think of her as he already knew her, as Andy's mom.

Sam couldn't help but appreciate the way she wanted to set his son's mind at ease. He also thought her more than a little perceptive about why Jason was upset in the first place. As he studiously avoided the distracting view of her denim-covered backside and called to Jenny that it was time to go, he just couldn't help but wonder why that sort of insight was there.

"We're all set," she announced, turning to face him. "They're coming here after school."

One dark eyebrow slashed upward. "Just like that?"

"No. Not just like that." Her voice dropped as she walked toward him. "There was some bribery involved. But at least he answered me."

"Bribery?"

"I told him about Grandma Crystal's cookies. She says they're magic. I told him they were just chocolate chip."

Jenny's little blond head popped up between them. "Can I have a magic cookie, too?"

"Of course you can." T.J.'s voice was as kind as her smile. "But not until we stop by her shop tomorrow."

"Are you gonna take us to school in the morning?"

"Yes," she replied.

"No," Sam said, overriding her. "Not tomorrow."

Puzzled green eyes jerked to his.

"It's Jason's first day of first grade," he explained. "I told him I'd take them."

Jenny tugged on her dad's pants. "I wanna be in first grade."

Sam bent down, scooped his little girl up in one arm. "I know you do, munchkin. But you're stuck in pre-school for a while."

Resigned, Jenny stuck her thumb in her mouth and rested her head on her dad's shoulder.

"Do you still want me to pick them up after?" T.J. asked.

"Please." Absently rubbing his daughter's back, he hesitated. "There's just one problem. I had to trade schedules with one of the other pilots so I could go in later. If I can consolidate one of his runs, I'll be back by six. If I can't, I'll be a little late."

The man had the build of a linebacker, a face that could make the gods weep and he looked completely at ease holding his angelic little girl in his big, strong arms. He'd also just told her it was his son's first day of big-kid school and that he was going to be there for him, no matter what he had to do to make that happen.

Her fingers snaked back around the crystal. "Don't

worry about it," she murmured, backing up to slip her arm around Andy. "We'll be here."

"He just picked them up and left?"

"What else was he supposed to do?" T.J. asked her mom.

Crystal eyed T.J. over her frozen yogurt. Maddy, taking a break from the café a block away, sat opposite Crystal on the bright yellow and orange sunflower bench in front of The Herb Shoppe and Video Store. Overnight, Main Road, which in any other community would have been called Main Street, had gone from wall-to-wall bodies to nearly deserted. The locals had once again reclaimed their space.

"He might have stayed for a cup of coffee," Maddy suggested.

"If she'd offered," Crystal muttered.

"I take it that you didn't," Maddy surmised with the arch of one perfectly penciled eyebrow.

From where she stood across from them, by a street lamp with its hanging basket of alyssum and pink petunias, T.J. smiled and shook her head.

"It was after nine o'clock when he got there. Jason and Jenny were falling asleep, and he needed to get them home and into bed. The kids all had school this morning."

"So you really had no conversation at all," Maddy concluded.

"Not really." The instant T.J. had opened the door last night, Sam had apologized for being even later than he'd thought he would be, then asked how the kids' day had gone. She'd barely had a chance to tell him she thought all had gone well before he'd hoisted Jenny into his arms and led a bleary-eyed Jason back to the door, thanking her on the way out for having watched them. "Unless you count him telling me he would be earlier tonight."

Apparently, that wasn't the sort of information Maddy was looking for. "So what time did he drop them off this morning?"

"About seven." He hadn't hung around then, either. Sam had kissed his children goodbye on her porch, distractedly told her what time he'd pick them up and left her to convince his offspring that cereal didn't need to have colored marshmallow bits in it to taste good.

"I don't suppose you asked him in for coffee then, did you?"

The forty-something owner of the café smiled as she posed her question.

T.J. smiled back. "I'm watching his children for him. That's all."

"There's no chance the two of you...?"

"None. Andy and I like our lives just the way they are."

"Forget it, Maddy." Crystal peered through the bottoms of her coral-rimmed bifocals and eyed a drip on her cone. "The girl's not interested."

"Well, I don't know why not." Exasperation flitted over Maddy's sharp features. "He's handsome. He's rich. He's—"

"Breathing," Crystal completed for her.

Maddy's mouth pinched at her friend. "I was going to say that he's nice," she insisted. "You know as well as I do that Sam Edwards has a lot going for him. Tina's been gone over three years now, God rest her soul. It's time he put himself back in circulation."

Crystal frowned. "You make him sound like a newly minted coin."

Maddy pulled a napkin from the pocket of her bib apron and held it out before the drip could run. "I just mean that he's an eligible man with a lot to offer a woman," she explained, refusing to acknowledge her friend's jibe. "If T.J. isn't interested, then how about Ardeth Carlisle's niece?" Caught up with the prospect of a match, her whole expression brightened. "She's taking care of Ardeth while she recovers from knee surgery. I understand she has a great personality."

The subject—or maybe it was its direction—had T.J. glancing at her watch, then up the street toward the school. Maddy and Crystal could debate Sam's future. All she was going to do was tend his children. "The kids will be out in few minutes. I better go." She held up a small brown paper bag and smiled at the woman in the headache-inducing swirl of lemon and hot pink. "Thanks for the cookies."

"Glad to do it."

"See you later, Maddy."

"Before you go," the red-headed restaurant owner called, rising from her perch on the bench, "are the Benders going to close the bookstore this winter?"

"They're thinking about it. Maybe January and February."

"If they do, would you be interested in helping me on weekends? Lunch on Saturday and breakfast and lunch on Sunday? Mary will be quitting to go back to school winter term."

"Be glad to."

"And maybe a couple of shifts during festival week in December, if the Benders don't need you?"

Crystal took another lick from her cone. "You can't have her then. November and December is my time in Hawaii. She's watching the shop for me."

The quick frown on Maddy's face made it apparent that she'd forgotten that. How, T.J. had no idea. Crystal's trip to the islands had become an annual pilgrimage. At least it had for the past several years. According to the grapevine, she had a male friend over there. Crystal herself justified it by buying exotic flowers and herbs for her shop. T.J. was more inclined to believe it was simply the easiest way she knew to escape the holidays.

Crystal never had been much on celebrating them.

The throaty whistle of the afternoon ferry gave a long, low blast, announcing the vessel's impending arrival. That meant potential customers for Maddy.

With a smile and wave, the bag of cookies in hand, T.J. headed across the street and climbed into her reliable old Jeep. Crystal Walker was the epitome of contradiction. She always had been. The woman had stayed up last night to bake extra oatmeal raisin cookies so there would be enough for Sam's kids, but she wouldn't have baked a Thanksgiving dinner or Christmas cookie had her life depended on it.

Gears gave an unhealthy grind as T.J. shifted. Giving the dashboard an encouraging pat, she tried again and headed for the brick schoolhouse a few blocks away. She had suspected for a long time now that Crystal's avoidance of what she called "establishment culture" was probably why T.J. tended to go overboard on those very holidays with her son. Granted, they cut their tree from the woods and many of their decorations were homemade because working part-time here and there didn't leave much for extras, but from October on, there wasn't a room in her home that didn't reflect the coming season.

Like Crystal, T.J. supposed she was one with the seasons in her own way. Even now, because school had just started, her refrigerator was covered with red paper apples and bright yellow letters of the alphabet. She'd cut them out with the children last night and left a space for art.

Within five minutes of unloading Andy, Jason and Jenny that afternoon, the empty space on her fridge was covered with a picture of what looked like a fire truck, which Andy had drawn, and something green with legs, which Jenny said she'd made just for T.J.

The decidedly quiet Jason wanted to give his picture to his dad.

Sam was late again.

He had told T.J. that morning that he would pick up his kids by six o'clock.

According to the digital clock on the dashboard of his truck, it was 7:33 when he turned off the coast highway and bumped his way along the dirt and gravel road leading into the forest and T.J.'s place.

The need to hurry had his jaw working and his foot pressing on the gas pedal a little more than it should. Every pothole jarred his truck and rattled the windows.

In deference to his front end alignment, he made himself slow down, which only made his jaw work that much harder.

He'd radioed Zach from south of Stewart, Alaska, a few hours ago and asked him to let T.J. know he was running behind schedule. The vacationers were gone for the most part, but people in the more remote places they served were starting to stock up for winter.

That was why he was running behind tonight. After his regular mail run, he'd had to deliver supplies to a recluse living in the middle of nowhere, which had also meant bringing the guy up-to-date on everything that was happening beyond his own little world. Sam had been

glad to do it. He'd have been a whole lot happier about
it if he'd had more time, though. The old coot had
seemed starved for company. On the other hand, the man
had seemed just as happy to see him leave when Sam
had told him that he really had to go.

Tipping his head to get the kink out of his neck, he
turned onto a narrower road carved though the towering
firs. He'd felt bad for the guy. But he'd felt a certain
empathy with him, too. No one understood better than
he did how a person could come to seek isolation. He'd
done it himself after his wife had died, though not for
nearly so long.

A week alone with his grief was all he'd needed to
realize that he and his children didn't need everyone else
trying to decide what was best for them. His parents had
wanted him to sell his share of the business and move
back to Seattle. His father-in-law had pushed the idea,
too, because it meant he'd get to see his grandchildren
more often. But Sam had already lost part of his dream
with the death of his wife. He couldn't let go of the rest
of it by deserting the business he'd worked so hard to
build or by taking his children from the security of the
only home they'd ever known.

The rutted path opened up, revealing the neat little
house with its colorful flowers on the porch and his kids
perched on the steps. He'd been so grateful then that he'd
had Jason and Jenny to come back to.

He was grateful now.

He only hoped that the woman he could see backing
out of the storage shed didn't mind that he'd left them
with her for so long. T.J. had only watched his children
for two days, but both days he had been late. It didn't
matter that yesterday she'd known he would be. Or that
he'd warned her that it could happen at any time. It didn't

even matter that he would eventually reciprocate with flights for her animals. He'd felt the pressure all day of rushing to get his work done so he could get his kids home, fed and ready for bed. No way did he want her to think he was taking advantage of her.

Drawing a deep breath, he pulled to a stop behind T.J.'s geriatric Jeep and climbed out of his truck. He would apologize for not being there sooner, get his kids and go. If he was lucky, he could come up with something to feed them and have them bathed and in bed by nine, which would give him a couple of hours to work on accounts receivable before he fell into bed himself.

The sound of his door slamming echoed like a gunshot in the still evening air.

T.J. jumped at the sound, her nerves far edgier than usual. Because she expected Sam, her heart hadn't jerked with dread at the sound of a vehicle pulling up the drive. But there was no denying the heavy sense of caution she'd felt before she'd actually seen his truck and known for certain it was him.

A small part of her was growing more anxious with each passing day.

She hadn't heard a single word from Brad. Not a phone call. Not a note. No one had caught so much as a glimpse of him since the day he'd first reappeared, either. Still, try as she might, she couldn't shake the foreboding feeling that he could show up at any minute and totally destroy the sense of security she'd managed to find for herself and her child.

Aware of the relief she'd felt at the sight of the man pushing his fingers through his hair as he headed for his children, she was forced to admit that Brad was already messing with that hard-earned peace.

"Daddy! Daddy! Lookit what we got!"

Embracing a large roll of chicken wire, T.J. emerged from the storage shed at the side of the house. She could easily imagine Jenny's grin lighting her cherubic face as Sam crossed the shaggy lawn. From the enthusiasm in the child's sweet voice, she fully expected the affectionate little girl to launch herself at her dad to show him what had her so excited.

When T.J. reached the side of the house, she saw that Jenny hadn't moved. Still grinning, she remained seated sideways on the weathered step, her pink sweater hanging off one shoulder and her little body hunched over the new friend she held in her lap.

Jason, who had been so enthralled with feeding the animals that he hadn't even seemed to notice that his dad was late, sat on the top step next to Andy. Both boys wore jeans and sweatshirts that hit their knees. Both had tiny gray bunnies slung in the extra fabric.

All three were stroking, petting or grinning at the little balls of fur.

From ten feet away she watched Sam lean down, kiss his daughter's head and ruffle his son's hair. He'd just given Andy a quick smile and turned a skeptical eye back to the animals when Jenny pulled on the leg of his khakis. "We're baby-sitting."

"Baby-sitting?"

Jenny gave a vigorous nod.

"For the Muellers," T.J. supplied, walking up to the porch. "They're in Seattle for a few days so we're watching their pets. Mom's up there." With a nod of her head, she indicated the molded plastic-and-wire dog carrier on the porch. Inside, a large flop-eared rabbit contentedly chewed lettuce leaves.

Sam's glance cut back to the woman beside him. She'd put sweaters and sweatshirts on the kids because the evening air held a hint of chill, but she hadn't bothered with a jacket herself. The thermal knit T-shirt she wore over her loose jeans was pushed to her elbows. The only reason he noticed that was because her arms were wrapped around a large roll of chicken wire.

What he noticed most, though, was that she didn't seem at all concerned that he was late. When she smiled, she simply looked distracted.

Distracted himself by the need to get his kids moving, he offered a faint smile of his own. It came as no surprise to him that she also tended other people's zoos.

"Sorry I'm late." He would throw sandwiches together for dinner, he decided. And heat up canned soup. Cleanup would be minimal, which would give him more time on the accounts. "I'll get my crew out of here so I can get them fed."

"We had dinner right after Zach called. They already ate."

"Macaroni and cheese," Jenny informed him. "'N' applesauce 'n' carrots."

T.J. caught his eye. "You don't mind, do you?"

Mind? he thought. "Ah, no. Of course not."

Rubbing his nose with his sleeve, Andy turned to Jason. "Do you wanna see how far they can jump again?"

Jason was halfway to his feet, the bunny held protectively to his middle, when T.J.'s glance skimmed the night-time stubble on Sam's jaw. Fatigue deepened the masculine creases bracketing his mouth, the lines fanning from his eyes. He seemed every bit as preoccupied as he had been when he'd hurried in last night to collect his children. Hurried and anxious to be gone. That was why she felt certain from his faint scowl that he was about to tell his son there wasn't time for any more play when she walked behind him to get rid of her load.

It wasn't Jason's arm he caught, though. It was hers.

Chapter Six

The beat of small feet pounding down the steps underscored Jenny's impatient "Wait for me!" as she scrambled off after the boys.

T.J. barely thought to ask her to slow down, to remind her to be gentle with her charge. The moment Sam's big hand encircled T.J.'s arm, her breath seemed to stall in her lungs.

He stepped in front of her, his big body blocking her view of everything but his broad chest. "Where are you going with that?"

His hand fell, but his heat lingered, oddly intense and as penetrating as his eyes when they locked on hers.

Her heart bumped her ribs, throwing her even more off guard. There had been nothing personal about his touch. It had only been a means to stop her. And there was nothing in his eyes but curiosity and a faint scowl—

both of which were directed toward the three-foot-by-two-foot roll of chicken wire she carried.

The thing was actually more awkward than heavy. What made it difficult to handle was that she was also carrying an industrial-size staple gun and a screw driver.

"Just over there," she replied, still disconcertingly aware of his heat.

She had barely nodded to the sawhorses on the opposite side of the porch when she felt the weight of the wire being lifted from her arms.

"I can do this," she insisted.

"I'm sure you can," he murmured back. "Let go before I pull and you get scratched."

Her instinct was to hang on. She was quite capable of fending for herself. She'd been doing it for years. But the instant she realized that her glance had slipped to the carved line of his mouth, she let go.

More aware of him than she wanted to be, she watched his eyes dart to his children, who scurried past them both. She didn't doubt that he wanted nothing more than to get his kids home and crawl into his cocoon for a while. He was just uncomfortable with the idea of her carting such a load when he was around.

He was simply being a gentleman.

Disarmed by the thought that helping her came first, she watched him carry the bulky roll to where she'd been working. But instead of calling to his kids when he set it down, his brow furrowed more deeply at the large frame she'd built and the tools lying in the grass.

"What are you making?"

"An animal enclosure. All the big ones I have are full right now. In case I get something else, I want to have room for it."

"Wouldn't it be easier to build it by your shed so you wouldn't have to cart everything over here?"

"I couldn't see the children from the shed."

A delighted squeal went up from Jenny.

Sam's focus immediately shifted to the three children now playing in the middle of the lawn. He still looked perplexed.

"Are they all right with those rabbits?"

"They're bunnies. Babies," she pointed out. "They're harmless."

"You're sure?"

"I wouldn't let them play with them if I thought they could get hurt. Either the animals or the children." He'd spoken nearly those same words to her when she'd been so anxious about her son and Sam's airplane. Remembering his understanding, she quietly offered him the same option he'd offered her. "Would you rather they didn't?"

"I don't know. They've never been around animals like that before."

"They've never had a pet?"

"Tina wasn't big on them. It wasn't that she didn't like animals," he quickly defended. "Domestic ones, anyway," he amended. "She was just afraid a bigger animal from the woods might attack it...or hurt the kids if they were outside playing with it."

Her glance skimmed the noble lines of his profile. "That wasn't an unreasonable fear to have."

Her claim seemed to give him pause.

"Larger animals prey on smaller ones all the time," she continued, a shrug in her voice. "It's not like it couldn't happen."

His expression turned considering as he looked from where Jenny, Jason and Andy now sprawled on their bellies watching the bunnies hop in the grass. He hadn't seemed to expect her justification of his wife's attitude. Or, maybe, given T.J.'s lack of fear about animals, he hadn't expected her understanding.

"I don't suppose it was," he murmured, thoughtful. "She'd never been in a place like this before we moved here."

"She was from the city, wasn't she?"

"Yeah. She was." A certain distance entered his voice, shadowed his carved features. "She loved it here after a while, but she was really out of her element with the local wildlife."

Sam's glance skimmed the enormous trees isolating the little piece of property and the neat cabin-like dwelling nestled only yards away from the dense foliage. The woman he'd married would never have been able to live as this woman did, with the woods so close to the house. That was why their sprawling log home had been built in the middle of cleared acreage.

Tina had loved the idea of living on Harbor, the romance of it, he remembered her saying. She'd just had problems with some of the island's less civilized realities.

"I can sympathize with that," he heard T.J. murmur. "When I was in the city, I felt out of my element with the wildlife, too."

Her easy response had Sam glancing up. He'd been thinking of Tina, trying to picture how excited and apprehensive she'd been when they had first found their property. But the picture wouldn't form. He couldn't remember any image of her anymore that hadn't been captured in a photograph.

Mercifully, T.J. had canceled that disturbing thought with her comment. Just as he couldn't picture his children's mother living up close and personal with nature, he couldn't imagine T.J. surrounded by high-rises and freeways.

"You lived in the city?"

"Seattle," she told him, "for a year."

"Doing what?"

"Going to college," she replied. "Would you hand me that screwdriver, please?"

One of the bunnies must have pulled into the lead. The boys were chanting, "Go! Go! Go!"

At his son's unexpected enthusiasm, T.J. saw a faint smile tug at Sam's mouth. The expression eased the tension in his jaw, curved the corners of his beautifully molded lips.

Rather than be caught staring at his mouth, she turned her attention to the staple jammed in the staple gun. "Why don't you get a pet for them now? Something small that wouldn't mind being kept inside."

"Because it would just be something else I'd have to worry about taking care of."

He worried. She knew that. Unable to offer him anything that would alleviate that burden, not caring to question why she wanted to, she focused on her task—and the fact that he no longer seemed at all in a hurry to leave.

She didn't question why that was. She suspected she already knew, anyway, though he would undoubtedly eat ground glass before he'd admit it. He was lonely. With his children already fed, he now had a few minutes to kill. So, he was sticking around because talking to her was a way to avoid going home to a place that had to make that loneliness even more pronounced.

The staple popped free enough to work loose.

Sam's glance narrowed on her slender fingers. Her hands were small. Delicate, he supposed, and undeniably feminine despite the lack of polish on her short nails and the tiny nicks that marred her knuckles. They were soft, too. Remarkably so. He knew that because he couldn't forget the feel of her skin slipping against his when she'd shaken his hand. He couldn't forget, either, the feel of her strong supple muscles when he'd caught her arm and the silken feel of her flesh burning against his palm.

She would be soft everywhere.

The thought had him jerking his attention to the wire cutters she'd dropped on the lawn. Picking them up, he told himself he shouldn't be thinking such things about her. He should be collecting his children and going home. T.J. seemed pretty intent on getting her project finished before it got dark, and he really should get his kids home and into the tub.

Something inside him rebelled at the thought. For the first time all day, all year, he didn't feel compelled to act on what he should do. Though he sensed a certain restraint in T.J., she didn't really seem to mind him or his children sticking around a while longer.

More importantly, hearing Jason actually laughing, Sam simply couldn't justify leaving now. His kids were having a great time. It seemed unfair to take them home when they were so obviously enjoying themselves.

Wanting to believe he was only thinking of his kids, he eyed the frame again, checking out the joints she'd made, their perfect alignment and interlocking cuts. He'd known professional carpenters who weren't as meticulous about their work.

"Where did you learn to handle tools so well?"

"By watching Crystal." Taking the wire cutters from him, she handed him the edge of the chicken wire to hold. "She always seemed to be the only person around who could fix anything when I was growing up."

"In the communes, you mean?"

"We didn't always live in those." Wire parted with a series of sharp snips. Setting the roll aside, she lined up the yard-wide section she'd cut with one side of the frame. "There were times when it was just three or four people living in an abandoned house. Or a tent," she added, matching edges.

"You lived in a tent?"

"Sometimes. Would you hand me the staple gun?" she asked, only to see that he already had it.

"You hold," he said, coming up beside her. "I'll staple."

Because her palm was already raw from sawing with a dull blade, she gratefully stepped aside, allowing him the space he needed while she held the wire where she wanted it.

"What was it like?" he asked, sounding casual, looking curious. The staccato concussion of heavy staples being driven into wood punched through the peaceful air. In the woods beyond them, leaves rustled as birds flew at the sound. "Living that way, I mean."

"In a tent?"

"In any of those places."

She gave a dismissive shrug. "Mostly what I remember is people coming and going." Rather like the ebb and flow of the tide, she thought. Constant. Predictable. "No one ever stuck around for more than a few months. Or maybe it was weeks," she amended, since time had seemed to blur. "Especially the men. We would just get used to having a guy around, and he'd be gone."

"What about your father?"

"I never knew him." Her brow furrowed as she pointed. "It needs another staple right there."

The pop of the staple gun sounded again.

"So you never had a father figure?"

"I had a lot of them. Until I was ten or so," she murmured, moving the frame for him so he could get a better angle. That had been when she'd finally figured out that men were just going to move on when the spirit or boredom moved them, anyway. And that their leaving her behind hurt.

She'd stopped letting herself get attached after that.

"I guess that was when I figured I didn't need one," she concluded for Sam.

Sam watched her from the corner of his eye while she lined up another section of wire. There was a sort of hesitation about her that hadn't been there a moment ago. Not wanting her to get quiet on him, he shifted the subject in a safer direction.

"So where were these places?" he asked, beginning to see where her insight into his son might have come from.

Her hesitation dissolved. "The first place I remember was in Oregon. On Mt. Hood. But Crystal said we were near Astoria for a while first. I was too young to remember that."

One place had been in the mountains. The other along the northern Oregon coast. "You call her Crystal?" he asked. "Not Mom?"

"I call her both. She's not really my mother," she explained, her tone utterly unconcerned. "My birth mother was one of the women who didn't stay for long. She left when I was about a year old. I guess I was sort of community property for a while and when the camp disbanded about a year later, Crystal took me with her."

They had finished covering the small end of the frame. Reaching for the wire cutters and the chicken wire, T.J. set to work cutting a larger piece.

Sam simply blinked at the lovely auburn-haired woman handing him the loose edge of the wire to hold. "So Crystal adopted you," he concluded, his entire perspective of the older woman undergoing a radical shift.

T.J. gave a preoccupied little laugh. "She would never do anything that conventional. She just let me live with her."

"But how did you get into school? I couldn't even register Jason last week without his birth certificate and immunization records."

She would have just gone through that with Andy, too.

"She told the school that she was my mother, but that she never registered my birth, then applied for a certificate after that. As far as I knew, she was exactly who she said she was. She didn't tell me what had happened until I turned eighteen, and she knew the authorities couldn't take me away from her."

"And you're okay with that?"

"What's not to be okay?" The green of her eyes lit with a genuine smile as she looked toward the woods where her animals were settling in for the night. Her smile slid to her child playing with Jason and Jenny and their furry playmates, then to the treetops hiding the setting sun that left the sky streaked with fading shades of salmon and purple. "She eventually brought me here. To Harbor. Of all the places we lived, I liked this best. That's why I came back from Seattle." The frame caught her attention again. "It's why we stay."

He couldn't believe how easily she accepted all that had happened to her, how comfortable she seemed with having been uprooted from one spot to the next. Mostly, he couldn't believe what little rancor she bore toward the woman who had so blithely abandoned her.

"Have you ever tried to find her? Your birth mother?"

"I wouldn't even know how to look. She called herself Firelight." From beneath the fringe of her dark lashes, she shot him a wry glance. "I seriously doubt that was her real name. It was probably something more like Ann or Mary. Smith maybe," she continued with a shrug. "Or Jones. I guess no one knew her last name. All Crystal remembered is that she was small and had curly red hair and green eyes. For a while, after Crystal told me about my mother, I'd look at every redheaded woman I saw and wonder if she was her. I even wondered about Maddy," she quietly admitted, still fiddling with the wire, "except her hair is as straight as a stick, her eyes are a clear green, and she was born here, married her high school sweetheart straight out of high school, and they had four kids four years in a row. One of them is my age."

T.J.'s focus remained on the frame, but she felt herself hesitate.

Of all that she'd just told him, she had no idea why she'd confided that last part. She seldom talked about her childhood. Mostly because the subject rarely came up, and those who knew thought little of it. It wasn't something she guarded. Like the fact that Sam had great shoulders it just…was. But the lost, floundering feeling she'd experienced after Crystal had told her about Firelight was something she had never confided to anyone before.

Apparently, Sam had picked up on that little nuance. "Maybe I should rephrase my question," he suggested, quietly searching her face. "Did you want to try to find her?"

"No." Her tone held utter certainty. She felt no need whatsoever to face another rejection should the woman not want to see her. And Crystal, for all of her eccentricities and lack of maternal skill, had been as good to her as she'd known how to be. "I like my life here. I wouldn't want it to be any different."

The conviction in her voice was mirrored in the feminine lines of her face. But it was the conviction that gave her away. To Sam, that adamant note made it sound very much as if it wasn't him she was trying to convince of her contentment. She was trying to convince herself.

"No different at all?" he prodded, intimately familiar with that need himself. No one knew better than he did how important it was to keep up the appearance of having his life under control. It gave everyone else less reason to worry. Or interfere. Which was why he wasn't all that inclined to believe T.J. now.

"We have everything we need. We're fine just as we are."

"Even without Andy's father?"

At the unexpected question, her glance shot to his.

A blink later, she looked away. "Yes," she murmured. The restraint he'd sensed in her before reemerged, cloaking her in caution and robbing her completely of her charming, disarming ease. "My relationship wasn't like yours, Sam. Definitely without him."

Edging back, she carefully brushed off her hand. "You know what?" she asked, hoping to change the subject without offending him. "It's getting dark and the kids really should be heading for bed. I can finish this myself tomorrow."

"T.J. Wait."

She'd barely taken a step back in the grass when his hand shot out, catching hers to keep her from bolting like one of her deer. But whatever he was about to say was forgotten when she sucked a hiss of air between her teeth.

Sam's dark eyebrows slammed together with the swiftness of a thunderclap. Turning over her hand, he saw his thumb pressing a raw spot near her palm. The small patch of angry red skin slashed at an angle in the soft flesh below her fingers.

He immediately adjusted his grip. Beneath his fingers, he felt the quick tension in her slender bones and muscles as she subtly tried to tug away.

"What did you do?" he asked, refusing to let her go.

"I rubbed the skin off while I was sawing wood for the frame."

Eyeing the abrasion, he absently skimmed his thumb over her wrist. Beneath his touch, her pulse leaped.

Aware of that faint betrayal, his eyes met hers. He would let her go in a heartbeat if he thought she was at all afraid of him. But it wasn't fear he saw in those lovely green depths. It was caution.

"You should wear gloves when you work out here."

"I do. Usually," she amended, her glance faltering once more. "I couldn't find them."

Her untamable cinnamon-colored hair spilled over her shoulders. A spiraling lock of it curled against one cheek. With her hand cradled in his, he could feel the incredible softness of her skin and the almost hesitant way her hand began to relax in his. Relieved by that, he reached toward that long spiral and slowly nudged it behind the delicate shell of her ear.

Silk, he thought, trailing his fingers down its length. Her hair felt like spun silk.

The thought had barely registered when he realized what he was doing. Surprised by the unquestioned way he'd reached for her, he drew back and released her hand.

"You should go in and take care of that before it gets infected. And T.J.," he said, capturing her glance again,

"I'm sorry. About bringing up Andy's father," he clarified, because that was when she'd closed up on him.

He didn't understand this woman. He especially didn't understand how she slipped past defenses that would have been there with anyone else. But his kids seemed comfortable with her, and she had a way of making him forget everything else he had on his mind. At least for a while. He didn't want her upset with him. "That was none of my business."

From behind her, T.J. could hear Jason and Andy starting to argue over who was going to open the door of the rabbit hutch to put the bunnies inside. Ahead of her, she was aware of Sam's big body inches from hers. He was so close she could see each tiny hair in the stubble shadowing the hard edge of his jaw. Close enough that all she had to do was lean forward and he could wrap her in his strong arms.

The yearning to be protected, to be held, sneaked up on her too quickly to be fought. The gentleness of his unexpected touch had unleashed it before she could even begin to question why it was there. But the need no sooner hit than Sam stepped back as if to let her know he meant nothing by his touch or his concern. Nothing more than a little neighborly friendship, anyway.

Unprepared for what she'd felt, embarrassed by it, she called to the children and told the boys that she would put the bunnies back in the hutch herself. They were to sit on the porch with them until she got there. Jenny already lay on the bottom step, yawning, a bunny cradled against her.

"It's not that it's none of your business." She glanced back toward him, needing him to know that it hadn't been a matter of overstepping bounds that had disturbed her. Especially after the way he'd spoken so easily to her about his wife. "It's just that thinking about him..."

"Upsets you," Sam concluded when her voice trailed off.

Just the thought of the man seemed to put a knot in her stomach. Noting the protective way she'd crossed her arms, Sam moved with her as she took a step back toward the kids.

"Yeah," she murmured. "It does."

His glance slid from her arms to the lushness of her lovely mouth, the flawless skin of her cheeks. The feel of her was still on his fingers, her scent still working in his bloodstream. Touching her had been a mistake. Now, he didn't have to wonder if her hair was actually as soft as it looked. He knew. He knew, too, that something about her touched a part of him that had felt dead for a very long time.

"Then we won't talk about him unless you want to," he assured her. "Why don't you rescue the bunnies, and I'll get my kids out of here?"

Her hold on herself loosened when she told him that was probably a good idea, but the smile she managed before she turned and opened her arms wide to her son held a definite hint of strain.

That strain obviously had something to do with Andy's father. Sam just wasn't sure why it bothered him so much that it was there. He wasn't sure, either, who he could ask about the man without having to answer a lot of questions he wasn't sure he could answer himself.

Even if Sam had known some disinterested third party he could question about the man who'd fathered T.J.'s son, there was no opportunity for extracurricular conversations the next day. Or the rest of the week, for that matter. The Indian summer everyone had anticipated was still holding on Harbor, but up north winter was breathing down the mountains. In some of the more remote reaches E & M served, early snows made the need to stock up even more imperative for the isolated residents there.

Sam took his share of those runs, which kept him flying from sunup to sundown. His only day off was Sunday and he spent all of that fixing a leak in his kitchen sink, doing laundry and taking his children with him to the grocery and hardware stores.

When supper rolled around that night, frozen pizza was the best he could do.

By the time the kids were settled with their slices of "plain cheese 'cause pepperoni is icky," and he was folding the clothes he'd dumped on the couch, his desperation for a housekeeper was growing by the minute.

His whites were pink. His pinks—all Jenny's—were dingy. Probably, he figured, from washing them with his and Jason's jeans and sweatshirts. Except for eggs, he couldn't cook anything that couldn't simply be heated. And he'd rather row to Seattle in a rubber boat than have to face cleaning the bathroom again with Jenny trying to help.

He knew his sweet little girl meant well, and her innocent, triumphant smile had made it impossible to be upset with her, but every time he'd turned around she was squirting disinfectant spray on whatever surface he'd just cleaned.

Bedtime that night brought the worst. That was when Jason reached under his pillow and produced assorted pictures of cats and dogs.

He wanted to know if he could have one.

"T.J. said a cat would be easiest to take care of,"

Jason informed him, watching soberly as Sam sat down on the race-car-print comforter to study his son's magazine cutouts. "But she said cats are inda...inda..."

"Independent?" Sam quietly offered.

"Yeah. So a dog would be more company 'cause they like attention, and I can teach it tricks."

Sam had no philosophical objection to his children having a pet. Though he'd respected Tina's concerns, he had never shared them. He just didn't want an animal now.

"A dog would have to be housebroken," he gently pointed out, thinking that was absolutely the last thing he had time for. "And someone would have to clean up after it until it was."

Looking hopeful, Jason tugged his pajama top back onto his shoulder. "I'd do it."

"Housebreak it or clean up after it?"

"I can do both."

"Do you know how to housebreak a pet?"

He didn't even hesitate. "No. But I think T.J. does. She can help us."

"She can, huh?" The woman knew he didn't need anything else to take care of right now. Yet, she'd clearly encouraged his little boy. The cutout of the terrier was far too neat to be his son's handiwork.

A surge of annoyance tightened his jaw. For his son's sake, he immediately let it go.

He also promptly copped out.

"Why don't we talk about this after we get a housekeeper to stay here with us? The way things are right now, there wouldn't be anyone home during the day to care for a pet. It might get awful lonely while you're at school."

Jason's mouth twisted as if he knew there had to be a

way around that particular problem. But to Sam's relief, he seemed to accept the logic.

"Yeah," Jason murmured, looking far too understanding for a six-year-old. His quiet voice grew quieter still. "It would."

It killed Sam to deny that bit of comfort to his son. And comfort is probably what a pet would have been to him, he thought, wrapping his boy in a hug. He remembered T.J. saying that was what the animals she had played with as a child had been to her. Comfort and companionship.

Weariness settled like a blanket of lead on his shoulders. Guilt compounded the weight. He wanted to give his children everything he could, and if a pet would make his little boy happier, he would find a way to make the addition work. As he kissed Jason's forehead and tucked him in for the night, he just didn't know how he could handle anything else right now. There were times when he felt as if he were barely able to keep everything together as it was.

By the next morning, Sam was more than ready to trade his house-husband duties for the responsibilities of his job. He was also running late. There'd been a search for a shoe to conduct, which was why he didn't take the time to tell T.J. she could stop encouraging the pet thing. He figured they could have that discussion when he picked the children up that night.

But that was before he found himself facing the day from hell and animals became the last thing on his mind.

The downhill slide started within minutes of his arrival at the office. He'd barely taken his first sip of industrial-strength coffee from the pot brewed on the filing cabinet when Dave Walsh, one of their pilots, called in with a head cold so nasty he could barely speak between coughs. With his equilibrium shot because his ears were plugged and on medication that was putting him to sleep, Dave couldn't possibly fly.

Zach took part of Dave's runs. Sam split the rest with Chuck. That meant hustling, but it worked fine until shortly after noon when Sam's plane developed mechanical problems, which left him with two cranky passengers on Stuart Island breathing down his neck because they just knew they were going to miss the flight they were to connect with at Sea-Tac International in Seattle.

He jury-rigged the cable causing the problem and got them there, listening to them worry and fret all the way, then spent three hours tracking down parts and fixing the thing properly, which set him farther behind. That was when he'd called T.J. and told her it would be at least nine o'clock before he could get back. She'd told him not to worry about it. That she'd feed the kids and see him when he got there.

That thirty-second conversation turned out to be the one bright spot in his day. Because he was so far behind schedule, and so far from where he was supposed to have been by then, Chuck had to pick up his Vancouver passenger for him, which made Chuck late getting home but put Sam back on Harbor before nightfall.

It seemed that the Fates weren't through with him yet, though. He walked into the office, starving because he hadn't eaten anything all day, hit the play-messages bar on the answering machine and heard the voice of the woman he was to interview on Saturday.

He wrote down the number she gave him to call, then heard a pause on the tape before she said she supposed calling her back wasn't really necessary. She had decided to move back east with the family she was currently working for. She was no longer available for his position.

So much for the housekeeper and nanny.

"What's the matter with you?" Zach asked, walking in just as the paper with the nanny's number sailed in a tight ball toward the trash can.

Sam pulled a deep breath. Blew it out. He didn't even know where to start.

Tossing his flight log on the map-covered counter, his partner planted his hands on the hips of his khakis and met him eye-to-eye. "Hey, buddy."

"It's nothing." A muscle in Sam's jaw jerked.

Noting the indisputable sign of tension, Zach's eyes narrowed. "Did the plane give you more trouble?"

"It's running fine."

"Then, what's the problem? You know, Chuck really didn't mind taking that run, if that's what's bothering you."

"It has nothing to do with work. It's...." Everything else, he thought. "The baby-sitter," he concluded.

"What's the problem with T.J.? I thought the kids liked her."

"They do." They adored her. His son was even quoting the woman. "And not her. The live-in I had scheduled to interview. She flaked on me."

The big man frowning at him wasn't yet a father, but he was practically an uncle to Jason and Jenny and close enough to actually being a dad himself to have a fair understanding of how the care and feeding of little people could complicate one's life. He was also a good enough friend to suspect that there was more to Sam's discontent than he was letting on. The less Sam tended to offer on his own, the more troubled Zach knew he was.

"If the kids are getting along with her, why can't you just leave them with T.J.?"

"Because that arrangement is only temporary."

"You can't make it permanent?"

The glance Sam shot his friend was as dull as the finish on the floor. "I'm not going to ask her to stay at the house."

"Why not?"

"Because it would be asking too much of her." He also wasn't sure at all how he'd feel with her sleeping just a short flight of basement stairs away. "She's got her own work and all those animals to take care of and a son of her own to think about."

Zach paused, a glimmer of suspicion glinting in his keen eyes. "So you won't ask her to help you out because you're thinking of how hard it would be for her."

His tone was utterly flat with conclusion. There also was a catch to his phrasing. Sam felt sure of it. He was just too preoccupied with his immediate problem to figure out what it was.

"I won't ask her because she already said she wouldn't cook and clean for me," he muttered. "And she's only watching the kids now until I can find someone else," he reminded his friend, who was well aware of the terms of their arrangement. "She's not an option."

"You're sure."

"I'm positive."

Zach finally looked convinced. He also looked a little speculative as he gave Sam a supportive slap on the back. "It'll work out," Zach claimed, adding two more quick pats for good measure. "It always does."

Shoving his fingers through his hair, Sam drew another long breath. "Right," he muttered. "It always works out."

He was seriously thinking of adopting that phrase as his new mantra. For years he'd lived by the philosophies of the success-in-business gurus who preached strategy, determination, focus. According to those brilliant and distinguished minds, there was no obstacle a man couldn't overcome as long as he had a plan.

That, Sam decided as Zach headed for the door, was the crux of his problem. He'd had a plan, but it had shattered into a thousand pieces three years ago, and he had been prepared for little of what had been required of him since. The only plan he'd developed in the meantime was to survive from one day to the next.

The term "flying by the seat of his pants" had taken on a whole new meaning.

"I need to check out and refuel," he called out as Zach headed into the hangar. "Then, I'm going to get Jason and Jenny."

"I'll refuel your plane after I finish mine," Zach returned. "Check out now and go get your kids."

Chapter Seven

A curtain of white lace covered the window on the front door of T.J.'s weather-grayed house. In the lemony glow of the porch light, Sam watched that filmy fabric edge back and a slice of T.J.'s face appear behind the clear glass. As agitated and preoccupied as he was, the only reason her expression registered was because the obvious caution in it struck him as so odd. He'd never seen her look so apprehensive.

It seemed as if he'd barely blinked, though, before that trepidation gave way to relief, the curtain swayed back into place and the door opened with its usual faint squeak. The delicious scent of cinnamon greeted him along with her welcoming smile.

"You're earlier than I thought you'd be," she told him, stepping back to let him in. "I already fed the kids. They're in Andy's room watching a video."

She took another step into the room, wiping her damp

hands on a pale-green kitchen towel as he closed out the evening chill. She definitely favored clothes that concealed, he thought, eyeing her baggy brown coveralls and long-sleeved beige T-shirt. She also seemed to favor green. He'd noticed the latter the first time he'd stepped into the comfortable, almost tranquil space.

A large, healthy ficus tree dominated the corner by the lace-curtained front window. In front of that paned glass, fringed pillows of ivory, verdigris and sage covered a thick beige futon. Emerald leaves dominated the botanical prints on the pale cream walls. Even the old trunk that someone had refinished and made into a coffee table, her probably, he figured, had been stained the deep shade of woodland moss. A beautiful clay pot swirled with the misty green of the sea, sat atop her bookcase.

She had brought the colors of the outdoors inside, surrounding herself with nature in a way that seemed to suit her perfectly. There was a calm almost serene feel to her home. He'd noticed it the first time he'd come in to pick up his children.

He found that he noticed a lot about her, whether he intended to or not.

"Are you okay?" he asked.

Surprised by the question, or maybe it was the concern, she looked up at him curiously. "What makes you ask that?"

"The way you looked before you opened the door. Like you were afraid of who you'd find on the other side."

"Oh." Her glance faltered. The man was beyond perceptive. Because she'd expected him to be much later, that had been exactly how she'd felt when she'd heard his knock. "I'm fine," she concluded, because she was desperately trying to be.

Trying, but not succeeding. She thought she'd seen Brad only a few short hours ago, and she had been mentally holding her breath ever since.

A tall blond man had been leaning against one of the gnarled old spruces near the playground when she'd picked up the children from school that afternoon. She'd noticed him watching the kids as they'd funneled out of the double doors and into waiting cars and the community's two school buses.

As far away as he'd been, she hadn't been able to see his face clearly, but there had been something about his long, lanky body and the lazy way he'd leaned against the tree that had seemed far too familiar.

There hadn't been a single red Jaguar in sight. And she knew whoever it was hadn't followed her because she'd checked her rearview mirror every ten seconds all the way home. Still, she hadn't wasted any time calling Maddy the moment she'd unloaded the kids and settled them on the porch with a snack.

Maddy hadn't seen him. Nor had she heard of anyone who had.

Crystal hadn't seen him, either. And neither woman had noticed his flashy car, which would have stuck out like a cherry in a bowl of vanilla ice cream when it had come off the ferry.

"Like I said," she concluded, wondering if paranoia hadn't finally settled in, "I just didn't expect you so soon."

A muscle in Sam's jaw jerked as he lifted his chin. He seemed to accept that he'd simply caught her off guard. He also seemed as agitated as she felt when he glanced toward her son's room.

Because she'd seen him do it before, she fully expected him to swallow his tension for his children's sake and do what he'd done the other nights he'd come to pick them up: go in, give them a hug and tell them it was time to go.

Instead he stayed right where he was and plowed his fingers through his dark hair. He looked as if he were ready to pace up the nearest wall.

Preferring to focus on his agitation rather than her own, she did the neighborly thing and motioned toward her kitchen. "I just brewed chamomile tea." Crystal swore the herb was soothing to the nerves. T.J. had brewed a double batch. "Would you like some?"

His eyebrows merged. "Actually, I'd prefer a double of anything with a burn to it, but I have to drive."

"Rotten day?"

"I've had worse...but it wasn't the best," he admitted, understating considerably. "The woman I was to interview Saturday about taking care of the kids decided to keep her present job."

"Do you have any other prospects?"

"Not a one." He jammed a hand into his pocket. "It wouldn't be so bad if it were this time next month," he said, verbalizing what had been eating at him all the way to her house. "I'll only be working thirty or forty hours a week by then, and it would be easier to keep up with everything."

He could probably even manage the house on his own, he thought, though he seriously doubted he'd ever master laundry. It wasn't as if sorting was for sissies, but the inability to get whites white had to be a guy thing. Not that he'd ever talked to another guy about it.

"I'd still have to take them somewhere during the day, and I don't know what I'd do if I got stuck somewhere," he said, "but at least I could handle the bulk of it until I can find someone else."

She flipped the towel over one shoulder, the airy gesture cutting him off even as she cut in. "Don't worry about it," she said with her disarming, dismissing ease. "They're getting along fine here. Jason would be disappointed if he didn't get to help feed the animals, anyway. He adores anything with fur."

His problem solved, she headed for the kitchen, bending to pick up a few stray Lego pieces on the way. "As for taking them somewhere else when your hours ease up," she continued, snapping the pieces onto a car one of the boys had created, "that's not really necessary. It would be easier on them if they kept staying with me before and after school, don't you think?"

It would be infinitely easier, he thought. Especially after the way his son had reacted when he'd first brought him to her. "You would do that?"

"For Jason and Jenny?" she asked, setting the car atop the stone fireplace mantel. "Of course I would. My hours have already been cut back at the bookstore, so I have more time now than I did before. Jenny doesn't even have to stay both sessions at preschool, unless you want her to. She could just do regular half days and spend the rest of the time with me."

Sam could hear cartoon voices coming from her son's bedroom as he blinked at T.J.'s retreating back. All the way over, he'd tried to think of how to approach the problem with her. Since hedging wasn't his style, he'd figured he'd just lay it out and hope he could convince her to keep watching his children until he could run more ads and find someone else.

But just like that, she'd stepped in, solved the problem and moved on. She hadn't even hesitated, he realized, only to remind himself that she apparently never did when it came to such decisions. When there was a need she could fill for a child or an animal, it didn't occur to her not to help. She simply jumped in and did it.

"How much do you want? A week, I mean. I'm going to pay you for this."

"No, you won't. All I want are more flights."

"You already have five."

"I have six," she corrected, reminding him that she'd kept the kids for him Saturday. "I want as many more as I can get. It's flights or the deal is off," she declared, and disappeared around the corner.

The children, variously sprawled on the comet-and-star-covered bedspread and the big blue rug on the floor, were so absorbed in their show that they didn't even notice him when he walked past the doorway and followed T.J. into her brightly lit kitchen.

He hadn't been this far into her home before. The walls were the same cream as the living room. The curtains, the same cotton lace. But the cheerful space with its sunshine-yellow cabinets and herbs hanging above the sink was unbelievably small. There was barely enough room for the well-used stove and ancient refrigerator, much less the little round table and two wooden chairs beside the window's bench seat.

As narrow as the area was, he felt big and a little awkward when he came to a halt beside the only counter in the room. Leaning a hip against the five-foot-long strip of ivory Formica, he debated pressing his point about the money and watched to see which cabinet she was headed for so he'd know which way to move.

She had a chunky, brown-and-blue pottery teapot in one hand when she reached past his left shoulder for two matching mugs.

"I cut this room in half," she said, sounding apologetic when he had to move down another foot. "That's why it's so small.'' The earthenware clunked against the well-scrubbed counter. "I needed an inside work area, so I closed in the dining space back there. Do you like honey or lemon in your tea?''

He never drank hot tea. He had no idea how he liked it.

"Sure,'' he said, not nearly as willing as she was to change the subject.

She had clearly moved past the child-care issue. He hadn't. He knew how she felt about her animals, but practical was practical. It wasn't as if she couldn't use the money, he thought, checking out the water stain on the ceiling where the roof had leaked. He doubted there was much of anything in her home that hadn't been repainted, refurbished, bought used or made by hand. Even the old relic of a Jeep she drove looked as if it was running on nothing but hope.

"What you said about having more time,'' he began, reminding himself that a practical argument would pretty much be wasted on her. "How far back did they cut your hours?''

"I only work weekends, now that the island isn't so busy. The bookstore is closed on Monday and the Benders handle the rest of the week. It's only open six hours a day now.''

"What do you do during the week?''

The tang of lemon perfumed the air as she poured golden liquid over the slices she'd dropped into the mugs. The cinnamon scent he'd noticed when he'd first come in drifted from a pile of crisp cookies that had cooled on wire racks.

Seeing what held his attention, she nudged the rack toward him, silently inviting him to help himself.

"You know how slow things are on the island during

fall and winter," she replied, stirring honey into his tea from a clear plastic bear. "There isn't much to do unless you have your own business or can run one from your computer. I use that time to work on my pottery and ship it to the stores that sell it over on Orcas and Lopez. And I fill in for Mom at her store and at the café."

His glance shifted to the teapot, the mugs. He'd forgotten about her pottery.

"Did you make those?" he asked, nodding toward the beautifully shaped and colored vessels. Azure blue swirled like the aurora borealis against a glazed background of mocha and bronze.

"This was a line I did a couple of years ago. Plates, mugs, serving pieces. I think I'll just do art bowls and pots again this year. I make more from them."

But barely enough to make ends meet, he thought, marveling at what she could create out of little more than a handful of clay. "So you make your pottery and take odd jobs," he concluded.

Looking as if she sensed a trap, she cautiously handed him a mug. "Pretty much. No one thing I do brings in quite enough, but everything together give us all we need. Besides," she felt compelled to mention, "I like the variety."

She truly did like the diversity her jobs provided. She and Andy really were quite comfortable. There was nothing of any consequence that they didn't have. She was providing her son the home she'd never had, permanence, a stable life. She had a place for her animals, enough money to feed and care for them and by caring for Sam's children, who needed stability, too, she had a means to get them veterinary care after the vet was gone.

She had the feeling Sam didn't see her life the way

she did, though. As he glanced around the tiny, admittedly modest space, she was afraid he only saw the lack.

He opened his mouth, undoubtedly ready to question her eclectic way of making a living, only to promptly close it again.

"What?" she asked, fully prepared to point out that she wasn't the one getting ulcers over how to juggle children and a job. Granted, he made far more than she did. More than she ever would, for that matter. But she and Andy didn't need a house as large and expensive as she'd heard his was. They didn't need lots of clothes. Or vacations. Or a new car. Not as long as the Jeep kept running, anyway.

As quickly as his frown had come, his brow relaxed.

"How were the kids today?" he asked, reaching for a cookie.

"They were fine." With her fingers wrapped around her own mug, she stepped back to the stove, leaving four feet of the linoleum she'd laid herself between them. "They even ate tofu burgers without gagging on them. But that's not what you were going to ask."

Half of the cookie was already gone. Preparing to wash it down, he watched her through the steam rising from his mug. "It wasn't?"

"No."

His frame seemed to take up a lot of space as he shrugged, sipped and the other half of the cookie disappeared. His *presence* seemed to take up a lot of the space, she thought, as he reached toward the rack again.

"In case you were thinking of pushing the point, I don't need your money," she insisted, more aware than she wanted to be of how he seemed to dominate everything around him. With his compelling features lined with character and experience, his carved jaw shadowed, he looked powerful, rugged and utterly, completely male.

The alpha, she thought. The unquestioned leader of the pack.

"I really can't think of a single thing we need that we don't have."

His glance pinned hers. "Not a single thing, huh?"

"No."

Half of another cookie disappeared. "If you insist, I believe you."

"Don't do that," she muttered, as the other cookie went the way of the first.

"Don't do what?"

"Try to placate me about the money. You don't believe I don't need it."

"I just said I did."

She didn't look convinced.

"Okay," he finally conceded. "I was wondering why you didn't get child support. But if I'd asked, you'd have to think about Andy's father and I didn't want you to do that." He lifted his mug in salute. "Great cookies."

Disbelief vied with something that made her chest feel a little tight. He truly didn't believe she was making it as well as she could. But he'd kept himself from pushing to protect her feelings.

"Thank you," she murmured, partly for the compliment, mostly for his consideration. She couldn't remember any man ever being that thoughtful of her. "But he's been on my mind a lot lately, anyway."

Her mug settled with a dull thump on the stove a moment before her arms snaked around her middle. No matter how hard she'd tried, she hadn't been able to get Brad off her mind at all. He was there more and more, preying at the periphery, robbing her of her sense of safety, robbing her of sleep.

Feeling helpless, hating it, she hesitantly glanced to where Sam remained, carefully watching her. She had no idea what went on in the male mind that made one man love his child and another pretend his child didn't even exist. If she could understand, then maybe she wouldn't feel so anxious. But to understand, she needed answers. And Sam was the only male she felt close enough to to ask. Desperate, it didn't occur to her to question what she'd just admitted to herself. Her voice lowered to nearly a whisper. "Can you tell me why a man would ignore his son for years, then suddenly show up wanting to know about him?"

Unprepared for the nature of her question, Sam said nothing. For a moment he simply watched worry wash over her fragile features while she tightened her arms around herself.

"After how many years?" He matched her quiet tone. "Did he ever have visitation?"

The overhead lights caught glints of garnet and ruby in her curls as she shook her head. "He's never even seen him." Unless, she thought with an inward shudder, that had been him today. "He left before Andy was born."

Sam glanced toward the open doorway. As occupied as the children were with their video, he seriously doubted they were being overheard. His kids, Jason especially, totally zoned out when glued to the television. He wasn't sure about Andy, though.

With his mug in his fist, Sam walked over, picked up T.J.'s mug and nodded toward the table. Without a word, she sat down in the chair he pulled back for her at the small disk of pale oak and clasped her hands on its shining surface. Wood quietly scraped against linoleum as he pulled out the other chair and lowered himself opposite her.

"You said he's shown up again. Is he here? On the island?"

"I don't know if he is now. He was here a couple of weeks ago. The day I came to see you about flying lessons," she explained. "I didn't even know he'd been here until Maddy told me the next day. She and some others saw him. And I thought I saw him today," she said uneasily, "but neither Maddy nor Crystal did, and Maddy sees nearly all the cars that come off the ferry."

"He's not an islander," Sam concluded, understanding now why there'd been such a difference about her the day he'd seen her at the bookstore.

"He lives in California. At least, that's the return address on the letters I've been getting. His family owns a winery in the Napa Valley."

Sam watched her rub her thumb over the top of the other one, the restrained motion restive.

He couldn't imagine abandoning a child of his own.

But he couldn't have imagined T.J. ever turning to him, either.

Unexpectedly touched by the fact that she had, he wrapped his hands around his mug, resting his forearms on the table. As small as the table was, his fingers were only inches from hers. "Do you want to start at the beginning?"

"The beginning as in when I first got the letters from him? Or the beginning as in when we met?"

"Whatever you're most comfortable with. But the beginning as in when you met might help explain what's going on now."

Focusing on his reasonable, practical tone, T.J. took a

deep breath. "Okay," she murmured, letting it out. "It's just been so long…"

"How old were you?" he asked.

"Nineteen."

"And you were where? In college?"

He was going to make it easy.

"I'd just come back after finishing my freshman year," she said, grateful, "and decided I was never going back to the city. Brad had just arrived for the summer from UCLA and decided he was never going back, either."

"He was dropping out?"

"Oh, nothing like that," she murmured, remembering the passion he'd had for his project. Seemed to have, anyway. "He was the son of a wealthy vintner. Who was also the son of a vintner," she recalled, though she had no idea why that detail mattered. "Brad had been groomed from the time he was a child to follow in his family's footsteps. But he didn't want to make wine. He wanted to save the whales. So he'd changed his major from viticulture to oceanography without telling them. When they found out at graduation, his family pitched a fit, and he came here to do the research for his master's degree."

Brad had told her that his family was controlling and narrow and that he didn't care what they thought of his choices. Since she knew little of what family was supposed to be, she hadn't seen where he would be losing anything of any consequence by walking away from them. She didn't mention that to Sam, though. She simply told him that she'd thought Brad's goal to save a part of the environment at the expense of his inheritance enormously noble.

She also told him that Brad had stayed on Harbor that

summer long enough to do his research, have her type his master's thesis and get her prcgnant before admitting that he'd never actually informed his family he wasn't joining the family business. He also told her that he was moving back to the mainland.

"I'd thought he was going to complete his master's program and return to Harbor," she quietly told Sam. "But he never said anything that night about coming back. Not even after I told him I was going to have his baby."

She frowned at her ragged cuticle, worried it with her fingernail. "All he did was try to talk me into having an abortion. When that didn't work, he denied being the father and left the next day." With the tip of her finger she smoothed the cuticle down. "I hadn't heard a word from him until he wrote a few months ago wanting to know if I'd had the baby."

Her voice was calm as she spoke, her account deliberately devoid of the devastation she'd experienced at the hands of a man she'd obviously trusted. But the sense of betrayal and abandonment she felt was still evident to Sam as he watched her focus on her work-scarred hands.

What her child's father had done was cowardly, irresponsible and totally inexcusable. Yet, incredibly, he couldn't detect a trace of accusation or anger in the young woman across from him. As he considered how Brad's betrayal would have compounded the insecurities inflicted on her by her birth mother—and all the other adults who had wandered in and out of her life—what he sensed in her most was fear.

"What kinds of things did he ask in the letters?" He could see now just how badly her sense of trust had been battered. Except for the decidedly eccentric Crystal, there didn't seem to have been anyone in her life that she'd ever been able to count on to be there for her. "What did he want to know?"

"Whether I'd had a boy or a girl," she softly replied. "If I'd married. Where the child went to school."

"What did you tell him?"

"I never answered." She hesitated, her already quiet tone dropping even further. "I didn't answer the letter that came a few weeks ago, either."

Something uneasy shifted through him. "What did that one say?"

"He knew by then that I'd had a boy. He said the least I could do was send him a picture."

Her fingers were still threaded together, her thumb rubbing the other one again. As Sam sat watching her, he wanted badly to believe his only concern was for how her problem might affect her care of his children. But he couldn't swallow that lie any more than he could deny the stirrings of protectiveness he felt when her glance lifted to his.

"I just don't understand why he's come back after all this time," she admitted, her luminous eyes beseeching his. "All Andy knows about his father is that he left before Andy was born. I don't want my son hurt if all Brad wants is to meet him to satisfy his curiosity, then disappear from his life again. But I'm not about to start sharing Andy, either, if that's what Brad has in mind."

Sam leaned closer and nudged his mug aside. As small as the table was, he'd barely have to reach to touch her. Seeing how anxious and bewildered she was, instinct had him doing just that.

"I'm sure you don't," he murmured, absently lifting his fingers to skim her knuckles. "But it could be that the guy got an attack of conscience and just wants to make sure his child is being properly provided for."

With his eyes on hers, he slowly traced the same path back. "You're doing a terrific job with Andy," he assured her, over the drip of the faucet and the cartoon voices filtering in from the other room. "He's a great kid. All anyone has to do is see the two of you together to know you're doing an amazing job."

Her quiet "Thank you" was barely audible as she lowered her gaze.

His touch was making her uncomfortable. He felt certain of it. Fearing she might pull away, not wanting to add to the discomfort she was already feeling, he drew back. "That would be the best case," he continued, clutching his mug again. "Worst is that he wants visitation rights."

Her head snapped back up. "But he has no right—"

"I'm not saying it's fair. I have no idea what a court would decide about what he's done. But there's a practical side to this. You can probably get child support. If his family has that much money, you'd at least have medical insurance and Andy's college taken care of." He paused, considering her circumstances. "You don't have insurance, do you?"

His tone was more conclusion than query. Still, she shook her head. There were a few things they did do without. But Andy was healthy, and she did everything in her power to keep him that way.

"I don't want his money."

"I know." Just like you don't want mine, he thought. "You want to be independent of him." Of any man, he would imagine, considering her history with them so far. If she didn't count on a man, a man couldn't fail her— as everyone who'd been in her life apparently had. "I don't blame you," he assured her, edging back further.

Without even thinking, T.J. felt herself lean forward

as he withdrew, only to catch herself and draw her hands closer to her body. She couldn't believe how badly she craved the support she'd felt when he'd touched her. Couldn't believe how much she wished he'd just hold her.

Afraid to let herself want anything as badly as she wanted his touch at that moment, she made herself stay right where she was.

"Maddy thinks he might have shown up out of guilt," she confided, all too aware of how Sam had pulled away, "and that he wants to do right by his son."

The twinge of protectiveness tightened Sam's tone. "I would hope so."

"But Crystal thinks he's just curious and that he'll disappear just like he did before."

If Crystal's experience with men was anything like T.J.'s, Sam thought, he could see where the woman might believe that. He seriously doubted that would happen, though. Especially if it had been Brad that T.J. had seen today. A man didn't come all the way from California just to catch a glimpse of his child, then return home. From the request in his last letter, and the fact that he knew she'd had a son, it didn't seem as if he was ready to crawl back under his rock. It sounded to Sam as if Brad were gathering information. Either himself or through an investigator.

Sam saw nothing to be gained by sharing those particular conclusions. T.J. looked troubled enough as it was. She sounded it, too, when she drew her hand through her hair.

"I just wish I could shake the feeling that I'm about to lose control of everything."

The anxiety shadowing the beautiful green depths of her eyes was almost tangible to him. He seemed to have no control over the way she drew him in, demanded that he feel when numbness had served him so well for so long. The need to make her anxiety go away was as undeniable and as real as anything he'd felt in a very long while. Yet, he couldn't do what he wanted to do and tell her everything would be all right. He had no way of knowing that, no way at all of predicting what her flake of an ex-boyfriend might do.

"I know the feeling." It was the best he could offer. "I wake up with it nearly every morning."

She glanced at him, looking desperate to know his key to survival.

If he'd had one, he would have shared it, but he didn't get a chance to tell her that. His daughter was walking through the doorway.

"Do you have *Little Mermaid?*" Jenny's tone was half query, half whine as she frowned down at the video case she carried. "All the boys want to watch is *Shrek.*"

With her bottom lip protruding enough to trip on and her high ponytail listing to one side, she glanced up.

Seeing the big man slowly rising from his chair, the pout vanished like stars in sunlight. "Hi, Daddy!"

"Hi, sugar."

His daughter flew at him, wrapping her little arms around his leg as he moved toward her. He had barely bent to pick her up when his son and Andy wandered in, both complaining that Jenny wouldn't give them back the video they wanted to watch before Jason noticed his dad was there. The child gave him a big smile. Since Sam never left Andy out of his greetings, he smiled, too.

Within seconds videos were forgotten and both boys were wanting to know if they could have another cookie. Not to be left out, Jenny wanted one, too.

"They've each had at least three," T.J. said to Sam,

leaving him to make the decision, since the majority of the kids were his, and headed for the closet to get the jackets and backpacks. The clock on the stove indicated that it was already the children's bedtime. She'd had no idea they'd talked for so long.

When she returned with her arms loaded moments later, all three children were chewing, crumbs were falling to her freshly swept floor, and Jason was going on a mile a minute about how he got to help release the doe and her fawn into the woods that afternoon.

"The doe is all better now, and they need turf before it snows."

"They need what?" Sam asked, reaching for his son's jacket.

"Turf," Jason dutifully repeated.

"Need to establish their turf," T.J. gently clarified, slipping one of Jenny's arms into her little turquoise sweater. "They'll probably hang out around here for a while, then work their way into the forest." A sad little smile touched her mouth. "We're going to miss them, but it was time for them to go."

"They eat berries 'n' leaves," Jason supplied, switching hands with his cookie to free his other arm. "And they can run really fast."

"How about you tell me more on the way home?"

Jason beamed.

"See you tomorrow, buddy," Sam muttered to Andy. He mussed the boy's chestnut-colored hair the friendly way he always did, then held his hand up, palm out.

Andy, loving the male attention, grinned back and gave him a high-five.

With the kids surrounding them and the hour growing late, there wasn't much else for him to do but usher his children toward the door and offer his usual "Thanks."

"You're welcome," she replied, following with Andy beside her. "And thank you."

His eyes caught hers. "I didn't do anything."

He wished he could have, though. He wished there were some way he could make her believe that her life would be as stable and secure as she'd managed to make it before Andy's jerk of a father decided to show up again and steal that sense of security from her.

No one knew better than he did, though, that it only took a second for a life to change. Someone could reenter a person's life. Someone could be taken away. Once that happened, nothing was ever quite the same.

"Yes, you did," she murmured. "You listened. I guess I didn't realize how much it was on my mind." Apology entered her tone, shadowed her smile. "But I won't bother you with it again. I promise."

"It wasn't a bother."

"Still…"

Her voice trailed off as she shrugged.

She felt she'd imposed somehow. Or maybe, he thought, now that he was leaving, she felt uneasy about having turned to him. Either way, she was doing what he suspected she'd learned to do very well. She was pulling away, pulling in.

With his kids tugging him toward the door, there wasn't much he could do to stop her.

Chapter Eight

"Good. I see you're wearing your stone." Crystal, resplendent today in shades of crimson and canary, flipped her long graying braid over her shoulder and nodded at the rock T.J. wore over her long black sweater. "You keep wearing it. I did your chart this morning, and your moon is in a new phase."

T.J. shook her head at the woman stocking bead bracelets behind the counter of The Herb Shoppe and Video Store. Crystal knew that T.J. didn't believe in horoscopes, tarot cards, tea leaves or any of the other mysticism her aging flower-child mother had delved into over the years. But it was a waste of breath to remind Crystal of that. The woman was who she was. She would do what she would do.

T.J. couldn't imagine Crystal any other way.

"You know, it might not even be my phase," T.J. mused, smiling as she plopped her denim bag on the counter. Her charges were behind her, searching for the perfect video game among the racks. "We don't know for sure when my birthday is. You made up June twenty-fifth."

"It was an educated guess," Crystal informed her. "You had the traits of a moon child and that's the date the sun enters that sign. Just keep in mind that the phase you're in right now could bring change," she continued, completely undaunted by logic. "What you've been doing all along may not be the right thing for you now."

T.J. wasn't sure what to think of that. Doing what she'd been doing was the only way she knew to survive.

"It's about growth," Crystal said, catching T.J.'s expression over the top of her half glasses. "The alignment of your planets suggests that something significant is about to happen. It could be good or bad, depending on how you view it." Plastic crackled as she shook a dozen blue power bracelets from their packing sleeve. For Longevity, the labels dangling from each wrist-size circle claimed.

"Instead of just letting it happen, it might not hurt to take the initiative yourself and do something to influence the direction of that change. Take the bull by the horns," Crystal added, untangling the lot, "so to speak."

With Crystal's head bent, T.J.'s glance narrowed suspiciously on the part in her hair. "This 'bull' wouldn't happen to be Sam, would it?"

"Might," Crystal replied, her tone surprisingly noncommittal. "Might not. I still think there's a reason your paths converged, but it looks like there are actually several males who could affect you right now."

A hint of unease slithered up T.J.'s back. She didn't believe this stuff. She truly didn't. And the phase Crystal had just described could have fit anyone at any time.

Odds were that half the people they knew were facing some sort of change in their lives. As for whether whatever was going on was good or bad, T.J. had always believed that a person's attitude directly affected their circumstances.

She wouldn't mention her skepticism, though. This was Crystal's way of taking care of her. The woman T.J. had always thought of as her mom would never say "I love you" or offer to fight T.J.'s battles. Independence was like a religion to Crystal. But she would do T.J.'s charts, give her the proper stone to wear for protection and keep a cookie jar filled for Andy.

"Speaking of Sam," Crystal muttered, now putting price stickers on the bracelets' brand tags. "I hear he's fogged in up north somewhere."

"Where did you hear that?"

"Maddy heard it from Mavis who got it from that skinny fellow who works for E & M. Chuck, I think is his name. Mavis took some packages over to have flown to her daughter on Orcas, and she heard someone call in on the radio. When she asked who it was, he told her it was Sam. Fog must be pretty nasty up there." She nodded toward the kids. "Guess that means you'll be keeping them tonight."

It certainly sounded like that was going to be the case. Sam had warned her that there would be times when he couldn't always get back from wherever he'd gone. Weather in this part of the country was always unpredictable. Especially farther north. Most especially with the approach of winter.

Crystal's sharp glance settled on T.J.'s face. "You don't look too pleased with the prospect," she observed, her tone low and curious.

"I'm fine with it." With a smile to prove it, she reached for her bag. "Andy will love the company."

"Then why did you look so disappointed?"

Because that was how she felt, T.J. realized, then lifted her shoulders in a shrug. "I didn't know that I did," she hedged, seeing no point in admitting it. "I was just thinking about the clothing situation. Jason can wear Andy's clothes to school tomorrow, but I guess I'll have to wash out Jenny's."

Pure speculation moved over Crystal's face. "You weren't thinking about clothes," she muttered, and mercifully let the matter go.

The woman was far too observant. Though T.J. had denied to Crystal any feeling of disappointment, she couldn't deny the dispirited feeling to herself. Until that moment, she hadn't realized how much she'd looked forward each day to seeing Sam.

There was something vaguely threatening about that realization. But simply looking forward to seeing someone meant nothing, she assured herself. After all, she knew better than to get attached to a man. She had only turned to Sam about Brad last night because he was a father himself. If she was feeling close to him at all, it was only because of his children.

"There's no way I can get out of here tonight. The airports are closed. Even commercial flights out of Anchorage are grounded." For as far away as Sam was, the connection was amazingly clear. The frustration in his deep voice rumbled over the line, as tangible to her as if he'd been standing six feet away. "I don't know how Jason's going to deal with this. He's never stayed overnight anywhere except at his grandmother's and his aunt's."

T.J. tucked the phone under her chin as she reached into the grocery sack she'd just brought in. "He's doing fine. He and Andy are thrilled with the idea of a sleep-over."

The crackle of the brown paper melded with the confusion in his tone. "How did you know the kids would need to stay with you?"

"I heard from Crystal that you weren't going to make it back tonight. She got it from Maddy, who got it from Mavis, who heard it from Chuck."

"The Chuck in my office?"

"Apparently."

For a moment the workings of the local grapevine met with nothing but silence.

"Then you and the kids are all right with this?" he finally asked.

You and the kids. The way he said it made it sound as if he worried about them all just the same.

Not about to let herself believe that he was actually concerned about her, she shoved the milk into the fridge and focused on his offspring. "Don't worry about the children. They'll be fine here. Do you want to talk to them?"

He said he did. So she called Jason to the phone first. Then Jenny. Then Jason had to talk to Sam again because the little boy needed to hear one more time that his dad would be back tomorrow for sure.

"I told him I'd be there as soon as the fog lifts," Sam told her when she took the phone again. "I didn't promise him exactly when because I have no way of knowing that for certain, but according to the reports, this should clear by afternoon. I'd appreciate it if you'd reassure him for me tonight," he told her, sounding as if he truly wished he could have offered more reassurance himself. "Maybe give him a hug from me? Jenny, too?"

His earnest request tightened her grip on the phone. "Of course I will." The children had already lost one parent. Sam didn't need to explain it for her to realize that his son, especially, worried when his dad didn't come home when expected. "Is there anything else?"

She was thinking of the children, of the rituals or routines they might have that would be of comfort to them sleeping in a strange place.

"Yeah. There is. How about you? How are you doing?"

Her grip grew tighter. "Me?"

She could almost hear the frown in his voice. "You sound surprised that I'd ask."

She was. Surprised, and uncertain about why he was doing it.

I am, she started to admit. "I'm fine," she told him.

"You haven't seen Colwood again?"

There had been concern in his voice as they'd spoken about his children. It was still there. Only, now it was for her.

"No. No," she repeated, craving that concern, desperately afraid to trust it. "Everything's fine."

"Are you sure?"

"Positive."

Standing between the twin beds in the Moose Jaw Motel with their ancient orange-and-brown-striped bedspreads, Sam frowned at the wall. Specifically, at a starving-artist-quality painting of a trout. He didn't doubt her assurance as far as his children were concerned. But he seriously questioned her assessment about herself.

He wouldn't push her, though. Despite everything she had told him last night, she had been careful to let him know that she didn't intend to impose her problems on him any further. She was accustomed to handling her life on her own. His concern wasn't necessary.

He supposed he should appreciate that. He had enough to worry about with his job and his kids, without worrying about her, too.

With that thought he finally thanked her for keeping his children for him and told her he would see her tomorrow. Yet, as he hung up, the concern was there, anyway. The protective walls he'd surrounded himself with for the past three years were nothing compared to those she'd built around herself.

He would pick up Jason and Jenny and go.

It was six o'clock in the evening, relatively early compared to the usual time he arrived to pick up his kids. Because he hadn't seen his children since yesterday morning, Sam wanted to give them a little extra attention tonight—maybe take them to Pelican Pizza and play the game machines with them. They would like that.

Letting out a long breath, he cut the truck's engine and reached for the handle of the door. He would have had a lot more enthusiasm for a night out with his kids had his mind and his mattress allowed him any rest last night. Had anyone asked what he really wanted just then, he would have told them nothing more than a hot shower and bed. The one he'd attempted to sleep on at the motel had felt like a sack of stones with a canyon in the middle.

Telling himself not to think about it, he climbed out of the truck and headed for the empty porch. When no one answered his knock on the door, he automatically headed for the woods.

He found his son inside a cage big enough for a cow, carefully filling dented pie tins with kibble from a coffee can while Andy lugged a bucket of water toward a small plastic tub. Occupied as he was, Jason barely seemed to notice he was there. His muttered, "Hi, Dad," indicated far more interest in the little raccoons chittering at his feet than the parent he hadn't seen since yesterday.

Jenny was crouched low a few yards away, poking nuts through chicken wire for an injured squirrel. She didn't come running to him, either. She just demanded that he come see what she was doing.

Rolling his shoulders beneath his heavy navy sweater to relieve the kinks in his neck, he dutifully crouched beside his little girl to watch as instructed. He was feeling a little thrown by their lack of interest in his presence when he heard T.J.'s soft voice behind him.

"Hi," she murmured, a twig snapping beneath her feet as she walked up the path. "We didn't know if you were going to make it back this evening or not." Continuing toward him as he rose, she tossed an empty pet food can into the wheelbarrow and gave him a hesitant smile. "I'd heard the fog was still pretty heavy up north."

"I found a hole in it." His glance skimmed the exquisite lines of her unadorned face as he pushed his hands into the pockets of his khakis. Realizing he was looking for signs of strain, not sure what he'd do even if he detected them, he jerked his glance to the dolphin on her Save the Sea Life sweatshirt. "Thanks for keeping the kids for me last night."

"I was glad to do it."

"Were they all right?"

She moved a few steps from the children, absently stroking the foot of a bunny in a hutch on the way. "Jenny was fine," she quietly said as he followed. "She had a couple of rough minutes just before bedtime, but

I let her sleep with me. Jason did better once Andy let him share Cat.''

Sam glanced back to his offspring. Both seemed blissfully content with the little zoo. It wasn't what they were doing that had his attention, though. It was the tug of guilt T.J.'s solutions had brought.

He already knew that his daughter never seemed to have a problem latching on to whoever took care of her. It seemed that she found her comfort in whoever was willing to offer it. His son, on the other hand, seemed to be withdrawing from just about every adult in his life and was now finding solace in things furred and four-legged.

Neither thought spoke of a secure and well-adjusted child. Neither evoked much confidence in his parenting skills, either.

A muscle in his jaw jerked. He needed to get Jason that pet. But all he could do for now was give his children his time. ''I'll take them for pizza before we go home.''

A flash of something that looked almost like disappointment washed over T.J.'s face. An instant later she glanced away.

''I'm sure they'd like that,'' she murmured.

That wasn't what she'd been about to say. Sam was sure of it. But he barely had a chance to wonder why that disappointment was there when Jenny poked her head between them.

''Not pizza, Daddy.'' A frown wrinkling her button nose. ''We already fixed dinner. It's like spaghetti. But it's not.''

Sam looked down at his daughter. He was totally puzzled. Not by what Jenny said, though he hadn't quite gotten that either. But by her choice. His children never turned down a chance to go out for pizza. Never.

"It might be easier for you if you stay," T.J. suggested, knowing for certain that it would be. It could have been the shadows, thick as they were in the trees, but the lines bracketing his mouth looked deeper to her, his eyes weary. Still, she assured herself that she was thinking mostly of the children's efforts. Not of his need for a break. And not of how much safer she felt whenever he was around. "It's almost ready. I didn't know when you'd get in, so I'd planned to feed the children. They helped make it."

His eyes narrowed. "It's not tofu is it?"

"It's eggplant parmesan with linguine."

"I picked it!" Jenny beamed a smile at her dad. "The plant and the tomatoes."

"Eggplant," T.J. gently corrected, smoothing her hand over the child's ponytail.

"Yeah, 'cept it doesn't have a yolk. An' it's purple. An' Andy 'n' Jason got to stir the sauce."

T.J. thought for certain that she would finally see Sam's smile. It was so rare that he didn't have one for his children. But his focus didn't seem to be so much on his child as it was on her. Specifically, on the way she absently stroked his daughter's hair.

Her hand moved slowly from Jenny's crown to the end of her short, curling ponytail. The motion was unconscious, a sign of the very real affection she was beginning to feel for his precious little girl. She had found herself smoothing her hand over Jason's head, too, on the rare occasions he would allow it, just as she so often did with Andy. Something about what she was doing, though, deepened the rugged lines of Sam's face, narrowed his eyes, creased his brow.

Slowly she pulled her hand away.

Jenny didn't notice a thing, but Sam did. The moment T.J. crossed her arms, his guarded eyes met hers. She couldn't tell if it was discomfort or disapproval she sensed in him. Either way, what she'd done definitely disturbed him.

Uneasy with the thought, unable to imagine why he wouldn't want her to care about his child, she watched him crouch down in front of his daughter.

"You helped make dinner?" he asked her.

With him at her level, Jenny nodded. "T.J. let us."

He nodded toward his son. "Jason, too?"

Her head bobbed once more.

Sam blew a long, low breath. He wanted to leave. T.J. felt certain of it.

His smile, reluctant as it was, finally emerged.

"Then, if you kids fixed it, I guess we'd better stay."

Jenny grinned at his agreement and promptly whirled around to finish the chore she'd been assigned. The boys were already outside the cage. Andy carefully latched the door to keep the raccoons from running out after them. Jason diligently put the coffee can he carried into the feed sack, rolled the top of the sack down so the oats wouldn't spill out and started dragging the garden hose back toward the house.

Sam rose, knees cracking, and watched his children go about the tasks. Both were clearly comfortable with what they were doing. More important to him was that they both seemed utterly content.

They were the way children should be, he thought. The way they would have been if they'd had their mother to do the sort of things T.J. did for them. A mother who let them pick vegetables in the garden. Who let them help her in the kitchen. A mother who would have let them

know by her touch and her presence that they were cared
for, secure. The way T.J. had when she'd stroked Jenny's
hair.

Sam wasn't sure why he'd been so struck by what
she'd done. As he reached for the wheelbarrow himself,
all he knew for certain was that he didn't want to think
about the nurturing his children had missed. There was
nothing he could do to change the past. The best he could
do was deal with the present.

"Where does this go now?" he asked, thoughts of the
past nudging at him, anyway.

"Into the shed," Jason told him.

The chores with the animals were almost finished.
Within minutes all that remained to be done was to re-
wind the hose and for the kids to pick up the baseball
and bat they'd played with on the lawn. Sam actually
wished there had been more to do. Something physical
that would have required concentration.

It wasn't often anymore that he let himself think about
what his little family's life would have been like had
Tina survived. But despite his best efforts to push away
the thoughts tonight, the natural way T.J. had with his
children made them impossible to avoid. The reminders
were everywhere as he watched her check the children's
hands after they'd washed, sending the boys back with a
rueful smile to do a better job. She washed Jenny's herself before handing the little girl napkins and eating uten-
sils and showing her where to set them on the table.

From where he leaned against the doorway of the
small kitchen, he watched her hovering over the children,
serving the plates, fixing his. The tantalizing scents of
tomatoes, thyme and oregano filled the air. Her smile
warmed the room. But when she motioned to the stools

she'd pulled up to the counter for the two of them, he felt himself taking a mental step back.

There was too much about the scene that was too comfortably domestic. Too much that suggested a family that...wasn't.

Glancing to where he hung back from the activity, she offered an apologetic smile. "I know it's kind of crowded in here," she admitted, adding extra linguine and sauce to his plate. "Maybe you'd rather eat in the living room?"

She was clearly thinking in terms of space.

He was thinking more in terms of escape.

"It's nice outside. Do you mind if I eat out there?"

"Not at all." With one eye on the boys, who were dangling linguine beside their chairs for Cat, she handed him his plate. "Just come back in if you want more. Andy? Jason? Keep your dinner to yourself. You don't eat mice, and Cat doesn't eat noodles."

"Eeeww, gross." Jenny dropped her fork onto her plate with a clatter. "Cat eats mice? Like Mickey?"

"Yeah." Andy nodded, lifting his noodle to dangle it above his mouth. "Snakes do, too."

Jenny gasped.

"How about we change the subject?" T.J. suggested.

"Maybe I'd better stay."

The look she gave him clearly questioned why that was necessary.

"Only if you want to," she told him, rather wishing he would go. The tension in his big body seemed to leak toward her, making her even more aware of him than she already was. "I've got this covered."

"Can I eat outside with you, Daddy?"

Nerves knotted, she grabbed for Jenny's plate as the little girl lifted it.

"I've got it." Sam took the plate himself, waited for Jenny to gather her napkin and her fork and let his little girl lead him to the front door. "It'll be easier if we separate them. I'll take her with me."

T.J. swore she felt her shoulders drop when the screen squeaked and slammed shut a few moments later.

She was accustomed to him being a little uptight when he first arrived. She had even come to expect a certain amount of strain in his smile and had thought time and again how truly devastating that smile would be if he ever really let it go. But, tonight, from the moment he had noticed her stroking his daughter's hair, there had been a distance about him that he hadn't been able to mask. Not even with his children.

She had the uneasy feeling she knew why that distance was there, too. Every time she'd glanced toward him, she'd found him watching her. It was almost as if he'd weighed everything she'd done, the way she acted toward his children, the easy way they acted toward her. As she picked at her own dinner while everyone else finished theirs, then sent the kids off to wash again while she cleared their dishes, she felt almost certain that Sam feared his children were growing too close to her.

Seeing no point in waiting for him to bring it up, not entirely certain he would since she was his only option at the moment for child care, she tossed the hand towel on the counter and headed for the door.

Jenny raced in as T.J. headed out, and disappeared into Andy's room where the boys had gone to build a fort.

Sam remained on the top step, kneading the muscles in the back of his neck, his feet planted wide on the step below. From the way he dropped his hand and reached for his and Jenny's plates, it appeared he was getting ready to come inside, too.

At the faint squeak of a board when she stepped onto the porch, his head jerked up.

"Leave them," she asked, slowly crossing the weathered planks. "I'd like to talk to you for a minute."

The sun had already set behind the trees, robbing much of the light from her patch of the woods and turning everything shades of gray. In those deepening shadows, she saw him frown.

"Is there a problem?"

"Not for me." Another board squeaked as she sat down on the step beside him. Crossing her arms against the faint evening chill, she warily met his eyes. "But I have a feeling there is for you."

He didn't even blink before he looked away.

That lack of denial spoke volumes.

"You know, Sam," she began quietly, "anytime you have a concern about what's going on with your children here, you should talk to me about it."

A quick frown flashed over his brow.

"I really like Jas and Jenny," she admitted. "I think they like me and Andy, too. But you don't need to worry about them getting too attached to us...if that's what's bothering you. I know how hard it has to be for them having people come and go. But we're not going away once you find your housekeeper. We'll be right here. They can come and play and feed the animals any time they want. And I hope you'll let them," she said, truly meaning it. "They will always be welcome."

For a moment Sam said nothing. The nature of T.J.'s concern had never occurred to him. Even after she had made him realize what was probably going on with his son because of the women who had come and gone from his life, he had never considered her to be one of the women who would leave.

He had no idea why that was. All he knew when he turned to see her toying with the frayed threads at the knee of her jeans was that he found it reassuring to know she wouldn't be leaving his life, either.

"Thank you," he said, touched by her sensitivity to his children. He was drawn, too, by how she'd sought to reassure him. "But I really wasn't worried about that."

"You weren't?"

"No."

"Oh." Looking puzzled, and maybe a little self-conscious, she barely murmured the word.

"I was thinking about the kids, though," he admitted, figuring he owed her at least that much. "I've never known them to turn down pizza."

Her soft smile held sympathy as she flicked at the frayed threads again. "They worked hard on dinner."

"I know. Jenny went into great detail. I didn't realize making their own meal could mean so much to them."

"Children love to help."

"I guess I don't do that many things I figured they could help with."

"That's why we have to teach them." She lifted a thread, smoothed it down. "I figure they can help with just about anything that doesn't involve sharp edges, fire or heights."

She sent a glance toward him, clearly pondering.

"I imagine it's a lot harder for you raising children alone than it is for me."

"Why?" His brow furrowed as he met her darkly lashed eyes. "Because you're female? Or because I have two kids and you only have one?"

"Because you were married and had a partner to share it all with," she replied easily, turning her focus back to her knee. "It has to be far more difficult with that taken away. I've had Crystal, and she's great," she explained, tugging out one of the threads, "but I've never had a real partner to share anything with. I'm used to doing everything all on my own." Her shoulders lifted in a shrug. "I'm not sure I'd even know how to share," she mused. She hesitated a little at the thought. "I don't have a clue what a good marriage is supposed to be like.

"Anyway," she murmured, getting herself back on track, "that's why I think it has to be harder for you. You did have someone. And from what I hear, your marriage was as good as they come."

The glow of the porch light had grown brighter as the light of the day continued to fade. The trees were black sentinels now, the color of their silhouettes nearly indistinguishable from the night closing in around them. Leaves rustled as an animal settled in somewhere for the night or a nocturnal creature ventured out. A lone cricket, a holdover from summer, called from beneath the steps.

Sam was barcly aware of the sounds. Caught unprepared for T.J.'s observation, it was a moment before he heard himself murmur, "It was."

"Maddy says that people who've been in good relationships are more likely to marry again than someone who has come out of a bad one." That didn't leave much hope for her, she thought, but at least he had a chance. "Maybe you'll find someone again."

He shook his head, the motion slow but certain. "I can't imagine ever having a relationship like I did with Tina. It's not like it was perfect," he admitted, to himself as much as to her, "but it was as close as it gets."

Close to perfect. T.J. couldn't begin to imagine what that sort of relationship was like.

Drawn as much by that unknown as she was by the

quiet note in his voice, she murmured, "What made it that way?"

For a moment she didn't think he was going to answer. Fearing he thought she was prying, afraid that she was, she started to apologize for asking. She didn't want to resurrect something he didn't want to think about, something that might hurt.

She'd just opened her mouth when she heard him say, "She did."

Another moment of silence passed. "She was a special person," he said, his voice low and thoughtful. "She was always going out of her way to make sure everyone felt comfortable. She remembered birthdays and anniversaries and everyone's favorite color. She cared about people," he concluded, "but she never took herself all that seriously. Even when she'd get frustrated with herself, she would laugh about whatever it was she'd done."

She sounded awfully nice, T.J. thought. She knew Tina had been. But T.J. also knew of a lot of nice people who'd wound up in truly lousy relationships.

"What else made her special to you?"

The thoughtful note turned quieter.

"She needed me."

From the corner of his eye, Sam saw the motion of T.J.'s fingers still for a moment before she went back to smoothing the threads. She would understand that need to be needed, he thought. It wasn't something he would admit to anyone else, but with her it was surprisingly easy. After all, she shared it. Whether she admitted it to herself or not, that need was undoubtedly part of why she couldn't say no to any animal or child she could possibly help.

"It was everyday stuff," he explained, aware of the nicks on T.J.'s knuckles. "She wasn't at all mechanical.

And she was constantly forgetting things so I would have to go and rescue her.''

He'd been her white knight, T.J. thought. ''What kind of things?''

''Keeping gas in the car, for one.'' Noticing the long scrape on her index finger, Sam reached over and absently touched beneath it. The light abrasions had been fresh the last time he'd seen her. They were healing now. ''And her keys,'' he remembered, carrying his touch below the next scratch. ''I can't count the number of times she locked them in her car. Or in the house. She lost the extra ones I kept at the office, so I finally gave Zach a set so he could help her if I wasn't around.''

T.J.'s voice sounded quieter, almost cautious. ''With two kids, she probably had a lot on her mind.''

''She was like that even before the kids were born. Always preoccupied with a dozen different things.'' Remembering, he shook his head and slowly traced soft skin to the base of short nails. ''She was involved with everything. The community. Her job. Her friends. And surprises,'' he said, the memory surfacing over the others. ''She loved planning surprises.''

His palm settled over the back of T.J.'s hand, his fingers still moving up and down hers. He'd forgotten about Tina's surprises until just then. As he followed the motion of his hand, he realized his children wouldn't be able to remember them at all.

''That's something Jenny and Jason don't even know about her.''

''Then you need to tell them.''

''Jason doesn't ask about her anymore. Jenny never did.'' He slowly shook his head. ''I don't know how to keep the memory of her alive for them anymore.''

The rhythmic call of the cricket filled T.J.'s considering silence. When she spoke, hesitation filled her voice. "Are those memories all still alive for you?"

The slow caress of his fingers faltered, only to resume with his contemplative frown. Memories were like feelings, he supposed. Some had faded and grown less detailed in their recollection. Just as some feelings had lost the sharpness of their edges.

Over the past three years he had learned that he could get through each day by thinking only of the next minute, because thinking of the next hour without her was too painful. He knew that he could wake up in the morning without first reaching toward the empty space beside him. And that even when he did wake with that void in his chest, he'd learned that the feeling wasn't going to kill him.

"I can remember the sound of her voice," he finally said, "but I can't remember her laugh. When I picture her now, the image I see is the one of her and the kids on my dresser."

"Maybe that's not such a bad thing," she suggested softly. "If all memories stayed fresh, a person would never be able to heal and move on."

Time heals.

He'd heard the phrase a thousand times. And a thousand times, he'd dismissed it as a platitude invented by someone who couldn't possibly know what he'd lost. There had been a time when he'd felt certain there weren't enough hours in creation to make the pain go away. Yet, as he sat beside T.J., surrounded by the sounds of the night and the melodious laughter of children drifting from inside the house, he knew that with the passage of time he truly had learned to live without the woman he'd married.

There was sadness in that realization—and an odd kind

of hope. Considering the wisdom in T.J.'s observation, he might have told her that, too, had he not just glanced toward her.

Her head was bent, her thick hair tumbling over her shoulders as she looked at their hands. Hers rested on her knee. His covered it, his thumb gently brushing the delicate bones below her wrist.

The unconscious motion stopped.

He couldn't remember when he had reached for her, but from the way her self-conscious glance lifted to his, he had the feeling she'd been aware of his touch far longer than he had.

Drawing back his hand, he clasped it with his other between his knees.

"I'm sorry. I can't believe I just told you all that."

He couldn't believe, either, how easily he'd sat there going on about one woman while thinking how soft another woman's skin felt. Or how much comfort he'd felt simply touching T.J. as they'd talked. When he'd touched her the other day, offering his support when she'd told him about her son's father, she had seemed uneasy with the contact. Yet when he'd needed the comfort himself, she had allowed his touch, for his sake.

"Please, don't apologize," she murmured. Tucking her arms around her middle, she gave him a forgiving smile. "I needed to talk about Brad the other night. You needed to talk about your wife. I guess we both just needed for someone to listen."

He had the feeling she didn't confide in people any more often than he did—and he rarely mentioned what troubled him to anyone. It hadn't been often that he'd even mentioned his concerns to his wife. As sensitive as Tina had been, she would get upset if she thought he didn't have a handle on everything. Instead of feeling better after confiding a problem to her, he would wind up having to assure her that there really wasn't a problem at all, that he had the answers, that all was under control.

Keeping his worries to himself had simply become habit.

Keeping her worries to herself was probably how T.J. kept from appearing vulnerable.

But she was. He could tell every time he touched her.

"Are you saying you want to call it even, then?" he asked.

"I suppose we could."

He didn't get the chance to consider if he wanted them to be even or not. The pounding of feet on the living room floor preceded the screech and bang of the screen.

"The boys won't let me play in the fort."

"It's no girls allowed," Jason informed his sister.

"Yeah," Andy echoed behind them. "It's a club."

"Sounds like it's getting close to bedtime," T.J. murmured. "Don't worry about the dishes," she said to him when he reached for his and Jenny's plates. "I'll take care of them while you get Jason and Jenny together."

It was time to go home. The thought held little of the appeal it once had, but Sam didn't let himself think about why that was as he rose beside her. With Jenny sulking and Jason starting to pout because he didn't want to leave, Sam's only thoughts should have been on getting the kids to cooperate. Instead, watching T.J. pick up the plates herself, he was thinking about the scrapes on her hands and the package in his truck that he'd all but forgotten.

"Did you find your gloves yet?" he asked.

"Not yet," she replied as he held the screen door open for her.

"Hang on," he muttered, and jogged down the porch steps.

He was back a moment later, instructing his children on his way through the living room to get their school things together and go get in the truck.

"Here," he said, laying a small sack on her cluttered kitchen counter. She was at the sink, a plate in one hand, the other on the faucet handle. "I bought these for you the other day. Okay, kids," he called, turning back to the living room. "Say goodbye. We're out of here."

It seemed like less than a minute to T.J. before Jenny had hugged her knees and the clamor of feet and voices gave way to the quiet of her dripping faucet.

"Lock the door," she called to Andy, wiping her hands.

"I already did," he replied, walking into the kitchen to pick up the sack. "What did Sam get you?"

Curious herself, she took the bag her son held out. Paper crackling as she opened it, she peaked inside and pulled out his gift.

"Oh," Andy said, totally unimpressed.

"Oh," she echoed, more impressed than she wanted to be.

He'd bought her gloves. The heavy, industrial kind with canvas backs and leather palms.

Something warm bubbled up in her chest. She hadn't received a gift from a man since Brad had given her a half dozen yellow roses for typing his thesis. And as gifts went, Sam's was hardly romantic. But it was practical. And thoughtful.

Because it was thoughtful, because he had been thinking of something she needed, it touched her far more than she should have let it. She was already guarding herself where Sam was concerned. But as she fingered the heavy fabric, she knew that if she wasn't even more careful, she could start caring for him in ways that could only lead to disappointment.

She was already starting to trust him, she realized, and that was something she hadn't done with a man in more years than she could count. But trust was only there because he had no ulterior motives where she was concerned. She'd known from the beginning that his interest in her was only as the caretaker of his children. After listening to him talk about his wife tonight, she knew that if he wanted anything else from her, it would only be friendship.

Chapter Nine

Sam crossed his living room with the telephone receiver tucked against his shoulder and dumped a load of freshly dried jeans and sweatshirts on the sofa. Jason and Jenny were in bed. As soon as he folded the clothes, he would head in that direction himself. In the meantime he was on the phone with his mom, returning the call he hadn't had time to take when she'd caught them walking in the door a couple of hours ago.

"I tried to call last night," she told him, "but I kept getting your answering machine. Lauren told me that the housekeeper you'd planned to interview canceled on you."

"She did," he confirmed, digging for matching socks.

"That's too bad," his mom murmured. "So," she continued easily, getting back to her other observation, "where were you last night? Did you take the children out for dinner?"

With a black sock in one hand, a blue in the other, he tossed them both onto the back of the sofa. He could have sworn his mother would have had more to say about the canceled interview. At the very least, he thought she would ask if he had anyone else in mind. "I got fogged in up in Alaska."

A pause filtered through the lines. "Where were Jason and Jenny?"

"With T.J."

"She kept them at her place?"

"They did fine, Mom. They like her. I told you that."

"Aren't you looking for a live-in anymore?"

"I'm still running ads, but I don't have any prospects yet."

"So you're still looking for someone else," she concluded.

"Yeah, Mom," he murmured, smoothing out a pair of small purple denims with legs the length of his forearm. As concerned as he knew she was about him not having a housekeeper, he'd felt certain she would get back to the subject sooner or later. "I'm still looking for someone else."

"I don't suppose you've given any thought to what I suggested?"

"That depends on which suggestion you're talking about." Every time he talked with her she had a new one.

"About dating again," she reminded him.

Matching up inseams, he didn't even hesitate. "I don't have the time."

"And you definitely aren't going to move back here?"

Sam hesitated. He hadn't thought a thing about the nature of his mom's questions. Next to his sister's pregnancy, her grandchildren were her favorite topic, so she'd simply sounded like her normal, conversational self. Yet, as he set aside Jenny's pants and turned from the rest of the load on the sofa, he began to suspect more than simple grandmotherly interest in her queries. It wasn't at all like his mother to move from one of her suggestions to the next without defending them along the way.

"I'm not moving to Seattle," he confirmed, realizing that she'd just run through his list of options. "Why?"

For a moment he heard nothing on the line. Just a long warning pause that told him she had come up with something else for him to consider.

"Well," she began, sounding as if she intended to present her idea as gently as possible, "after Lauren told me about that interview, I got to thinking about what we might be able to do to help the three of you. Your father and I know how hard it is for you raising those babies. And we know you're trying to give them as stable a life as you can. But you haven't been able to find full-time help for a while now, and it doesn't seem likely that you will soon."

"Why doesn't it?"

"Because you've been through nearly everyone there, dear. Even if you do manage to find someone else," she continued, her tone utterly reasonable, "how long will it be before that one moves on? Or you discover that she isn't good with the children, and you find yourself looking for someone all over again?

"I'm thinking of Jason and Jenny," she explained, "and what would be best for them in the long run. That's why I think they should come live here. At least with us, their care will be consistent."

In the three years since Tina had died, Sam had seldom cared for any of the ideas his mom had come up with for the care and feeding of his family. But he wasn't at all prepared for what she'd suggested this time. The thought of sending Jason and Jenny to live away from him struck at the very heart of everything he'd tried to do for them as a family. He took no time from them that wasn't necessary. Everything he did, he did to keep them together.

Defense moved into his voice, adding an edge he tried his best to mask. "Their care is consistent right now."

"Sam..."

"It is," he insisted, trying not to be angry. "I'm here in the evenings, and we're together on weekends." They would be together on weekends soon, anyway.

"You weren't there last night," she pointed out. "They were with a stranger."

"T.J.'s not a stranger. The kids have known her for a long time." He took a deep breath. T.J. was right. It was harder for him raising kids alone than it was for her. She didn't have to deal with his mother. "Their staying with her last night was no different from them being here with a housekeeper."

"Who would also be a stranger."

"Only until they got to know her." The edge of defense slipped through. "Are you going to do this with Lauren when she takes her baby to daycare?"

"She has Zach," she replied, failing completely to see his point. "I'm only trying to help, Sam. You're a single father with a business that requires almost all of your energy and attention."

"Things slow down in the winter. You know that."

"But what about next summer?"

She didn't know what she was asking. He was only now looking ahead a few weeks at a time, instead of a day or an hour. "I'll worry about next summer when it gets here."

"That's only a matter of months."

"My kids belong with me," he told her, cutting her off before she could truly argue her point. "And they're doing okay," he assured her, wanting badly to change the subject. "I'm even thinking about getting Jason a dog. He really wants one."

"Oh, Sam, do you know how much work an animal is?"

He released a beleaguered sigh. Dropping the pair of pants he held, he decided that the clothes could wait. He'd just dump them all back in the dryer in the morning to get the wrinkles out.

"You know," he muttered, "I think I hear Jason calling. He probably wants a glass of water."

"He'll wet the bed if you give him too much."

Plowing his fingers through his hair, Sam headed for the end table to hang up the phone. "I know, Mom," he said, forbearance dripping from his tone. "I've got to go. Say hi to Dad for me."

"Sam, please don't do that. It's just that I worry," she reminded him. "About both you and the children. I thought this might be easier for you."

The faint plea in her voice tugged at his conscience. The past few years hadn't been easy for any of them. "I know you worry," he assured her. "But I've got it covered. Okay? Thanks, anyway," he muttered, and quietly added, "good night."

He didn't know if his mother said goodbye or not before he set the receiver back on its base. All he knew for sure was that there wouldn't be much of anything he could say to her that she wouldn't find fault with. He really couldn't deal with that right now. He was having a hard enough time believing he was still doing his best for his children.

Because of T.J., he knew what the transience of care-givers could ultimately do to his son's sense of trust.

Because of her, too, he was beginning to see that it hadn't been his children's needs that had wedded him to the idea of them being taken care of only in their own home. It was his own.

They were far more adaptable than he'd wanted to think. He was the one clinging to the familiar.

The thought had him sinking to the sofa. The home he'd built, his life on the beautiful rugged island, the business he'd nurtured all these years. Those had all been part of his dream. Not theirs. He had clung to his dreams, too, finding comfort in them, finding purpose and escape. But just as he'd had to let go of the life he'd known with the woman he'd married, maybe it was time to start letting go of the rest of it, too.

Maybe, for his children's sakes, he needed to rethink what his mom and dad had first suggested: that he sell his share of the business to his partner, get a job with regular hours with a major airline and move back to where his kids could be close to their grandparents.

The thoughts added a sense of futility to his frustration and put a knot the size of a fist in his gut. As much as he hated the thought, he knew he could no longer close the door on that option. Despite what T.J. had said about her always being there for his children, he hardly expected her to help him raise them.

He headed down the hall, flipping out lights behind him. As he did, his last thought only added to his concerns. His little Jenny was definitely getting attached to T.J. And Jason had opened up to her far more than he had any woman in a very long time. But they needed more than for her to be there for them as a neighbor and a friend. They needed a mom.

He didn't want to raise his children alone. He never had. And T.J., he knew, had their best interests at heart. She just wasn't someone he could look to for a relationship. He doubted she would ever let a man get that close. Considering her history with men, he figured the only reason she hadn't backed away from him by now was because of the kids.

As much as he found himself thinking of her, wanting her, he had the feeling that if he ever made a serious move, she would freeze up on him like a shallow pond in the dead of winter.

The uncertainty Sam felt over considering the move was still there when he dropped off Jason and Jenny at T.J.'s the next morning. It was there that evening, too, making him edgy, restless and oddly defensive. As he and his children headed off for pizza, he conceded that his conclusions about T.J. weren't helping his agitation much, either.

In some ways it was almost too easy being with her. In others, far too difficult. When he was with her, listening to what the children had done that day or catching signs of worry that she refused to discuss with him, he found himself wanting to reach for her, to touch her. When he thought about touching her, his thoughts inevitably drifted to her lush mouth, her high firm breasts, the softness of her skin. He could only guess at her shape, hidden as it was beneath the baggy clothes she tended to wear, but he found himself trying to imagine that, too.

As much as he liked being with her, as much as he found himself wanting a little more than the friendship that had developed between them, it seemed wiser to keep his distance and protect the relationship they had.

That was why he didn't let himself hang around after

he arrived to pick up his children that evening. He didn't hang around much the rest of that week, either. Or the next. Only once did he stay for supper when she invited him, and only then because his children had helped prepare it, but he wasn't alone with her at all—until the weather changed.

He'd just had his first full weekend off since the beginning of summer—which he'd spent replacing a few missing shingles on his roof, chopping firewood and trying to teach Jason and Jenny how to run a vacuum cleaner—when the wintry weather up north dropped lower, pelting all of Puget Sound with rain and blustery wind. One of their pilots, Dave, only worked for them in the summer, so he'd already gone back to his teaching job on the mainland. Without Dave around, Chuck and Zach were as late getting in as Sam that evening.

The fact that Zach was in as much of a hurry to get home as Sam was, was actually a relief to him. He had planned to finally talk to his partner, to test the waters and see what Zach thought about buying Sam out. The weather had simply saved him from having to invent yet another excuse to postpone that particular conversation.

Every time Sam thought about approaching Zach, something inside him balked. The problem with taking that first step was almost like the problem he had finding the right dog for Jason. He'd asked T.J. to help him find a suitable puppy and, while the children were in school, she'd checked out a couple of litters. All he wanted was a good-natured animal his son could sleep with, since that seemed to be important to him. But one breed had been the high-strung variety that required constant brushing and grooming. The other had been the sort that did better outside than in.

Finding the right dog shouldn't be that difficult. Neither should making the decision about what was right for his children.

T.J. had actually made that decision even harder.

When he'd mentioned the possibility of selling out and moving last week, she'd simply blinked at him and, in her usual pull-no-punches way, said the decision shouldn't be hard at all. If he was happy, his children probably would be, too.

He was still mulling over her amazingly simplistic philosophy, and wondering when the last time was that he'd felt truly content about much of anything, when he pulled into her drive and caught the glow of her windows through the blowing rain. Within seconds of running into the warmth of her house, however, his dilemma was the last thing on his mind.

When he'd called to tell her he would be late, he'd thought she sounded a little hesitant. Or maybe it was distant. As hurried as he'd been, he hadn't given it much thought.

He did now.

She was wound as tightly as his best fishing reel.

''Are the kids okay?'' he asked, immediately aware of her evasive glance when he closed out the cold. Her arms were crossed tightly over the gray fleece pullover she wore over her loose jeans. Her features seemed pale and drawn.

''They're fine. They're asleep, actually.''

Droplets clung to his hair, and rain darkened the shoulders of his brown bomber jacket. ''You're a little damp,'' she murmured, the observation making her sound far more normal than she looked. ''Do you want to warm up? I can make tea.''

''As late as it is, I think I'd better just get the kids and go.''

She had a fire going in the potbellied stove in the corner. Wood shifted and snapped inside. Warmth radiated to every corner of the comfortable room. The place was a snug and cozy refuge from the rain pounding outside. Yet the way she held herself made her look as if she were freezing.

"You could just leave them for the night," she suggested, an odd strain marring her delicate features. "It doesn't make a lot of sense for you to wake them, just to have to wake them in the morning to bring them back again."

"What about clothes for school?"

"You can drop them off on your way to work."

He could, he supposed, but those logistics were forgotten as he studied her face. There was something going on with her. Something she was trying to work around. Or trying to hide, for all he knew, and doing a lousy job of it. He'd seen that look in her eyes before. It was the same apprehension he'd noticed when she'd sat across from him at her kitchen table and told him about Andy's dad.

Part of him wanted to let the observation go—the self-protective part that had decided to play it the way she did and keep the focus only on what affected his kids. They were doing fine within those boundaries.

The part of him that had never failed to be drawn to her ignored that logic completely.

"If the kids are all right, what else is wrong?"

Her glance faltered. Lowering her head, she turned away.

"T.J.?"

"I said I wouldn't bother you with it again."

That could only mean Colwood. Since she hadn't mentioned the guy at all lately, Sam had almost begun to believe that Andy's father had crawled back under his rock after all.

"Bother me with it, anyway."

He thought for sure she would claim it was nothing. He'd known her to insist before that everything was fine when he could see for himself that it wasn't. It was almost as if she believed saying it would make it so.

This time, though, that stubbornness failed her. Either that, or she was no longer brave enough to pretend.

Her uneasy glance made it as far as the evening stubble shadowing his jaw before she slipped into the little hall and closed the door to Andy's bedroom. When she returned, her hold on herself even tighter, her voice dropped to nearly a whisper.

"I got another letter."

"From Andy's father," he concluded.

She gave her head a negative shake, her shining, spiraling curls dancing against her shoulders. "From his attorney."

Sam's brow lowered. "What did it say?"

She didn't reply to his flat demand. Instead she dug her purse from a cabinet in the kitchen and pulled out an envelope with a Registered sticker on it and the remnants of the return receipt still glued to the back.

"I had to sign for it," she said, her hand shaking as she held the envelope out to where Sam had stopped beside her.

The ivory envelope bore the name and address of a prestigious-sounding San Francisco law firm. When Sam opened it, he discovered matching ivory letterhead.

He had already sensed that what he was about to read wasn't good. Even as shaken as T.J. clearly was, he didn't expect the two pages of allegations and incredible demands—or the quiet rage that built as he scanned the formal language and boiled it down to its essence.

Andy's father wanted custody of his son. Not joint custody. Or even reasonable visitation. He wanted Andy.

According to the letter, Bradley Preston Colwood IV asserted that Tierra Jade Walker, "whose actual surname was unknown," had hidden the child known as Andy Walker from him for nearly seven years. He claimed that he had fathered the child, that he was willing to take blood tests to prove it, and that she had deceived him about the child's existence by claiming she'd had an abortion.

The letter went on to state that if Ms. Walker gave him full and complete custody of the boy without legal challenges that Mr. Colwood would refrain from bringing it to the court's attention that she was an unfit mother. His basis for that claim was that she had no full-time job, or prospects for one, that she had no relatives or husband to help her provide a stable environment for his son and that she "constantly exposed his son to danger by keeping wild animals within his proximity."

The letter concluded by stating that it would be in the best interests of the child for her to meet with the firm's co-counsel in Bellingham to handle the matter amicably—and without having to involve Children's Protective Services. A meeting had been set for Wednesday at one o'clock to sign the necessary documents and arrange for a transfer that would cause the least trauma to the child. If she didn't attend, CPS would be called.

That gave T.J. less than forty-eight hours.

She was as pale as snow when he looked up from the crisp sheets.

"Brad called about an hour ago," she told him, her voice raw with apprehension. "He wanted to know if I'd received the letter. I asked him why he was doing this, but all he said was that if I'd answered his letters, he might have been able to leave the family's attorneys out of it.

"I never hid Andy from him. Never," she insisted, searching Sam's face as if to beg him to believe her. "When I reminded him that he was the one who walked away from us, he said he was afraid I was going to make up something like that.

"He said he was afraid all along that I'd lie," she expanded, sounding even more desperate. "He's making me out to be the liar, and it's him, Sam. He's the one who isn't being honest. He left us. He was the one who wanted me to have the abortion. I never—" her voice dropped, loath to have her sleeping son awaken and over-hear "—I never even *considered* one," she practically whispered. "Not for a single minute. Before Brad left he'd even tried to make it sound like I'd slept around and that Andy might not even be his. Now he's saying he'll take a blood test to prove he is the father."

Sam's jaw had grown tighter with each contradiction. Easing the pressure before he shattered his teeth, he slipped the letter under the purse she'd left on the counter. "What else did he say?"

As if caught by a fresh sort of pain, T.J.'s breath shuddered in. "He said he's married to a woman from a well-respected family and that he and his wife can take much better care of Andy than I can. He said he's seen how I live."

T.J. felt sick. It *had* been Brad that she'd seen at the school a couple of weeks ago. He had apparently even been to her home when she wasn't there, or at least close enough to know about the animals. He could have been on her porch, looked in her windows.

She had never felt more violated or more frightened in her entire life as she had in the hours since she'd received that letter.

He wanted her child.

"What are you going to do?"

Sam's husky voice sounded deadly calm to her. The look in his deep blue eyes simply looked deadly.

"I don't know." She had no experience with anything like this. Her life was simple. Unsophisticated. Uncomplicated. "I've been trying to think all afternoon," she said, her mind desperately seeking possibilities. Unable to remain still any longer, she turned to pace her tiny patch of a kitchen. "All I know for sure is that I'm not going to that meeting, and I'm not signing any papers. I'll take Andy and move to Canada before I'll let anyone take him from me. I'll go tonight if I have to."

She whirled around, her eyes colliding with his. "Would you fly us there?" Hope flashed as she grasped at the idea. "We could go to Victoria. Or to up into British Columbia. It's not that far, and I don't think it would get you in any trouble because it's not like there's a warrant or anything out for me."

"T.J." He stepped closer, starting to reach for her, deciding against it. As agitated as she was, she would just pull away. "Even if the weather wasn't as lousy as it is, I wouldn't take you up there now. You have to go to that meeting. Or have someone go for you. Running is the worst thing you can do."

"But if I stay, he could get Andy."

The desperation in her eyes struck him like a physical blow.

It was obvious from the intimidation tactics Brad's attorneys used that they were playing hardball. It was just as clear that Andy's father was prepared to lie through his teeth to get what he wanted—and that he felt T.J. didn't have a chance.

"I don't have the money to fight this, Sam. Even if I did, I can't even counter some of what he claims." Desperation merged with panic. "Except that I'm not unfit," she insisted, her voice raw. "I'm always with Andy when he's around the animals. I've never once let him near one that I thought could hurt him."

Her fear of the flagrant accusations had Sam reaching for her anyway. "I know that," he assured her, resting his hands on her shoulders. "And you have to fight this." Beneath the soft fabric of her shirt he felt her trembling. "You can borrow the money."

"And if I lose? Sam," she said, looking into his eyes as if to make sure she had his full attention, "I was raised by a hippie who swears by horoscopes and tarot cards and wears crystals to enhance her aura. And I'm only guessing at what a stable home life is supposed to be. What if a court thinks Brad is right? What if someone comes in here to do a report or whatever it is they do and they think I'm endangering him or not raising him right?"

What little color she had drained beneath her collar. "What if someone from Child Protective Services comes and takes my son away?"

Sam didn't think about what he was doing. Unable to bear her awful anxiety, he circled her with his arms, pulling her closer.

"They're using that threat as a power play, T.J." He was surprised by how thin she felt beneath the baggy knit. And by how badly she was shaking. He'd noticed the trembling of her fingers when she'd handed him the letter and felt it at his first touch. Now, holding her close enough for his thighs to brush hers, she felt as tremulous as a leaf battered by the wind. "No one can just walk in and take a child from his parent without an investigation or proof of neglect or abuse. There's no way he can even come close to proving anything like that with you."

At the reassurance, or maybe in spite of it, she slowly dropped her forehead to his chest. At the touch of his hand to the back of her head, he felt some of the stiffness leave her body.

He remembered how he'd felt when his mother had suggested sending his children to live with her. His mom's heart had been in the right place, but even the intimation that he was failing his kids and the thought of not having them with him had been enough for him to taste the sick sensation she had to be feeling now. He could only imagine how it felt to know that someone was out to deliberately rob her of her child.

He drew her closer. He hadn't had a woman in his arms in longer than he could remember. He hadn't soothed a woman in even longer than that. Yet, as good as she felt, as near as she was, all he cared about at that moment was easing her fear. That need was the strongest he'd experienced in a very long time.

"People here know you," he murmured. "And anyone who knows you, knows what a great mom you are.

"Then, there's Andy." He looked down at the auburn curls cascading from the top of her head. The light herbal scent of her shampoo filled his lungs with each breath. "All anyone has to do is talk to him to know how he feels about his mother. The first time I saw the two of you together, I knew he adored you."

The quivering breath she drew made him even more aware of the delicate bones in her shoulders, her spine. He had never thought of her as a small woman. Or frail in any way. If anything, he'd been impressed by her supple strength. Yet, as he held her, she seemed far more fragile than he would have ever suspected.

"I trust you with my own kids," he reminded her, smoothing his hand over her hair. He slowly trailed it down the length of her wild curls. The loose ringlets and waves felt like spun silk. Their rich color reminded him of the depths of the finest port wine. "I'll vouch for you myself," he murmured, drawing on one shining curl. The spiral curled around his fingertip and clung tightly. "If you want me to."

For a moment she didn't move. She just stood in his arms, not pulling away, but not letting herself totally relax against him. Though her forehead rested between the open sides of his jacket, she seemed as alone to him as she would have standing ten feet away. It was almost as if she couldn't let herself truly lean on him. Or as if she didn't even know how.

The fire in the stove snapped as she pulled back her head. With her arms still snugly around her middle, she lifted her face to look up at him.

Her jade-green eyes were luminous with unshed tears, and clouded with doubt.

"You would do that?"

Something inside him started to ache. It was painfully apparent that she couldn't believe a man would be there for her. As he watched her warily study his face, he realized she probably didn't believe she had anyone she could really count on. She'd told him herself that all she'd ever had was Crystal. It was just her and her son.

"Of course I would." Lifting his hand to her face, he smoothed her hair from her cheek, brushing his thumb along the corner of her eye. A tiny tear clung to her lower lashes, hanging on as if falling would be to admit defeat. To save her the struggle, he caught it for her.

Something about what he'd done caused another to spring into its place. She looked down, not wanting him to see what she'd clearly never intended to let leak past.

"Hey," he murmured. Tipping her chin back toward him, he found the moisture still there.

T.J.'s breath stalled in her lungs. Sam lowered his head, the carved lines of his face turning to shadows before her eyes closed. She felt his lips touch the corner of her lashes, the sensation as light as air.

From the moment she'd read the letter, she had wanted desperately to talk to him. He had been her first thought after the disbelief and the panic had hit. But she'd been afraid to turn to him. Even when he'd asked what was wrong, she had wanted to deny that she needed his strength, his wisdom.

Now, feeling him carry that breathless touch to her temple, she wanted to deny that she needed his incredible gentleness. She couldn't believe how seductive it was. Or how very much she craved it. There was solace there. And caring.

His lips brushed her cheekbone, then the corner of her mouth. The caress was a mere whisper of skin against skin that turned into a breath of a kiss before it drifted away.

Cradling her cheek in his hand, he touched his lips to hers once more.

There was no demand. No expectation. Only tenderness and a quiet sort of comfort so foreign to her that she had no defense against it.

She drew closer.

His breath entered her lungs, filling her with his essence. The heat of his hand as he coaxed her to open to him warmed the chill deep inside. But even as she felt herself responding to that warmth, the brush of his tongue against hers sent liquid heat straight to her womb.

She heard his breath hitch. Or maybe the strangled sound was hers. Needs long denied bloomed inside her.

The backs of her eyes burned. She desperately wanted the comfort. She just wasn't prepared for the need. As vulnerable and uncertain as she felt, she didn't trust it. Didn't trust where it could lead. As precarious as her world was just then, she couldn't bear to complicate it more.

Feeling more conflicted than she had in her entire life, she squeezed her eyes shut against the burning and turned her head.

Sam slipped his hand from her cheek and let it drift to the curve of her neck. He swore he'd felt her inner struggle. He could feel it even now. She looked just like she'd tasted, soft, sweet and scared. But all that mattered to him just then was that she made no attempt to move away.

His hand was steady as he skimmed his thumb over the hollow at the base of her throat. Inside, he felt as shaky as she had a few long moments ago. Somewhere between smoothing his hand over her hair and catching that one telltale tear, he'd found himself wanting to bury his fingers in that silken tangle and his body in hers.

The demands of his body were what he'd tried to ignore when he'd tasted her—the raw hunger, the need for more.

He was doing his level best to ignore them now.

Before she could pull away from him, he eased her back himself. With his hands on her shoulders, he gritted his teeth against the ache in his groin, drew a deep breath and nodded toward the stove.

"Do you still want to make that tea?"

T.J. blinked up at him. Her arms were still crossed tightly, pulling the fabric of her shirt across the soft swells of her breasts. "Do you want it?"

No, he thought. What he wanted was her. In bed. Naked in his arms and straining against him.

"Yeah," he told her, thinking it best to get his mind— and hers—off what he'd done. "I do. You're right about the kids. It doesn't make any sense to take them out in this, so I'm in no hurry." Pushing his hands into his pockets, he stepped back and leaned against the doorjamb. "Do you know an attorney?"

An attorney? she thought, jerking her glance from the front of his jeans. Her eyes had been drawn there when he'd fisted his hands in his pockets. If he'd intended to conceal the bulge straining against his zipper, he'd only been marginally successful.

"No. No," she repeated, shaking her head. The feel of his lips against hers had pooled heat low in her belly. The knowledge that she'd affected him the same way did it again. "Even if I did, I can't afford one. I already told you that."

"You can't afford not to have one."

"Well, I can't borrow any money," she pointed out, despite his suggestion to the contrary. "Lenders tend to want things like a credit record and a steady job. I don't have either."

It had been easier when she'd been in his arms. Even though the pull she felt toward him frightened the daylights out of her, he didn't scare her nearly as much as the battle he insisted she face with Brad.

The struggle continued. Sam could see it as he studied the shadows beneath her eyes. Touched by it, he considered drawing her back to him and telling her he would take care of the money himself. Fearful as she was of losing her son, she would probably even take him up on the offer.

But he was still conscious of how she had turned from him. And he knew how protective she was of her independence. That was why he figured it would be wiser to stay where he was—and for her to simply use what she'd accrued.

"You're right. They do. But you don't have to borrow. You can use the flights you've racked up with me."

Incomprehension joined anxiety. "I don't understand."

"A round-trip flight to a vet on another island would cost anyone else just under a hundred dollars," he explained. "For every hundred dollars you need for attorney's fees, you can take a day off the flights I owe you, and I'll take care of that part of the bill. If you look at it in terms of dollars instead of flights, I figure you have around two thousand dollars in credit by now." He dipped his dark head toward the metal teapot on the back burner. That amount would barely get her started if she wound up in a court battle, but there was no need to mention that now. "Are you going to make that tea?"

From where she remained in the middle of the room, T.J. frowned at his logic and her own reluctance. It seemed to her that she should have some sort of argument about why she shouldn't cash in her flights, but there was nothing in her life more important to her than keeping Andy with her.

"I'd just be using what I've already earned?"

"Absolutely. Does that work for you?"

She was too in need of the solution he offered to refuse it. She needed to be fair about it though.

"You're overpaying me to watch the children. I had no idea the flights were that expensive." Looking as troubled as she sounded, she picked up the poppy-red pot from the stove and headed for the sink. "I haven't earned nearly that much, but I'll take part of it."

"T.J.," he said flatly. "We made a deal. One flight for one day of child care. It's not like I don't owe you. You're just cashing in."

He was doing it because he owed her. Grateful as she was, she didn't know if that made her feel better or worse.

The turmoil inside her sucked at her energy, subduing her motions as she reached for the faucet.

"So now what are you going to do?" he asked, not trusting her silence.

She'd do what she had to do. Just like she always did. "I'll go to the meeting and find out why Brad is doing this." A dull ache filled her chest. She couldn't imagine what she had done to him that would make him do something so hateful. He was clearly willing to destroy her to take the son he'd never wanted. "Then I'll find an attorney."

The strain in her voice had Sam moving toward her. He wondered if she was even aware that she was standing with her hand on the faucet and had yet to turn on the water.

"I think you might want to do that the other way around. Talk to the attorney first," he suggested. Reaching out, he took the teapot from her. "You'll know better how to handle that meeting if you know what legal legs Colwood has to stand on."

Confused by what he'd done, she watched him set the pot aside.

"The tea..."

"You're tired, T.J. Forget the tea and go to bed. We can worry about all this later."

We. There was something terribly seductive about that word. Hearing it made her feel a little less alone. But what he'd just said made her realize that in a few minutes she would be.

"You're leaving?"

His glance narrowed on the disappointment she couldn't seem to mask.

Caution touched his tone. "Would you rather I didn't?"

Yes, she said to herself. I need you to stay. She couldn't stand to be alone with the awful sense of powerlessness she simply couldn't seem to shake. What if someone came? What if Brad decided he wanted Andy now?

Rain ticked against the window above the sink. Wind rattled the shutters.

"It's miserable out there," she said, because using the weather for an excuse was infinitely easier than admitting how completely helpless she felt.

Aware of the anxiety in her eyes, Sam lifted his hand and tucked back a curl brushing her cheek. "True," he said, not overly thrilled with the idea of heading into it himself.

"Tell you what," he continued, his grip on her arm totally impersonal as he turned her and steered her through the doorway. "Let's check on the kids. Then give me a blanket and I'll sack out over there."

He pointed to the pillow-strewn futon that served as her sofa, deliberately overlooking how short the thing was. "If you need me, that's where I'll be."

T.J. came to a halt. Sam hadn't been fooled for minute. He knew she didn't want him to leave because she didn't want to be alone with her fears.

He was going to stay simply because she needed him.

By making it clear where he would sleep, he was also letting her know he wasn't about to take advantage of the awful insecurity she was living with.

"Are you sure you don't mind?"

"I'm positive."

"You can sleep with Jenny in my bed, and I can sleep out here," she suggested. "It's only a double, but it's bigger than the sofa."

"I'll be fine."

He started past her.

"Sam," she said, stopping him. "I owe you one for this."

"T.J.," he murmured back. "I've stopped keeping track. As many times as you've rescued me, this is the least I can do."

She'd stopped keeping track, too. She honestly didn't even know how many flights he owed her. "Baby-sit a grown woman?"

"Stay close for a friend."

Near as she was, she could see the little chips of green in his incredible blue eyes. Near enough that all she would have to do is reach out and touch his hard biceps, feel the solid wall of his chest.

She couldn't believe how desperately she wanted him to hold her again. She just wanted to be in his arms. That was all.

She was afraid to want anything more.

She would settle for his presence, though, and be enormously grateful for it. It was as precious a gift as any man had ever cared to offer.

Chapter Ten

The rain had softened to a lulling beat on the roof by the time T.J. widened the crack in her bedroom door the next morning and moved silently down the hall.

She felt as if she had barely slept. Curled under the blankets in her bed with Jenny sleeping beside her, she had spent what felt like hours running through possible scenarios with Brad's attorney. She'd spent those same hours trying not to think about how Andy would believe she'd abandoned him if his father took him away. Or what Sam would do if he were to find her standing over him, asking if he would mind holding her for a while.

She was imagining reaching for him when an unfamiliar sound jerked her to awareness moments before her alarm clock gave the quiet click that announced it was about to go off.

She'd hit the snooze button and slipped from bed without waking the little girl sprawled in the middle of the mattress. T.J. had obviously slept a little, after all. But whatever rest she'd managed hadn't erased a single worry or thought.

She could still feel the chill that had settled inside her when Brad's intent had sunk in. And, wise or not, she still wanted Sam's arms around her.

Her last thought trailed off like mist in the wind as she came to a halt in the living room. Snuggling her old plaid flannel robe around her, she stared at the sofa.

The pale light from the hallway slashed across the darkened space. The pillow she'd given Sam lay atop the neatly folded quilt. And on the pillow was a note.

Moving closer, she found that he'd written it on the back of his business card.

"Went to get kid's clothes," it read, in bold, slashing script. "Back by 8:00."

Hearing the engine of his truck kick over outside, it seemed safe to assume that the sound that had wakened her had been the closing of the front door.

"Where's Daddy?" With her curls forming a blond halo around her head, Jenny emerged from the hall wearing one of T.J.'s thermal T-shirts and rubbing her eyes. "Isn't he here?"

Pushing back her own wild tangle of hair, T.J. slipped the card into her pocket. "Good morning," she murmured, heading for the sleepy-eyed child. "He just left to get your school clothes."

"Where did he sleep?"

"Right here," she said, motioning behind her.

"Did you sleep here with him?"

"I slept in my room with you. Just like the other night. Remember?"

Easily accepting T.J.'s hug and explanations, the innocent little girl murmured, ''Oh,'' and climbed onto the sofa where her dad had been.

Watching her pull the quilt over herself, T.J. added a new concern to her growing list.

It had been perfectly understandable that Sam would want to check on his children before he'd gone to bed. But all of the children had stirred, and Jason and Jenny had each wakened enough to ask if they had to leave now.

Sam had told them both the same thing; they didn't and they were all spending the night right there. Then he'd tucked his children back in, Jason with a groggy Andy and Jenny in T.J.'s old brass bed.

All three children had been asleep again in minutes.

As she headed for Andy's room to wake up the boys, she now wished they hadn't awakened at all.

As literal and open as children were, one of them could easily say something to a teacher or an aide about Sam having been there all night. Something that could easily be misconstrued. One never knew what a child would come up with for show and tell.

Ordinarily, T.J. would have shrugged off that little concern and figured that any gossip would be relatively short-lived. Maddy would give her a bad time about Sam being there, but Maddy would undoubtedly understand about the late hour, the weather and the kids, and any talk would die before it got started.

Under the circumstances that morning, though, the last thing she wanted was to provide any more fuel for Brad or his attorney should they have someone out there looking for more ammunition against her. The way Brad had twisted the truth, she didn't doubt for an instant that he would use knowledge of a man spending the night to allege loose morals, no morals or, at the rate he was going, that she was running a house of ill repute.

"Rise and shine, boys," she said, smiling, when smiling wasn't at all what she felt like doing. "Breakfast in ten minutes."

It actually took far longer than that to get the children up and moving. By the time she had the teakettle boiling for tea, water boiling for oatmeal and had herded the children through the bathroom to wash, brush teeth and get rid of the sleep spikes from the boys' hair, thirty minutes had passed. Fifteen more and the children were finally at the table eating their cereal, which allowed her time to change into a black pullover and loose charcoal pants before the rumble of a vehicle engine in the drive announced they had company.

Andy leaped from his chair, practically knocking it over to run to the door. Intercepting him in the kitchen doorway, T.J. caught his arm to stop him.

"I'll get it, sweetie," she murmured, doing her best to keep the strain from her voice. No way did she want him to open the door and find some stranger there. She wasn't expecting anyone but Sam. Odds were enormously in favor of it being him, too, since he was due back any minute. But despite the assurances he had given her about Brad's attorney using Child Services as a scare tactic, she wasn't taking any chances. If Brad's goal had been to intimidate her, he had thoroughly succeeded. "You finish breakfast. Then go get dressed. I'll get the door."

Agreeable as always, her little boy turned on his heel and marched like a good little soldier back to rejoin Jenny and Jason. Just the thought of him being taken by a stranger made her ill. The reality would be unbearable.

The surge of anxiety lasted until she nudged back the

curtain of lace covering the window. Something she didn't care to examine too closely eased the grip of anxiety as she opened the door to a mountain of muscle in brown leather, a beige sweater and dark khakis.

Without a word Sam stepped inside. Cold, moist air swept in with him, along with the clean scents of soap and shaving cream.

He couldn't have been out of the shower long. Closing the door behind him, she noticed that his dark, neatly combed hair was still damp. The hard line of his jaw was freshly shaved.

He also looked far more rested than she felt, when he turned to face her.

"I think I have everything." His keen glance swept her face, his assessment quick, bold and unnervingly thorough. Seeing something he apparently didn't like, his eyes narrowed as he handed her a small stack of clothes. "How are you doing?"

She didn't get a chance to lie and tell him she was doing fine. The children barreled in from the kitchen, saving the response he probably wouldn't have believed anyway.

Affectionately ruffling his son's hair, he did the high-five thing with her son, then swept his little girl up in his arms so she could wrap a hug around his neck.

"T.J. has your clothes," he told his children, hugging his daughter back. "How about you go get ready for school?"

"Come on, Jason," T.J. said. Clutching a pair of purple jeans and a pink sweatshirt, she handed over a pair of navy sweats. "Let's get you into these."

"They can dress themselves." After planting a kiss on Jenny's forehead, he lowered her to her bare feet. "You're big enough. Aren't you, guys?"

His bundle in hand, Jason assured his dad that he was and promptly disappeared with Andy and Cat into Andy's room.

Jenny looked a little less willing to be left on her own.

"Why don't you go get dressed in T.J.'s room?" her dad suggested.

"By myself?"

"Yes, by yourself. You're a big girl."

"I didn't finish my breakfast."

Taking her by her narrow little shoulders, her dad turned her around. "Then go finish it now. T.J. can help you get dressed later. I have to go to work in a minute, and I need to talk to her."

Jenny turned right back around, blue eyes so like his own blinking up at him. "Is it big-people talk?"

"Yes," he replied, and pointed her in the right direction once more.

The little girl with the freshly combed pigtails hoisted up the T-shirt that was long enough for her to trip over and headed off with her little mouth twisted to one side. She was not terribly pleased to be dismissed.

Certain she'd get over it by the time she reached her chair, Sam slid his attention back to the woman clutching his daughter's clothes. He wasn't terribly pleased himself. The strain he could see around T.J.'s eyes was far more pronounced than it had been last night.

"Didn't you get any sleep?"

"I got some."

"Not enough," he muttered. "Why didn't you come talk to me?"

"Were you awake?" she asked, wondering if he had any idea how tempted she'd been to do just that.

"No. Actually, I slept better than I have in a long time." He sounded slightly baffled by that, too, considering what he'd slept on. "But that wouldn't have mattered."

He didn't seem particularly surprised that she hadn't come to him.

He didn't seem interested in pursuing why she hadn't, either. "What's your schedule?"

She had been preparing to thank him, to tell him how much she appreciated what he'd done for her last night just by being there. No man had ever simply stayed near for her before.

Seeing him check his watch, she echoed him, instead. "My schedule?"

"For today," he clarified. "Where will you be?"

"I'll take the children to school in about half an hour," she told him, knowing that he needed to go. "Then I'm working at the bookstore. Mrs. Bender asked me to cover for her today so she can get a perm and go to Ester Jackson's eightieth birthday tea," she explained, since this wasn't her normally scheduled day. "I'll be there until I pick up the children at three." Between her fingers, she worried a thread hanging from Jenny's folded shirt. "Why?"

"I want to know where to reach you. Since you don't know a lawyer, I'll call the one Zach and I use in Seattle. If he can't help, he can probably give me the name of someone who can."

He was calling his own attorney for her.

Instinct had her starting to protest, to tell him he didn't need to do that. He didn't need to go out of his way any more than he already had. The need to protect her heart had become as basic to her as breathing, and he was already undermining her defenses. But a far greater necessity kept her protest silent. What she needed didn't matter. She had to protect her son.

"Thank you," she murmured, hugging his daughter's clothes to her middle. "Thank you for everything."

"No problem," he replied, frowning at the way she'd made it sound as if she expected his help to end there. "As soon as I talk to him and explain what's going on, I'll call you with his number and you can talk to him yourself. I'm sure he's going to want a copy of that letter." The frown changed quality. "Is there a fax at the bookstore?"

"The Benders just got a new one."

"Good."

She paused, looking hesitant. "Do you have to go very far away today?"

"I'm doing the big mail run. I'll be up and down a lot, but I won't be farther than 150 miles."

There was the regular mail run, which involved the major islands. Then there was the one he referred to as the big run, which hit dozens of the little dots on the map scattered through the San Juans with their weekly mail delivery.

T.J. knew those days tended to be longer than most. Now that the rains had set in, they could easily be longer.

As if reading her mind, he tipped his head to catch her eyes. "There's nothing in the forecast for fog or ice, T.J. I don't plan to get stuck anywhere."

He hadn't even left, and she was concerned about when she'd see him again. She didn't take that as a very good sign. She especially didn't think it good that he seemed aware of it himself. She couldn't worry about it now, though. Jason had wandered back in looking for socks.

Sam produced a pair from his pocket, then strode through to the kitchen to kiss his little girl goodbye. Heading back in, his long legs covering the distance in a dozen strides, he buzzed another kiss across his son's head and stopped with his hand on the door.

She thought for a moment that he might tell her not to worry, that everything would be all right. She thought he might even do what part of her ached for him to do and reassure her with a touch. But since she'd turned from him last night, he'd shown no interest in touching her again.

"I'll call you," was all he left her with before he headed into the early-morning light.

The day proved no easier than the night had been. Sam had no sooner walked out the door than T.J. heard Jenny's cereal bowl shatter on the floor. On the way to school, the car started making strange noises, which meant she had to stop by the hardware store for the can of oil she'd meant to add last week. That was all before nine o'clock and, even as rushed as she was, the specter of what Brad was doing to her life loomed in the back of her mind like the dark and ominous threat it was.

That threat affected everything she did.

She was sure Andy's teacher thought T.J. was nuts when she went back to get him to keep him at the bookstore with her. And she started jumping again every time she heard the bell ring over the bookstore's door. Not that there were many customers. She and Andy spent most of the day unpacking and shelving the extra stock Mrs. Bender had ordered for the upcoming holidays— and listening for the telephone.

Sam had said he would call as soon as he spoke with his attorney. But the only calls that came that morning were either personal calls for Mrs. Bender or people inquiring about the availability of certain books.

The only call she made herself was to Crystal. Waiting

until Andy was in the bathroom at the back of the store, she called to ask her to watch the children for her tomorrow. When Crystal asked why, T.J. hurriedly told her about the letter.

Crystal said nothing at first. She simply listened. Then, sounding as protective as a mother bear defending her cubs, she assured T.J. that she would pick up the children after school and keep them with her. T.J. wasn't to worry about anyone taking Andy. She would take him to Canada herself before anyone else would get him, and T.J. could follow. In the meantime, true to the way Crystal dealt with everything else, she said she would check T.J.'s horoscope and look for the weak spots in Brad's. She would also research the appropriate stone for Andy to wear.

Her mom's heart was in the right place, and T.J. thanked her from the bottom of her own heart for the help. She also confided that Canada had been her first thought, too, then asked Crystal not to take Andy anywhere if someone showed up but to call the sheriff first.

Sam was right. T.J. needed to face this down. And she would. But heaven only knew what a court would decide if Crystal were called as a character witness.

The thought of facing Brad's attorney alone, however, turned into a more frightening prospect with each passing hour.

By noon she hadn't heard a word from Sam.

He hadn't called by the time she had to leave to pick up the children, either.

She was desperately hoping that he'd left a message for her at home as she pulled into her drive with Andy, Jason and Jenny chattering away about who would get to feed the animals and who would water.

Rain fell in a steady drizzle. Because of the weather,

she was about to tell them she would handle all the feed-ing chores by herself when she caught sight of taillights ahead of her. Beyond the steady motion of the windshield wipers, she immediately recognized the vehicle near her shed.

The nature of her concerns changed like a shift in the tide.

There was only one vehicle like that on the island. The pea-green Volkswagen bus with the rounded orange flowers on its back bumper had a faded-yellow peace symbol on the front and a peeling sticker that once pro-claimed Flower Power but was now missing its conso-nants.

The aging bus belonged to Shenandoah Adams, the gentle, middle-aged hippie who taught yoga and medi-tated on the boulders overlooking the sea. Over the years, Doe had brought T.J. several of the wounded and or-phaned animals she had cared for and released.

As lousy as the weather was, T.J. had the sinking feel-ing that an injured animal could be the only reason the woman was there now.

The moment T.J. pulled to a stop, Doe scrambled out of her vehicle. With the hood of her heavy, striped serape pulled low over her head against the drizzle, she hurried to where T.J. climbed out of her Jeep.

The woman's sharp, narrow features were taut with concern, her kind eyes filled with it. Seeing the boys jumping from the back seat and the little girl waiting to be lifted over a puddle, she lowered her voice to nearly a whisper. "I'm bringing you a deer. I found it out by my place. Someone hit it and just left it on the side of the road in this rain."

T.J. winced. "How bad is it?" she whispered back.

"I can't tell. It opened its eyes when I came up to it.

And I know it had to hurt when I pushed the blanket under it because it made this little crying sound. I used a blanket to drag it up a board and into the back so I wouldn't have to move it so much.''

Thoughts of the hurt and suffering animal had T.J.'s heart stinging as she gave Doe a quick nod. ''Let me get the children inside.''

Doe didn't say another word. She simply hurried back to wait in her little green bus while T.J. carried Jenny through the rain and unlocked the front door so the boys could go in.

''What does she want, Mom?''

''She's bringing us another animal to take care of.'' T.J. wasn't about to tell them what Doe had just told her. Until she knew more, that was all the children would get. Andy always worried when a new tenant arrived. As sensitive as Jason was to their furry and feathered friends, she had the feeling he would worry, too. ''I need all of you to be good and fix your own snacks. Can you do that for me? And listen carefully to any messages if anyone calls?''

Jason's handsome little features had already filled with concern. ''Is it hurt bad?''

''I don't know yet. But we're going to do what we can to help.'' She tucked back his soft blond hair, the motion as reassuring as she could make it. ''We can do that best by you and Andy and Jenny taking care of each other in here while I help the lady outside. Okay?''

He gave her a solemn nod. Seconds later she hurried through to the kitchen to grab glasses and pour milk.

The children would be fine with their peanut butter and crackers while she worked on the animal in her pottery room. It would be warm in there and if the poor thing was in shock, which she figured it probably was, it would fare better inside for a few days than it would out in the cold and the rain. With Doc Jackson's vet practice gone and Sam flying heaven only knew where, she could only pray that the animal hadn't suffered anything worse than bruises or a simple broken bone. That she could handle. She'd been setting broken bones since she was thirteen.

Coats were scattered over the living room floor, and the children were at the table worrying about the animal and who was getting more crackers when T.J. hurried out the front door with an old blanket so Doe could take hers home.

The mild-mannered woman met her at the back of the bus and quickly threw open its doors.

The moment she did, T.J. felt her heart stop.

Even in the dim gray light, one glance was all it took for her to recognize the pattern of brown and black on the still, sweet face. She knew this beautiful creature. She had cared for her before. Her and her precious little fawn.

Placing her hand on the doe's cooling chest, she also knew there was absolutely nothing she could do to help.

T.J. was wet and so cold that her teeth chattered as she pushed the wheelbarrow back into the shed and closed the latch on the door. Sam had just pulled in. His headlights cut a beam through the rain as she hurried up to the porch.

She didn't know what time it was, but there wasn't a scrap of daylight left. Doe, bless her, had stayed to help and had left about twenty minutes ago. That was when T.J. had last checked on the children. She'd caught them in a bouncefest on Andy's bed and had planted the boys in front of a board game at the kitchen table and Jenny on the sofa with a book. All were given strict orders not to move. When she'd checked on them the time before that they'd gone through the entire jar of peanut butter, the last of the milk, and she'd found them trying to get the cat to lick the jar lid.

Now she needed to feed them dinner.

She needed to wash up. To dry off. To get warm.

She needed to stop thinking about the deer.

Mostly she needed desperately for this day to be over.

As much as she wished for that, the thought of what the next day might bring had her trying to blank her mind completely. She was afraid that if she focused on any one thing too closely, she would lose the battle she'd been fighting since yesterday and fall apart completely.

"Did you get my message?"

Sam's deep voice carried on the cold breeze as he jogged up the steps behind her.

"I did." With her back to him, she stripped off the gloves he had given her and her dripping yellow rain slicker. The slicker went over the back of the fir branch rocker. The gloves she kept to dry by the fire. "Thanks for trying."

"I played phone tag with him all day," Sam said, brushing rain from the arms of his leather coat as he repeated the message he'd left on her answering machine.

"He was in court when I called him this morning," he explained, catching the screen door above her head when she opened it. "I was in the air when he returned the call to the office. When I called him from Waldron Island, he was with a client." He crossed the threshold behind her, entering the warmth of her inviting house. "He called back while I was on my way to Remos, but when I called from there, he'd left for the day."

He wanted her to understand why he hadn't called

earlier. As frustrated as he was by his inability to connect with the guy, she had to be even more concerned.

"It's all right," she said, when what she really felt was that nothing would ever be right again. "You tried."

Her dismissive response gave Sam pause. "I'll try him again in the morning."

Acknowledging him with a seemingly indifferent nod, she laid her gloves on the stone pad under the potbellied stove and held out her hands to its warmth.

"Can we move now, Mom?" her son hollered from the kitchen.

"I'm hungry," came Jenny's plaintive little voice from the corner of the sofa.

"How come it took so long?" Jason called. "You said it would be faster if we didn't help with the animals."

From where he stood by the sofa, Sam noticed the defeat in T.J.'s stance. "You can move now," she called, her back still to him.

That was all it took for a half dozen little feet to hit the floor. Seconds later two of the children headed for him. One for T.J.

The gray furball of a cat wiggled in Jason's arms.

Andy and Jason cranked their necks back to look up at him. "Can Jason spend the night again?" Andy asked, his arm slung over his little pal's shoulder.

Jenny tugged at the knee of T.J.'s wet pants. "T.J.? Can we make bisgetti?"

Looking down at the two hopeful faces staring up at him, Sam couldn't help but notice how much less solemn his towheaded little boy was. Or how easy it was for Andy to make Jason smile. The lines of affection were definitely beginning to blend between the adults and the children, but he didn't bother to be concerned about it just then. He was more interested in the subdued woman skimming her cold-reddened hand over his daughter's hair.

T.J. had left her rubber boots on the porch with her parka, but the bottoms of her pants were soaked. She had obviously just come in from taking care of her animals and had yet to start supper. Since it was nearly seven o'clock, he had the feeling she was considerably behind her normal schedule.

According to Jason, they always took care of the animals right after school. And she tended to feed the kids around six.

"It's a little late for spaghetti," she said to Jenny, shivering. "If your dad wants you to stay for supper, how about soup?"

She had yet to make eye contact with him. Wondering if she was feeling let down about the attorney or upset with him because he hadn't called sooner, he crouched in front of the boys. "Let me talk to T.J., fellas. Then I'll get back to you. Okay?"

"They can stay if you want them to," she said. "Just let me wash up, and I'll get them some supper."

Drawing her hand from Jenny's head, she looked down at the child. "I'll be right back," she murmured and headed for the bathroom.

Rising, Sam followed her into the short hallway that separated her room from Andy's.

The bathroom was at the end of the hall. The small, utilitarian space was just large enough for the white tub, sink and commode. A painted wood rack above the commode held stacks of green-and-cream colored towels and a basket of herbal lotions and shampoo. A small fern flourished from a macramé hanger near the high, white-curtained window.

Since she left the door open, he could see her already

at the sink, her head lowered as she turned on the faucets and reached for a bar of soap.

He came to a halt in the doorway. She had let the matter of the attorney go far too easily. And just now she hadn't even waited to see whether or not he wanted her to feed his children.

"What's going on?" he asked. "Are you upset with me because I didn't call sooner?"

Her head jerked up. In the mirror, he saw a flash of consternation in her otherwise emotionless features. "No. No, I'm...no," she repeated, lowering her head again. "You said you'd call after you spoke with him. You didn't speak with him, so..."

Her voice trailed off, her shoulders lifting in a small shrug.

"Did you hear from Colwood or his attorney again?"

She shook her head, her focus still on her hands as she lathered and scrubbed. "I didn't hear from anyone."

"Then what's wrong?"

Her only response was another negative shake of her head. With her focus hard on her hands, she rinsed off the lather. She didn't reach for the towel, though. She lathered up again.

"T.J.?" he prodded. "Hey," he murmured when she said nothing. "Talk to me, okay?"

His gentle insistence did what simple query had not.

"Someone hit the doe," she finally said, her voice suspiciously tight as she continued scrubbing. "Shenandoah Adams brought it to me."

Shenandoah Adams. He knew her. She was the vegetarian who'd refused to baby-sit his children in his home because he had leather furniture. "The doe?"

"The one we released a couple of weeks ago."

"The one Jason was always talking about?"

She gave a tense little nod.

Brow furrowing, his glance slid to the wet cuffs of her pants. There must have been leaks in her boots. The toes of her socks were wet, too.

Caution crept over him. "How is it doing?"

The tones of her soft voice were already low. They dropped even farther. "It's not. The children don't know," she said, quickly meeting his eyes in the mirror. There was a plea in hers. Or maybe it was pain. "Jason was getting so attached to her I didn't want him to have to deal with this. I'm sure it would remind him of losing his mom, and he doesn't need...I mean, I know children have to learn to accept things like this, but I just..."

Cutting herself off again, she glanced down once more.

Sam moved closer. "Where is it?"

"We buried it."

That was why her chores had taken so long, he thought. That was why she was so wet and cold, and why she kept scrubbing. It also explained the short streak of mud on her jaw where she'd apparently pushed back her hair or rubbed an itch. She and her friend had been out there long past dark digging in the rain, burying what others would have left for scavengers and tending the other animals in her care.

He stepped beside her. Seeing that she'd rinsed her hands once more, he turned off the water before she could reach for the soap again and pulled the hand towel from its rack on the wall. "I'm sorry," he murmured, folding the towel over her dripping hands. "I really am," he said, because he knew what her animals meant to her.

He didn't doubt for a moment that she had been thinking about his son and worrying about how such news would affect him. But she was affected, too. The unemotional tones of her voice, the benumbed way she moved seemed intimately familiar to him. It was as if she were trying to shut herself down, trying to shut everything out. With all she'd been forced to deal with, it was probably the only way she could cope.

"What did you tell the kids about the deer?" he asked, his voice low.

She swallowed, blinked hard at his chest. But when she looked up, her eyes were clear. He saw only strain.

Her tone echoed his. "All they know is that a lady brought me another animal to take care of."

"Then I'll take care of any questions that come up. Go get out of those wet clothes and get in the shower. You're freezing."

"But the kids—"

"Will be fine," he concluded for her. "I'll take care of them."

He would take over. He would feed them and answer their questions and relieve her of having to act as if everything was fine when everything was as far from fine as it could possibly get.

The thoughts echoed in her mind as she watched him cradle her hands in the soft terry cloth. She couldn't feel his skin against hers as he dried her fingers and palms, but there was tenderness in what he was doing and a kind of gentle concern that threatened to put a serious crack in the calm she was pretending.

"If you're sure," she murmured.

He lifted the towel and wiped a damp end over the drying streak of dirt.

"Take as long as you need," he said and, catching himself, handed the towel back to her before he walked away.

Chapter Eleven

T.J. wasn't in the habit of turning her responsibilities over to anyone else. She rarely asked for help. Since she kept her needs to herself, help was seldom offered. Yet, unfamiliar as it felt to let Sam take over for a while, she couldn't deny how badly she wanted to get rid of the chill that had settled in her bones.

She intended to hurry, to take advantage of his offer only long enough to warm up, get dressed and get into the kitchen. But it seemed to take forever for the steam of the shower to take the edge off her chill. Even after she'd nearly drained the hot water tank, pulled on her warmest sweats and dried her thick hair, she could still feel it lingering deep inside her.

It was still there, an icy void beneath her breastbone, when she entered the living room. Through the kitchen doorway she glimpsed an unwashed pot and dishes piled by the sink. Sam had her attention, though. He was crouched in front of the sofa. With his back to her, all she could see of him was his dark head and the back of his beige cable knit sweater.

Jenny lay half-asleep, the colorful quilt pulled to her neck and her head resting on the pillow Sam had used last night. The boys sat in front of him with their hands clasped between their dangling legs. They were hanging on his every word, too interested in what he was saying to bother looking in her direction.

It seemed that questions about the deer had finally arisen.

As he'd said he would, he was fielding their questions and doing a far more rational job than she probably would have, considering how angry she was at the person who'd hit the defenseless animal and left it to die. She knew that accidents happened. She knew animals could bolt into the road before even the most responsible driver could hit his brakes. But she wasn't feeling terribly rational at the moment about people who parted parent from offspring. There was now a fawn out there that would have to face the winter completely on its own.

"Was it a big deer or a little deer?" Andy asked.

"I didn't see it," Sam admitted, "but it sounded like a big one."

Jason's brow furrowed. "Like the one we let go?"

"Like that one." He didn't mention that the animal under discussion was the very one they had petted and fed. There was no need. "It was hit by a car and hurt too badly to survive."

Jason's frown stayed in place. "My mommy was hit by a car."

Andy's expression mirrored his little friend's. "She was?"

Sam cupped his hand over his son's knee and gave a

comforting squeeze. "Another driver ran a red light and hit the car she was driving," he told Andy.

"Did the one who hit the deer run a red light?" asked Jason.

"We don't have stop lights on Harbor." Sam gave his son a pat. "Remember?"

"Oh, yeah."

"Mom says we have to be careful by a road and look both ways," Andy somberly informed them. "She says some drivers are idiots."

"Well," Sam muttered, "some of them are. And she's right, you always have to be careful when you're near a road. All of you."

"We won't let Cat go by the road," Jason informed them. "And when we get a dog, I'll teach him to look both ways so he won't get hit, either."

A smile entered Sam's voice. "How are you going to teach him that?"

Jason's shoulders lifted in a shrug that nearly reached his ears. "T.J. can show me."

"My mom knows everything," Andy blithely informed him.

T.J. was dead certain that Sam was smiling now. Reaching out, he tousled her son's hair. "I'll bet there's something she doesn't know."

Andy giggled. "What's that?"

"I'm not telling you."

"Will you tell me, Dad?"

The hopeful look on Jason's face earned him a tousle, too. "Maybe later. Right now you both need to get ready for bed."

"Jason gets to stay?"

"I get to stay?" Jason echoed.

"You can at least start out sleeping here." Planting

his hands on his powerful thighs, he pushed his big body upright. "It'll be a while before I'm ready to go. No roughhousing, though. I want you quiet and in bed. I'll be in as soon as I see how T.J.'s doing."

"I'm doing fine."

T.J. watched Sam turn as the boys darted past her. He'd pushed the sleeves of his sweater to his elbows. Dark hair dusted his strong forearms. He looked very large standing in her little living room and far more in command than she felt.

It was his eyes she noticed most, though. Their intense blue boldly swept her face as he walked over and stopped in front of her.

Without a word, he picked up her hands and folded them in his.

"Better," he finally said, feeling their warmth. "Tell you what. You can take care of the dishes, and I'll supervise those two. Or I'll do dishes and you get the kids."

The warmth of his own hands had barely registered before he'd released her. He had done that a lot lately. He would touch her, then withdraw before she could react. It was almost as if he refused to give her a chance to withdraw herself. Or, maybe, she thought, curling her fingers over her palms, he was simply getting her accustomed to the contact.

The thought that he wanted her to be comfortable with his touch collided with the realization of what he was doing at that moment. He was helping. Sharing responsibility.

Sharing.

Something in her weary, wary heart wanted that desperately.

"You're being great with the kids," she murmured. "I'll do dishes."

She didn't wait for him to say anything else. She was afraid to. She simply flipped out the overhead light in the living room and headed for the milk glasses on the table.

It seemed infinitely safer to focus on what needed to be done. She wasn't sure why Sam was choosing to stay. She was too tired and too unsettled to question it. All she knew for certain was that every passing minute brought her that much closer to tomorrow's meeting, and that she needed Sam's sometimes unnerving presence far more than she should.

She had the dishes washed and the counters and table scrubbed when Sam told her that the boys were ready for her to say good-night.

Twenty minutes later she was back in the kitchen drying the last bowl when Sam walked in again.

"I think they're both out," he said. "We read about cocker spaniels."

"I need to find a puppy for you to give him," she murmured, sounding guilty that she hadn't already. "He wants one so badly."

"He'll get one."

"I should check Jenny."

"She's fine. She's asleep."

"The boys' dirty clothes. I should throw them in the wash."

"T.J.," Sam murmured, catching her arm when she started past him to do just that. "How about just staying here for a minute?"

She wanted to keep busy, to not have to think.

It seemed that Sam wasn't going to allow her that luxury.

"The only thing you need to do right now is stay here and talk to me about tomorrow."

Cautious, T.J. let her glance skim the hard line of his jaw as he coaxed her back from the doorway.

"What about it?"

"Who's watching the kids tomorrow?"

A hint of defeat tugged at her. She should have mentioned her arrangement to him already. Of course he would want to know who would be caring for his children. "Crystal," she replied, wondering what other details her preoccupation had made her overlook. "She'll meet them at school, then take them back to the store." She hesitated. "Is that all right with you?"

"If you trust her, it's fine with me. Now, about the meeting," he continued, moving on as if he had some sort of mental checklist, "do you know if Colwood is going to be there?"

"The letter said the meeting was with an attorney." She hadn't considered that Brad might actually be there himself. Concerned about the possibility now, she met Sam's eyes. "Do you think he will be?"

"He sounds like the type who would leave someone else to do his dirty work. It isn't logical that he'd stick around to face you with his version of the story."

Distress was joined by uncertainty. "Is that a yes or a no?"

"I don't know," he admitted. "The man obviously thinks you can't fight him. He also must have an ego the size of this house to believe his deceit will get him what he wants. I don't know that logic applies here."

She knew that Sam was the analytical type. She knew he liked to weigh points, to think things through. As admirable and as...male as that was, his approach wasn't doing a thing to ease her mind.

She was about to tell him that when he moved on.

"What are you taking with you?"

"Taking with me?"

"What kind of documentation," he clarified. "Do you have Andy's birth certificate?"

She hadn't even thought about that. "It's in my bedroom."

"Who is named as father on it?"

"Brad is." She couldn't imagine any other person so easily asking her such a question or any other person she would so easily have answered. "If it ever became important to Andy, and I wasn't around to tell him, I didn't want him to have to wonder about his parentage."

She hadn't wanted her son to wonder who his father was, the way she had wondered about her mother. Sam had no problem understanding that at all.

"You might want to take it with you." It was clear that Colwood's threats and tactics had subverted this normally bright and dauntless woman's usual ability to judge. He wanted her armed when she walked into that room. In case he couldn't come up with a lawyer for her, he wanted her as prepared as she possibly could be. "If you show the attorney that Colwood's name is there that will help prove that you weren't trying to hide that he was the father. Don't take the original. Take a copy."

"I'll have to go to the library and make one."

"Give it to me. I'll make one at the office in the morning and bring it back to you before I go to work. How about letters? Do you have any correspondence that can defeat his claims? Anything you can use to prove he's lying?"

There had been no letters. All she had was the birth certificate that she kept with her high school diploma in the bottom drawer of her white wicker nightstand.

Quietly, not wanting to disturb the children, Sam followed her into the darkened hallway.

With a faint click, she turned on the small lamp beside her bed. Her room was neat and utterly feminine. The brass bed frame had been lovingly polished, the white eyelet comforter piled high with lacy pillows. T.J. had never impressed him as being one for frills, but here, in her private space, she indulged a sense of the romantic that she kept hidden from the rest of the world.

She kept a lot hidden, he thought, watching her kneel in front of her nightstand. She kept even more locked inside.

She pulled out the drawer and dug past a stack of Andy's artwork to the white envelope she kept in the bottom.

Without a word she held it up to him.

There was something about the gesture, the unquestioned trust in it, that plowed past Sam's intentions to remain on the periphery. He'd told himself he would help her find counsel. He would help her pay for it, if need be. But he had no intention of getting directly involved. It wasn't his battle to fight. She hadn't even asked for his help, except for last night when she'd finally let him know she wanted him to stay, and a few week ago when she'd asked how a father's mind worked.

"Thank you for thinking of this," she replied, rising to face him.

She tried to smile.

It didn't work.

"T.J.," he said, tipping her face back toward him when she turned away. "I said I'd try to get you an attorney." He'd really thought he would have been able to reach the man today. The fact that the guy was so busy didn't bode well for tomorrow. "If I can't, do you want me to go with you?"

T.J. opened her mouth and promptly closed it again. Her eyes searched his long moments before her glance fell.

"You don't have to do that, Sam."

"I know I don't have to." With the tips of his fingers, he nudged her chin back up. Breathing in, he caught the gut-tightening scents of her soap and herbal shampoo. "Maybe I just want to."

He wanted to be there. For her.

The thought put another crack in her defenses.

"Would you rather go alone?" he asked.

She had been doing fine until he'd so gently touched her face. She could handle just about anything except his tenderness. All evening she'd managed to keep moving from one task to the next without breaking the emotional grip she had on herself. It wasn't fair that such a simple question and such a simple touch could so easily threaten that tenuous hold.

"Honestly?" she asked, praying she could get through this night without falling apart. "I'd rather none of this was happening at all. I wish that…"

"What do you wish?" he coaxed, when she cut herself off.

She should move, she thought. She should stop torturing herself with his nearness and seek distance. "That I could go to bed and wake up and find that this had all been some hideous dream."

His free hand slipped to her shoulder. The weight seemed reassuring somehow, supportive. "What else do you wish?"

Seeking what distance she could, she crossed her arms over her faded emerald sweatshirt. She'd barely tightened her hold when her throat started to burn. Silently she swore, something she never did, as her eyes began to sting.

She'd tried not to think about it. She really had.

"That I knew what happened to her fawn."

Sam saw the telltale brightness enter her eyes and the quick way she blinked to hide it. All evening he had been aware of her holding herself back, holding herself in. But her distress over a fawn had finally sneaked past that grip.

He thought she would fight back the tears as she had so stubbornly done before. And she tried, he was certain of it. But a crystalline drop broke free and rolled down her cheek. Another promptly followed.

It seemed she could allow them for anyone but herself.

Another tear leaked down the other cheek. Wiping it from her chin with the pad of his thumb, he murmured, "Your friend didn't see it around anywhere?"

Her skin slipped against his as she shook her head.

"So that probably means it wasn't hit, too," he quietly concluded.

"Probably."

"Is it old enough to survive on its own?"

"Barely."

"But it could?"

Considering that, she finally gave a little nod. "It's possible."

"Then, let's hold that thought. Okay?"

Her nod came quicker this time. So did the silent tears.

Wanting to get her beyond that worry, he asked, "What else do you wish?"

Somewhere above their heads a board creaked as the house contracted against the cold. It was an ordinary sound to T.J., familiar because she knew all the squeaks

and groans of her little home. What she was feeling beyond her sadness for the little fawn was familiar, too—
though there was nothing ordinary about the fear and
uncertainty holding her in its grip.

It had been years since she'd felt so helpless, so completely unable to control her own destiny. Once again
she was at the mercy of someone else's decisions. Only
now those decisions would affect her son, too.

"T.J.?" he coaxed.

There was such kindness in his eyes. Such concern.

Her voice fell to a defeated whisper. "I wish you
would hold me."

She didn't know what he thought of the admission.
His face blurred before his hand slipped from her shoulder and he gathered her in his arms.

She never cried. Crying only made her feel more
alone. She was already so tired of feeling that way. Yet
last night and now, she had come as close as she had in
years.

She tried to swallow past the tightness in her throat.
She couldn't. The sob broke loose. Hating that she'd lost
even that much control, she tried to bury the one that
followed against his chest.

Sam covered the back of her head with his hand. "It's
okay," he told her. "Go ahead."

She shook her head against the soft knit of his sweater,
squeezing her eyes against the stinging. "No, it's not."
Her breath shuddered in. The scent of sea air and citrusy
aftershave came with it. "It won't help."

"It won't hurt."

Yes, it will. It already did. "It'll just make my nose
red."

"Let me see."

"No."

He didn't listen. Nudging her chin up, his glance swept her face.

"It's barely even pink," he murmured, looking into her shining green eyes.

He almost smiled, until he caught the glistening of tears on her cheeks. Seeing the droplets edging to the corner of her mouth, something shifted in his expression.

His arms slipped from around her. Before she could begin to miss them, his hands slipped up the sides of her neck to cradle her face. With his thumbs, he brushed away the dampness shimmering on her skin.

One thumb had barely grazed a bead of moisture from her bottom lip when his head lowered and his mouth covered hers.

A sound caught in her throat, half sob, half moan. He drank it in, his tongue slipping past her lips to tangle with hers. The minty taste of him mingled with the salt of her tears. His heat slowly seeped toward the cold void in her chest.

She almost felt as if the edges of that lingering chill were melting when he lifted his head.

His hands still cupped her face.

"That isn't what you asked for."

"No," she agreed in a whisper. "It isn't."

"Does it make it better or worse?"

It would only be worse if he let her go. She had never felt as tired as she did at that moment. Tired of being frightened about tomorrow. Of the cold void inside her. Of being emotionally alone.

More than anything else at that moment, she was tired of fighting the longing she felt for him.

"Better."

She didn't know what he saw in her eyes. Need, prob-

ably. But his eyes turned diamond bright in the moments
before his mouth covered hers once more.

She kissed him back, tentatively at first, her tongue
shyly meeting his. She was afraid to want him too much,
to let him know how very much she needed him. Then
she felt his fingers spread below the small of her back,
and she forgot to wonder why that was.

"Put your arms around me," he murmured. He
pressed her forward, slowly urging her toward him. Heat
pooled low in her stomach at the feel of him hard against
her. "It'll work even better that way."

Slipping her arms around his neck, she drew herself
closer. Her knees melted a little at the solid feel of his
chest, the incredible strength in his arms. She was thinking that he was right, that it did work better, when she
felt his arms tighten around her. The powerful muscles
of his shoulders rose with his deeply indrawn breath.

It was the moment of stillness in his body that she
recognized, that instant when a person suddenly achieves
what he has longed for. She'd felt it herself moments ago
when he'd wrapped her in his arms. He felt it now, when
she'd reached for him.

He needed to be held, too.

The knowledge shimmered through her, touching her
in a way his hands never could. He needed the same
comfort she did, the comfort of being in the arms of
someone who cared.

The chill beneath her heart slowly disappeared. So did
the tentative quality of her kiss. The thought that he
needed her, too, had her opening to him, kissing him
back as deeply as he was suddenly kissing her.

Sam bit back a groan as she shifted against him. The
hem of her sweatshirt had risen when she'd lifted her

arms. Feeling her sag against him, he slipped his hand under it, urging her closer still.

Her bare skin felt like warm satin. Splaying his hand over her back, he slid it up the delicate bones of her spine, then down to curve it around her tiny waist. With her mouth soft and giving beneath his, he shifted himself to align her more completely with him. He wanted to feel her. All of her. Everywhere.

Desire tightened its hold. Heat raced through his veins.

She felt incredible in his arms, all sweet curves and powdery warmth, and he was so hard he hurt. She tasted like honey, felt like heaven. As he dragged in air, her scent filled his lungs, seeped into his blood. He had no idea how he was going to let her go. He only knew that he would if he had to. He would never do anything to violate the trust she had in him. On the other hand, he would do absolutely anything she would let him.

His fingers traced over the silk of her skin, skimmed up her side. The moment he reached the slight curve at the side of breast, he felt her go still.

She wasn't wearing a bra. He'd suspected it when he'd first seen her in the hallway after her shower. Now, knowing there was nothing between him and her tantalizing fullness, the heat in his groin turned molten.

"Do you want me to stop?" His voice was a tight whisper against her skin. His lips touched her cheek, her temple, his hand still curved on her ribs. "All you have to do is tell me to stop and I will." It would kill him, but he would.

"Okay," she murmured.

His mouth grazed the corner of hers. "Okay stop? Or okay don't?"

The small negative shake of her head brought her lips to his. "Please. Don't."

The plea in those breathless words sent a jolt of raw need ripping through him. Her mouth softened beneath his. In his hand her nipple bloomed against his palm.

He was wrong. He'd thought he could do whatever she would allow. He couldn't. Not without wanting more. The way she had caught her breath at his touch, the feel of her responding to him, made him want her writhing beneath his body. He had gone too long without. And he had wanted this woman in his arms from the moment he'd noticed her smile.

Gritting his teeth against the need clawing inside him, he eased his hand down her side, forced himself to gentle his kiss.

T.J. felt the tension in his big body change quality. Beneath the feel of his amazing hands, he had awakened sensations she had forgotten, desires she had long denied. Now, sensing his withdrawal, she was afraid she had been too greedy, that she had felt too desperate for his touch. But before she could draw away herself, he cupped her face in his hands once more.

"I want you," he told her, his blue eyes dark and glittering. "I don't want to just hold you. I want to close that door and take you to bed, and if we don't slow down, that's exactly what's going to happen." The tightness in his voice reduced it to a growl. "You didn't ask for that, either."

He wasn't pushing her away. He was warning her.

Without thinking, she glanced toward the door. Beyond, all was quiet.

Her heart hammering at the promise in his words, she looked back to the taut lines of his chiseled features. She recognized the hunger in him. She felt it herself. But it was the sense of refuge she felt in his arms that she truly craved.

"I have to ask?"

At her quiet question, the hunger turned beautifully feral. Without a word, he stepped to the door.

The latch slipped into place with a quiet click.

His eyes were locked on hers when he walked back to where she stood in the pale circle of golden light.

He slipped his arm around her, possession in his touch. The last thing she saw before he reached behind her and turned off the light was his dark gaze fall to her mouth. A pulse beat later, she felt the hem of her sweatshirt slide up her back.

The room was cool. She felt the chill of air on her skin as he coaxed her arms from her sleeves and drew the fabric over her head. Then she was aware only of the heat of his lips trailing down her throat and the shiver racing after it. Cupping the weight of one breast in his hand, his hot mouth closed over her.

She gave a tiny gasp as heat licked deep in her core. He encouraged another as he gripped her hip and drew her closer. He carried that debilitating caress to the other side, his touch at times unbearably light, at times unbearably greedy.

Her knees threatened to buckle. When she grasped his shoulders, he must have felt her shiver. "You're cold," he concluded, carrying his kiss back up her throat.

She didn't tell him she'd forgotten about the temperature, that it was his touch that caused her to tremble. With one arm braced at her back, he pulled away comforter, blanket and sheet in one tug, pillows tumbling. Turning her, he lowered her to the bed.

He let her go long enough to pull off his sweater and boots. They had barely landed by her sweatshirt before he was over her, and she was in his arms again. The rock wall of his chest brushed her sensitized breasts. His mouth sought hers. Rolling them to their sides, he caressed her back, her hips, the length of her thighs.

Their mouths clung, tongues slowly tangled. Clothes were pulled off, tugged down, tossed aside. Blankets were jerked up.

Cocooned under the covers, soft skin met rough. Gentle curves met hard angles. He could be incredibly tender. She knew that because it was his tenderness that had drawn her. But he could also demand. That was what he did now as he buried his fingers in her thick curls, kissed behind her ear, down her neck, over her stomach. He demanded that she not hold herself back from him, that she meet his need with her own.

T.J. didn't question what he wanted or how totally she abandoned herself to him. All that mattered was that he wanted her, that she needed him.

She loved him. Body, mind and soul.

She'd never truly been in love before. The realization should have stunned her, slammed defenses into place. Instead while she caressed him as he caressed her, the feeling that swept through her was one of profound relief. She could finally admit to herself what she had attempted to deny all along. Later she would worry about how she'd let it happen. Later she would remember why she shouldn't have let him into her heart. Now she wanted only to cherish the knowledge that he was there for her at that moment and that it was her name on his lips.

She whispered his name back.

He whispered hers again, the sound as urgent as the demand of his body seeking hers when he tucked her beneath him. He had no idea how he'd lasted as long as he had. Every nerve felt tripwire tight. Every cell in his body screamed for release.

That was what he found within a few white-hot seconds of slipping inside her. There was no holding back. She wouldn't let him. She was right there, racing with him, joining him in the sweet oblivion that erased any thought of where he left off and where she began.

Sam hadn't wanted to fall asleep. He had intended to hold her, to let himself simply savor the peace that had seeped inside him until T.J. fell asleep herself. The first time they had made love, it had been over far too quickly. The next time he'd savored her with slow, fluid strokes that had her begging before they'd collapsed in each other's arms.

When he'd last glimpsed the clock on her nightstand, it had been nearing midnight. Catching the glow of numerals claiming it to be 6:03 in neon green, he realized he'd fallen asleep anyway.

T.J. lay curled against him, her back nestled to his chest and their legs comfortably tangled. Holding her, listening to her breathing, he became aware of something far more significant than the hour.

For the first time in longer than he could remember, the numb feeling in his heart was no longer there. It wasn't as if it had just disappeared. Now that he thought about it, the feeling hadn't been there yesterday, either. Or the day before. It was as if it had been gradually fading all along and that only now, holding her, was he completely aware of its absence.

Lifting his hand, he gently touched her incredible hair.

From the moment he'd met her, she had been pulling him out of the protective cocoon he'd built around himself, around his life. She'd made him get involved with her, her cause and her child, whether he wanted to or not. With every passing day she had worked her way a little further under his skin, a little closer to his heart.

Now, knowing he could never get enough of her, he realized that she had worked her way into his heart far more deeply than he would have ever expected.

The knowledge hit hard as he eased his arm from around her shoulders and slipped from the warmth of her bed. He knew he could never go back to simply being her friend. He just had no idea where they were going from there.

"Sam?"

"Right here," he murmured, groping for his clothes. "I didn't mean to wake you."

"You didn't."

"I don't think it would be a good idea for the kids to find me in bed with you." Fabric rustled. His belt buckle clinked. "I'm going to run to the house and shower and go make your copy."

T.J. felt the mattress sink beneath his weight as he sat down on the edge of it. It took a moment for him to pull on his sweater and boots, but when he turned, even in the dark, he had no trouble finding her. His hand skimmed her bare shoulder, slipped up the side of her neck.

"I won't be gone long," he said, and pressed his lips to her forehead. "I'll bring clean clothes for the kids, too."

She didn't know how long she'd lain awake before she'd felt his hand smooth her hair. She remembered fighting sleep, though. She'd wanted to remember the feeling of being in his arms, of lying close to him, of just holding and being held. But somewhere between cherishing the moments and drifting in and out of sleep, the reasons she should never have fallen in love with him had intruded.

She knew he cared about her. And last night he'd left

no doubt in her mind about the physical desire he felt for her. But Sam had told her himself that he couldn't imagine ever again having the kind of relationship he'd had with his wife.

More than anything on earth, that was exactly what she wanted.

She reached for him, but he had already moved away. Slipping from the bed, she grabbed her robe, tugged it on and flipped the light on low. In the soft glow, she turned to the big man behind her.

No man had a right to look as appealing as he did at such an hour. He needed a shave. His hair was a mess from the pillow and her fingers. But he managed to make even the sleep crease in his cheek look attractive.

"Can you wait a minute?" she asked, rather wishing she'd left off the light as she pushed back her own tangled hair. "I need to talk to you before the kids wake up."

Brad was already threatening her world. Now, more than ever, she needed to keep her relationship with Sam in perspective.

"Are you still going to call your attorney?" she asked.

Sam stepped closer and nudged back a curl of her hair. "As soon as his office opens."

"I'll take the eleven-o'clock ferry over, so I'll be here until ten-thirty. If I haven't heard from you by then, I'll know you didn't reach him."

With a faint frown, his hand fell. "If I don't reach him, I'll come with you."

"You don't have to do that," she murmured, her voice going even quieter. "I really appreciate the offer, but you and I both know how much work you have to do."

She also knew from experience that it was far easier

not to count on someone than to count on him and have him fail her.

The memories shouldn't have been so clear. Not after so long. But she could still remember being a child and waiting for people she'd become attached to in the communes to come back after they'd left. She could remember waiting for Brad to return even after he abandoned her. At least Sam had warned her. It would be her own fault if she let herself rely on him too much.

"You're doing enough by calling him and making that copy for me," she continued, "and I really don't want to impose on you like that." She managed a faint, almost brave, little smile as years of self-preservation kicked into place. "I'm used to handling things on my own, anyway."

Sam's eyes narrowed to slits on her sleep-flushed face. She was clearly trying to let him off the hook. She was also trying to mask the agitation that had probably kept her awake half the night, and make it sound as if his work was her concern.

He didn't believe for a second that she was thinking of him or his job. She was trying to push him away before he could do it to her.

He wasn't sure what he felt at that moment. But a healthy dose of anger at all the people who'd destroyed her sense of trust was fairly high on the list. So was anger at the injustice of what she was choosing to face alone.

She was already withdrawing from him. Afraid she might withdraw completely, he didn't bother arguing with her. There was nothing he could say that would make any difference. But there was something he could do.

Chapter Twelve

The law office of Michael L. Chapman, Esquire, overlooked Bellingham's bay and absolutely reeked of stuffy propriety. Mr. Chapman's secretary simply looked stuffy.

Considering what the compact, bottle-blonde had probably been told about her, T.J. wasn't terribly surprised by the woman's cool manner when she pointed T.J. to a chair and said she'd let Mr. Chapman know she was there. T.J. could have sworn the woman waited a full two minutes before she picked up her phone.

Mr. Chapman was more civil. Marginally so, anyway. After leaving her with her growing anxiety for a few minutes more, the distinguished-looking, gray-haired gentleman emerged from behind a set of carved wood doors. Closing them behind him, he greeted her with a professionally polite smile.

The nerves jumping in T.J.'s stomach prevented her from smiling at all. As she rose from the edge of the plush club chair she'd stiffly occupied, the best she could do was nod.

"You have no counsel?" he immediately asked.

"No. I don't," she added, clasping her hands in front of her so he couldn't see them shaking.

"You really should have, you know."

"I…thank you, but I wasn't able to get an attorney on such short notice."

She hadn't heard from Sam since he'd dropped off the copy she carried in her denim shoulder bag and asked for the letter Brad's San Francisco attorney had sent her. She wished now that she hadn't been so knee-jerk in her reactions this morning. Even without his attorney, she would have given anything for the support Sam had offered her.

"I'm not sure how any of this works," she admitted, telling herself she needed to think logically, the way Sam did. She couldn't let this man know she was afraid. Some predators scented fear a mile away. "I only came because the attorney who wrote the letter about this meeting said someone would call Children's Protective Services if I didn't.

"I'm not going to give up my son," she informed him, fingers knotted, voice calm. "I never tried to hide Andy from Brad, and I'm not an unfit mother. I don't care what he told you, he's the one who abandoned us."

"Miss…Walker," he said, as if he'd had to refresh his memory with her name, "perhaps we'd best have this discussion in the conference room."

"Unless you can tell me why Brad is doing this, I don't know what else there is to discuss. I'm not signing anything, and he can't have Andy."

"Miss Walker." He spoke her name patiently as he held out his hand. The jacket of his three-piece suit opened when he did, revealing a curving watch chain on his vest. He gave the impression of a man who had seen and heard it all, but who would gracefully bear it one more time. "If you'll come this way, please?"

Except for the secretary, they were alone in the paneled reception room with its huge bouquet on the center table. Still, she felt horribly awkward with the woman at her desk pretending not to listen. Hating the feeling, she followed him to the set of closed double doors—and froze when he opened the nearest one.

"Mr. and Mrs. Colwood," the man said, touching the small of her back to nudge her inside, "Miss Walker is joining us. If you'll take a chair over here," he said to T.J., pulling out one of the matching barrel chairs lining the long, oval conference table, "we can get started."

Brad rose from the chair opposite the one intended for her. The motion was automatic, she imagined, a result more of breeding and a desire to appear a gentleman than a gesture of respect for her. He'd always had good manners. Oddly, that was one of the first things that had made Crystal suspicious of him.

Wishing for the thousandth time that she'd listened when Crystal had said that a man from his kind of money never turned his back on it for long, T.J. clutched her shoulder bag and moved to where she'd been directed.

Brad looked as if he had stepped straight from the pages of *Gentleman's Quarterly.* His blond hair was neatly cut, a screaming departure from the shoulder-length ponytail he had once worn. His Nordic good looks and long, lean body were enhanced by a navy suit that had a hand-tailored look about it. His tie looked silk. The watch and tie tack had the gleam of real gold.

The last time she'd seen him, he'd been wearing a Greenpeace T-shirt and an earring. The earring had gone the way of the ponytail. So had the boyish smile that had once so thoroughly charmed her.

"T.J." He said her name as a greeting, his brown eyes barely meeting hers before sweeping from the auburn curls she'd restrained with a clip to the serviceable denim jacket she wore over her long corduroy jumper. "You've hardly changed at all."

Adjusting the button of his suit jacket, he nodded to the woman sitting beside him.

"This is my wife," he said, sounding far more comfortable than he should be in the presence of his spouse and a former lover. "Amanda," he said to the pretty woman in the dove-gray sweater set and pearls, "this is T. J. Walker."

The look in Amanda Colwood's pale blue eyes was more cautious than cool. As she nodded, the stylish wedge of her golden hair gleaming, T.J. caught a hint of sweetness about her that almost spoke of naiveté. She had a finishing-school look about her. Or maybe it was more a look of privileged society.

Feeling totally out of her element with her more natural, comfortable approach to makeup and dress, T.J. seated herself and folded her cold hands in her lap.

Mr. Chapman took the chair beside Brad, pitting the three of them against her, and nudged aside the official-looking document in front of him.

"Miss Walker," he began, "as in so many disputes where emotion can become involved, it's not uncommon for a person to overstate or overreact when first confronted with a demand. It is not my client's wish to become involved in a long legal battle that will drain your resources or bring up matters which could prove painful for you in court. His only interest is in what is best for his son."

Had she not already been so unsettled, she would have bridled at the man's patronizing manner. He almost made it sound as if she should thank Brad for being so thoughtful.

"Andy is fine where he is."

Brad drummed his fingers on the table. "In a shack in the woods?"

The attorney touched Brad's arm, the signal clearly telling him he would handle this. "Miss Walker..."

Refusing to let the comment go, T.J. lifted her chin. "It's not a shack. It's our home. And he's happy there."

Mr. Chapman tried again. "I take it there will be no challenge to the child's paternity?" he asked T.J. "You aren't denying that Mr. Colwood is your son's father?"

"I never denied that he was. I told you out there," she said, motioning to the reception room, "I never hid Andy from him. I've lived where I have ever since he abandoned us."

Brad kept drumming. "I told you she would say that."

"That is only your word against his," the attorney pointed out to her.

"Not necessarily." Fabric rustled as she opened her big denim bag and drew out the envelope Sam had given her. "If I hadn't wanted him to find out that he was the father, I wouldn't have had his name put on this."

Brad's brow furrowed as he watched the man to his right extract the white sheet of paper. The first words out of his mouth were, "That's not a certified copy. She could have changed it."

The attorney frowned.

"I didn't change it," she insisted to Brad. "Just like I never told you I had an abortion. That was your—"

"Look," he muttered, holding up his hands to cut her off before she could say anything he didn't want heard,

"I know we can do this amicably. Our only interest is in what's best for my son. He's not safe where he lives. He's being raised in the middle of the woods, miles from nowhere, in a place where you only associate with a handful of people who are…eccentric to say the least."

"He is safe," she insisted, thinking it best to let the eccentric part go. "And he's being raised by a mother who loves him. You don't know him at all."

"Then there's the economics," he continued, as if she hadn't even opened her mouth. "You can barely support him. You work how many jobs? Two? Three? With us, he'll have a beautiful home with a full staff. He'll associate with the right people, attend the best schools."

Leaning forward, he clasped his hands on the table, his expression so sincere that anyone who didn't know how he was manipulating the truth would have bought his every word. He looked as thoughtful and honest as he had when he'd told her he'd given up his inheritance to save the whales.

"Amanda is from an old Boston family with connections to the state senate and Harvard. My family owns one of the finest wineries in California. He has chances with us he'll never have with you." He leaned back, trying not to look too impressed with himself. "He also has a right to know his grandparents. He's the next generation of Colwood vintners."

"If you want to expose a child to all that," she said, thinking of how he'd once claimed to loathe the pressure his family put on him to do something he supposedly hated, "have one of your own."

"We can't," Amanda murmured. A touch of genuine sadness entered her soft eyes. "I was thrown from a horse a few years ago. When we tried to get—"

"Amanda," Brad muttered. "That has nothing to do with what's best for Andy."

Amanda fell silent.

"What is best for him," Brad continued, sounding as confident as he probably did in the winery's corporate boardroom, "is the proper environment. I really don't want this to get ugly, T.J. But it will if you don't give me custody of my son. I can prove you unfit. If that happens, you'll be lucky to get to see him at all. If you make this easy for all of us, we'll work out some kind of supervised visitation. But I'll do what it takes to get him where he belongs."

T.J.'s gaze froze on the resolute face of the man she obviously never truly knew. After the way Brad had left her, she had realized that his sole interest had been in whatever was best for himself. She didn't believe for an instant that he was thinking of Andy now. That was just the tactic he'd chosen to employ to get others around him to cooperate. He couldn't have a child of his own with his sweet little society wife, so he wanted the one he'd abandoned. No doubt his parents were breathing down his neck for another heir.

His family had money. They had power. They had position. She could call him a liar, but he had already primed his attorney and his wife to believe that she was the one who couldn't tell the truth. They would question whatever she said. If he got to the Protective Services people, she could only imagine the doubts he would plant in their minds. She would have to go before a judge with contrived evidence stacked against her, and her little Andy...

Drawing a shaky breath, she blanked the thought out, unable to consider what her child might be put through. She had been a fool to think she could handle this alone. She had nothing to fight Brad with but her love for her son. "You're not taking him."

The attorney cleared his throat. "Mr. Colwood. It's apparent that we aren't going to get anywhere today. And you, Miss Walker, need an attorney of your own."

Brad muttered, "She can't afford one."

"There's always legal aid. As for the environment the child is living in," the gray-haired gentleman continued, "if you feel he is in that much danger, perhaps we should call the authorities. The only information I have is what was forwarded to me by your attorney in San Francisco last week."

It was evident from Brad's faintly superior nod that he liked the leverage the threat of a call to the authorities gave him over T.J. It was also as clear as the huge diamonds in his wife's wedding ring that he felt he could charm, buy or barter a decision in his favor, too.

The knot of panic in T.J.'s stomach was the size of an apple when a knock sounded on the door. Startled by the sound, she felt as if that knot had lodged in her throat when the door opened and the secretary's head popped in.

"Pardon the interruption, Mr. Chapman, but a Mr. Edwards and a Mr. Deerborn are here. Mr. Deerborn is from Deerborn, Crowley and Cates in Seattle," she explained, walking over to hand him his business card. "He's representing Miss Walker and apologizes for being late."

"I thought you said you didn't have counsel," Brad's attorney accused.

"I...didn't."

"Then Mr. Deerborn isn't your attorney?"

If Sam was with him, then she supposed he was. "Yes. He...is."

Mr. Chapman's forehead pleated like the old Venetian

blinds in Harbor's library. Looking more curious than annoyed, he rose and adjusted his jacket. "Please, send him in."

"Mr. Edwards, too," T.J. requested, a moment before the secretary opened the door wider.

Considering that they were standing right there, the two men had clearly expected to be admitted. For a moment, T.J. noticed only the dark-haired pilot in the black sweater, slacks and sport coat. There was an aura of power about Sam, an unquestioned masculine confidence that had the other men in the room straightening the way males faced with competition usually did.

It was his eyes she noticed most, though. The look in those laser-blue depths as he walked in seemed to tell her everything was going to be all right, before he glanced away.

The gentleman with him, Peter Deerborn, as he immediately introduced himself to Mr. Chapman, was a shade under Sam's six foot two, but he had nearly the same no-nonsense impact. He was all of forty, with thinning dark hair, an athletic build and an impeccable taste in suits. After shaking hands with Mr. Chapman, Peter introduced Sam, skimmed an assessing glance over Brad and his wife and rested his hand on the back of T.J.'s chair.

"Do you want to go first?" he asked Sam. "Or should I?"

Sitting down a chair away from T.J., Sam said, "You start."

T.J. could have sworn the attorney gave her a wink before he popped open the leather briefcase he'd set on the table.

From it he took a copy of the letter Brad's attorneys in San Francisco had sent to her.

That was why Sam had asked for it this morning, she thought. To give to his attorney.

"Ordinarily, I would ask to speak with my client, since we haven't actually met," Peter said, with a pleasant smile in her direction. He pulled a pair of glasses from his shirt pocket. "But I have a deposition back in Seattle in two hours, and time, as we say, is of the essence.

"Since this is a rather informal meeting and the accusations and demand are quite straightforward," he continued, seating himself, "why don't we just address these points one at a time and see where we stand?"

"This is ridiculous," Brad muttered.

From beside his client, Mr. Chapman's bushy eyebrows shot up. "You have a problem with that?"

"She should have said she had a lawyer." Clearly disgruntled, he motioned toward Sam. "And who is this guy?"

Sam's gaze was direct, his voice deceptively calm despite the way a muscle in his jaw jerked. "Just think of me as the representative of a few people who couldn't make it here themselves."

"Mr. Colwood," Brad's attorney said, "I took this case as a favor to a friend at Brickman, Westover and Myer. Your family is apparently one of their largest clients, and he assured me that this matter was quite straightforward. If it's not, I want to know."

"Bradley?" Amanda asked.

Brad ignored his wife, along with her questioning glance.

"So, Mr. Colwood," Peter Deerborn began, peering down at his copy of the letter through his half glasses, "this first item where you state that Miss Walker hid your son from you. I understand there is a birth certificate with your name on it.'' He glanced over the top of the gold rims. ''Have you seen it?''

Brad leaned back as if he had absolutely nothing to worry about. ''I saw something she purports to be my son's birth certificate,'' he replied, clearly refusing to acknowledge its validity. ''But if you want to address the facts here, let's start with those animals.''

''The ones she rescues,'' Peter clarified.

''Everyone knows an injured animal is dangerous.''

''Only when it's in pain.'' Knowing nothing she said would matter to Brad, T.J. directed her response to Peter. ''That's the first thing I try to alleviate when a bird or an animal is brought to me.''

''Admirable,'' Brad muttered, ''but beside the point.''

''Actually, that is the point.'' Sam rubbed the side of his nose. ''She alleviates the pain, and the animal is then safe for her son to be around.''

Brad's eyes narrowed. Beside him, his wife thoughtfully fingered her pearls. ''She's endangering him,'' he insisted, clearly miffed that he was being challenged. Apparently, people didn't challenge him often. ''No responsible parent is going to allow a child around an injured animal.''

Sam's shoulder lifted in a deceptively casual shrug. ''I allow mine to be around them, and I consider myself very responsible. I've never known her to allow a child near an animal who could cause harm. If anything, a child learns compassion and patience from them. Working with those animals has even helped my son.''

''Now,'' Peter continued, seeing the tips of Brad's ears turn pink with annoyance, ''about your claim that she told you she'd had an abortion.'' He glanced to T.J. ''Since we haven't spoken directly, perhaps you should address this.''

She was actually fine with him and Sam doing the talking. With Sam, especially. It meant the world to her to know that he saw improvement in his little boy. It meant even more to hear him standing up for her. But she understood what her attorney wanted. Sam had obviously passed on to the lawyer what she had told him, but Peter hadn't heard it from her mouth. It wasn't that he didn't trust what he'd been told, he just wanted to make sure everyone had their facts straight.

She looked to the one person in the room who wouldn't have known a fact if it had bitten him in the backside. "The idea of an abortion was yours, Brad. You know that. When you brought it up, I told you it was out of the question."

The anger building in his dark eyes made it hard to keep looking at him. Needing to keep her own feelings toward him in check because she wasn't sure if she wanted to go for his throat or turn from him in disgust, she looked to the man representing him. "That was when he denied that the baby was his," she told Mr. Chapman. "He accused me of sleeping around, and he disappeared the next day. He was the one who left us."

"We've already heard that story," Brad muttered.

"Are you going to address what she just said?" Peter asked.

"Why? She knows that's not what happened."

"It *is*, Brad." T.J.'s glance jerked from him to his wife. "He knew the baby was his," she insisted to the woman who had married him, "and when I wouldn't get rid of it, he left us. He's even admitting now that he knew Andy was his, but the only reason he wants him is because he needs an heir.

"You know what it's like to want a child," she continued, clearly remembering the sadness she'd glimpsed in the woman's eyes minutes ago. "I can't honestly say I was ready when I discovered I was pregnant, but once I knew I was, there was no way I was going to harm my child. Can you imagine how it felt when he demanded that I get rid of it?"

The muscles in Brad's face were drawn tightly with some emotion T.J. didn't care to name as he reached for his wife's hand. "Don't listen to a word she says," he demanded, covering her diamonds with his palm. "I told you she'd say anything to defend herself."

The woman Brad had married looked like someone T.J. would have liked very much had she not been part of Brad's scheme. An unwitting part, T.J. was beginning to suspect from the questions she could see forming in his wife's expression.

Her eyes clouding with doubt, Amanda slowly pulled her hand away.

"You obviously don't want to answer," Peter interjected easily, "so how about this one? You claim Miss Walker deliberately hid the child from you. Did you ever go back looking for her?"

"Of course I did."

"When?"

"I don't remember the first time. It was a long time ago."

"Think back, then. Was it five years? Four?"

"I told you," he said tightly. "I don't remember."

"Why don't we give Mr. Colwood's attorney that paper, Sam?"

Looking happy to oblige, Sam reached for the pocket inside his sport coat and withdrew a letter-size envelope. He held it out to Peter so he could pass it on, but he addressed Mr. Chapman.

"This is a statement signed this morning by the mayor,

a minister, the vet who treated Miss Walker's animals before he moved and about fifty of Harbor's more prominent citizens. It attests to the fact that T.J. has lived on Harbor since before the birth of her son and has never left. Every one of these people is also prepared to offer testimony about what kind of mother they perceive her to be.'' He sent a flat glance toward Brad. Under that deadly calm and knowing gaze, Brad actually shrank back. "Me, included."

As Peter handed the letter to the very interested Mr. Chapman, Amanda turned pale.

"Bradley?"

Brad opened his mouth, shut it again.

Thinking he looked a bit like a poleaxed guppy, T.J. watched that momentary slip dissolve into pure defensiveness.

"You said you'd never mentioned your son before this summer because it was too painful for you," Amanda continued. "You said you'd actually spent years trying to track her down, and when you finally found her, you couldn't bear what was happening to your son."

"We'll talk about this later," he growled, sounding like the trapped animal he was.

"You said she was alone," she accused, refusing to listen to him the way he'd refused to listen to T.J. "You claimed she was a recluse who hid her child from everyone. You had me believing that poor little boy was going to be scarred for life if he wasn't mauled to death before we could rescue him."

The growl dropped lower. "Amanda."

"You didn't think she could defend herself, did you?"

"You and my parents want a kid," he hissed, looking as if he couldn't believe she was questioning him as she was. "I found you one."

The pretty woman in dove gray looked as if he'd slapped her.

"Excuse me," she said. Doing a commendable job of gathering her composure, she rose and swept a glance across the table. "I need to get to the airport in Seattle. You said you're going back there yourself," she said to Peter. "Would it be possible for me to get a ride with you?"

"Actually, I'm being flown back. Is there room, Sam?"

Sam stood, too, partly because a lady was standing, mostly because the meeting suddenly seemed to be over.

"Certainly." He glanced at his watch, skimming a guarded glance past T.J. as he did. "If we leave now, I can have you there in half an hour."

"Amanda." Brad was also now on his feet, his tone dripping patience. "We have a rental car," he reminded her.

"*You* have a rental car," she clarified, gathering her suede bag and cashmere coat before she headed around the table, "I'm catching an earlier flight home."

Mr. Chapman followed her to the door. "I would say it's been a pleasure meeting you, Mrs. Colwood, but the circumstances have turned…"

"Awkward?" the woman offered, continuing through to the reception room.

Mr. Chapman gave her a sympathetic smile. "I'm sure you understand that I will no longer be part of this action," he confided, clearly feeling put-upon by the attorney who had referred the case to him, "but if you find yourself in need of personal legal assistance in the near future, I would be happy to help."

At his significant glance toward the man they'd left fuming at the table, Amanda gave the lawyer a tight little nod, then turned to where T.J. was coming through the door with Peter and Sam.

"I'm really very sorry," she said to her. "I can only imagine what this has put you through, but I'm going to be selfish and tell you I'm actually grateful it happened. I realized a couple of years ago that Brad didn't really want children. What he wanted was my social connections. I just didn't realize the lengths to which he would go to hang on to them." Forcing a small and practiced smile, she glanced to the men flanking T.J. "I'll wait for you gentlemen in the hall."

T.J. watched her walk out the door, marveling at Amanda's composure. T.J. did her level best to maintain her own. Behind her the attorneys were doing the professional thing and telling each other that it had been a pleasure, that they would summarize the meeting in a letter and agreeing that this particular matter had been put to rest. Sam had most of her attention, though. He stood a few feet away, waiting for Peter to conclude his business and say goodbye to her, which her attorney did a moment later.

Peter held out his business card. "I'm sorry we didn't have a chance to meet earlier, but I think things worked out rather well."

"They did," she murmured, conscious of Sam's eyes on her as she took what the smiling man offered. "Thank you."

"Don't thank me. Thank Sam. He's the one who pulled the rabbit out of the hat. But keep that card," he said, nodding to what she held. "Sam indicated that you don't want anything to do with your son's father. And frankly I understand why. After this stunt I can't see where you'd have to worry about any court siding with him on visitation. But at some point you might want to pursue the matter of your son's inheritance. If you're feeling the need for a little reprisal, you could probably also threaten Colwood with a little jail time for stalking, harassment, defamation of character and whatever else I can dig up.''

She wasn't feeling vindictive. All she felt was relief. Relief and gratitude beyond belief toward the big man moving behind her.

Taking the first full breath she'd drawn in nearly an hour, she started to do what her attorney suggested— thank Sam. She was astonished by what he had done, the trouble he had gone to for her, and at a loss as to how she could possibly express what it meant to her that he was there. But he had just opened the door.

Thinking he only wanted to get them out of there, having no problem with that idea herself, she preceded Peter into the office building's wide hallway. Amanda stood in front of the elevator, thirty feet away.

Giving her a nod, Peter headed for the elevator himself a moment before Brad stalked out.

Seeing them all, he immediately headed in the opposite direction. Taking twenty flights of stairs to the street was clearly preferable to facing people who knew he had absolutely no sense of honor.

T.J.'s glance had fallen to her feet as he'd passed.

''Are you okay?''

Sam's deep voice held a wealth of concern. Lifting her head, she saw the same concern she had seen so often before.

''I'm doing…great,'' she replied. She would be doing even better if he would return her smile. Better yet, if he would pull her into his arms. She couldn't think of anyplace she'd rather be just then. Except home, hugging Andy.

The possibility of Sam reaching for her didn't seem likely, though. He'd just quite deliberately pushed his hands into his pockets.

"You're okay to get back to Harbor, then?"

"My car's only a block away. By the ferry terminal. I can catch the 3:10."

"Good." Sounding as if there was nothing left to discuss, nothing that interested him, anyway, he started toward the elevator. "Let's get going. I have to get Peter back to Seattle."

"Sam?" Her fingers curled over his arm, drawing him to a halt. "Thank you," she said, preparing to tell him how inadequate those words were.

"You're welcome," he replied, robbing her of the chance. Beneath the concern a disturbing guard remained in his eyes, touched his voice. "If you're sure you're all right, we really have to go. I'll see you tonight when I pick up the kids."

T.J. expected Sam to be even later than usual. He had obviously spent his entire morning and afternoon on her, and whatever work he'd missed still remained to be done. That was why she didn't expect anyone to be pulling into the drive at five o'clock in the afternoon.

She had just pushed the wheelbarrow into the shed. Latching the door, she pulled off her gloves and glanced toward the drive. It wasn't raining at the moment, but it had been a while ago. Being the Northwest, she knew it would be again soon.

In the respite, she shoved back the hood of her yellow slicker and watched a red Suburban pull to a stop behind her faithful Jeep.

She didn't recognize the vehicle. She recognized Sam, though. He was still wearing the same black sweater and jacket she'd last seen him in, as he climbed out and started for the house. Now, as then, he gave an impression of power and utter masculine confidence.

She also sensed a hint of the distance she'd felt when they'd parted.

Hating the feeling, not sure what to make of it, considering all he'd done for her, she motioned toward the big vehicle. "Is that new?" she asked, heading for the porch since that was where he was headed himself.

"I've had it for years. I brought it because we won't be able to get us all into the truck."

With that puzzling response, he jogged up the steps, pulled open the screen and pushed open the door. Since he was clearly waiting for her to enter first, she tossed her wet slicker over the porch rocker and slipped past him.

The fresh scent of sea air and pine was left behind as they entered the room that smelled of cinnamon, herbs and warmth. All T.J. really noticed was Sam when he closed the door. She turned to face him.

His appraising glance swept her face quickly, as if he needed to assure himself that she had escaped the day unharmed. An instant later he nodded toward the hall. "I'm going to get the kids."

Unease shot through her. She had no idea what was going on with him, but there was no way he was going anywhere until she'd done what he hadn't allowed her to do before.

"No."

At her unusual abruptness, he went still, one dark eyebrow slowly rising. "No?"

"No," she repeated. "I need to thank you."

"You've already done that."

"Sam, please." She held her ground. He could have

easily stepped around her. Instead, looking intrigued, he crossed his arms over his broad chest and narrowed his too-blue eyes on her face. "It must have taken you hours to collect those signatures."

"It only took me about thirty minutes. I wrote out the statement and asked Zach if he'd sign it. After he did, he suggested I take it to Maddy at the Road's End. Once I told her what was going on, she had signatures for me in no time."

"But how?"

"She took it to the principal of the school," he said. "After it made the rounds there, she took it to the bookstore, and Mrs. Bender took it to the library. I think that's where it went," he muttered, as if it really didn't matter now. "Then Crystal got hold of it and one of the patrons at the video store went out to the Mother Earth spa, and Shenandoah got more signatures and brought it back to Maddy."

T.J. could clearly picture the owner of the café, all redheaded fury and indignation on a mission. The fact that the mission had been about her, and that so many people had made it their concern, too, touched T.J. profoundly.

"But Doc Jackson. How did you get his?"

"He's living just north of Seattle. I stopped by his house before I picked up Peter."

Which meant he'd had to fly in, rent a car, drive out to the doctor's house and go back into the city for the attorney.

"I can't believe you did all that." Bewildered, she shook her head, pushing back a few errant curls as she did. "No one has ever done anything like this for me before."

"There are a lot of people who would be there for you

if you'd let them be, T.J. Me included," he said easily. "I'll be there the next time you need me, too. Just like you've been here for me with my kids."

He stepped past her then. The smile that wouldn't form for her came quickly for the children who'd come from Andy's room when they'd heard his voice.

"We need coats," he told them, doing the high-five thing with both boys. Bending a little, he reached down and placed his hand on the head of the blond little girl tugging at the knee of his slacks. "All of you."

"Me, too?" Andy asked.

"You, too, sport."

"Am I going to your house?"

"Maybe later."

"We got to go to Grandma Crystal's house today." Jenny grinned up at him. "She did my hor-something and made Andy wear a rock."

"See?" Andy said, holding up an amber-colored stone suspended from his neck by a kaleidoscope-colored cord.

Jason nodded. "And she gave us magic cookies."

"Oh, Lord," he muttered.

"Chocolate chip," T.J. explained.

"Right," Sam murmured, clearly relieved. "Why don't you tell me all about it later?" he asked his little girl. "Go get your coat."

"What are you doing?" T.J. asked when the kids all raced for where they'd left their jackets on the kitchen chairs.

"I figured we needed to celebrate, so I'm taking us all out for pizza." His eyes locked on hers. "And I'm giving you time. I could ask you to marry me now, but I won't."

T.J. couldn't have imagined anything else he could have said that would have nailed her so completely to the spot where she stood. She couldn't move. For a moment, she didn't even think she could breathe.

The look he gave her seemed to indicate he'd pretty much expected her reaction.

"Wait," she said, her motor skills kicking back in when he started past her. Grabbing his arm, she stepped in front of him. "What did you say?"

"You heard me," he told her, looking remarkably calm, remarkably certain. "If I asked you to marry me now, you'd probably think I was only doing it because it's the most practical thing for us to do."

"Practical?" she echoed, when practical wasn't what she was feeling at all. Hope and longing collided with a heavy dose of wariness.

"Sure." He gave an annoyingly casual shrug. "Marrying me would solve problems for both of us. We'd need to sell my place and maybe rent out yours and find a place we all like, but you'd have the stability and security you've always wanted for yourself and your son, and I'd have a mom for my kids. You'd have access to a plane for your animals, too. Not that you'll need it," he qualified. "One of the passengers Zach took for me today is a vet from California. She wants to take over Dr. Jackson's practice."

T.J. smiled instantly at that news, but the confusion she felt over all Sam was saying immediately overrode that bit of relief. She scanned the carved lines of his face, suddenly cautious. Her heart pounded at the prospects he offered.

Cautious herself, she met his eyes. "Why shouldn't I think you were just being practical?"

It was the caution that touched him and the vulnerability she had never failed to let him see. All day he had craved the feel of her. Now, seeing the hope she couldn't hide, he did what he'd been dying to do and let himself touch her face.

Skimming his fingers along her cheek, he tucked a curl behind her ear.

"Because I love you," he told her, simply, honestly. "Because I'm in love with you."

Her glance shied away. Catching her chin, he tipped her face back up.

"What?" he asked, suddenly uncertain.

"You said you couldn't imagine ever marrying again."

"I couldn't," he said, without hesitation. "Not until you." He spoke the admission quietly, sounding as if he'd never truly expected to find anything better than what he'd had. "I loved Tina. But in a different way than I love you. She was great for my ego, T.J. She needed me to be her white knight. But that meant I was responsible for nearly everything, including her. That's not a bad thing," he admitted, skimming his fingers along her jaw, "that's just the way it was.

"I think you need me, too," he continued after a moment, "but it's different with you. You make me feel as if I'm not doing it all alone."

Since this lovely woman had always been so independent, he didn't know if he could ever explain how important that was to him. But he had to try. There was so much about her that completed him, so much he really didn't want to live without.

"You feel like a partner, T.J. An equal. You feel more like a helpmate than someone always in need of assistance," he explained, wishing he could be more romantic about it but not really knowing how. "I like that I can talk to you. I like that you can talk to me." His finger brushed her mouth. "I like what you do to me in bed," he admitted, his eyes darkening at the thought. "But more than anything I just like being with you."

T.J. felt the caution slowly fade as hope bloomed bright in her chest. He loved her. He'd been there for her. In the depths of her heart she knew that if it was humanly possible, he always would be. Just as she always would be there for him.

She touched his face as he touched hers. "I like all of that about you, too. I love you, Sam." She murmured the words, her eyes on his. "And you know what?" she asked, the enormity of the events of the day hitting as she finally let her smile break free. "Whenever you want to propose, I'll say yes."

Something bright flashed in his eyes as he slipped his arms around her. "Then say yes, now."

"You haven't asked," she said with a teasing smile.

His beautiful mouth curved, his smile nearly stealing her breath. She had been right. The real thing was incredible.

"Will you marry us, Tierra Jade? You and Andy?"

"Yes," she whispered, and felt her smile melt when his mouth came down on hers. He kissed her thoroughly, completely, altering her breathing and weakening her knees. There was promise in his kiss. There were promises in hers, too, as she slipped her arms around his neck—and suddenly became aware of three small children staring up at them.

A little girl with blond curls who'd poked her head between them was grinning. Two little boys, one fair-haired, the other with auburn hair like his mother, had their fingers in their mouths and were making gagging noises.

"Nice, guys," Sam muttered, slipping his hands from where they'd tangled in T.J. curls.

"That means they love each other," Andy informed a now-grinning Jason.

Sam watched T.J. smile, her heart in her eyes. "It certainly does," he murmured. "It certainly does."

*   *   *   *   *

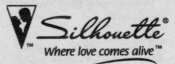

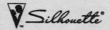

SPECIAL EDITION™

Coming in August 2002,
from Silhouette Special Edition and

CHRISTINE RIMMER,

the author who brought you the popular series

CONVENIENTLY YOURS,

brings her new series

THE SONS OF
CAITLIN
BRAVO

Starting with

HIS EXECUTIVE SWEETHEART
(SE #1485)...

One day she was the prim and proper executive assistant...
the next, Celia Tuttle fell hopelessly in love with her boss,
mogul Aaron Bravo, bachelor extraordinaire. It was clear he
was never going to return her feelings, so what was a girl to
do but get a makeover—and try to quit. Only suddenly,
was Aaron eyeing his assistant in a whole new light?

And coming in October 2002, MERCURY RISING,
also from Silhouette Special Edition.

**THE SONS OF CAITLIN BRAVO: Aaron, Cade and Will.
They thought no woman could tame them.
How wrong they were!**

Where love comes alive™

Visit Silhouette at www.eHarlequin.com   SSESCB

If you enjoyed what you just read,
then we've got an offer you can't resist!

Take 2 bestselling love stories FREE!

Plus get a FREE surprise gift!

Clip this page and mail it to Silhouette Reader Service™

IN U.S.A.	IN CANADA
3010 Walden Ave.	P.O. Box 609
P.O. Box 1867	Fort Erie, Ontario
Buffalo, N.Y. 14240-1867	L2A 5X3

YES! Please send me 2 free Silhouette Special Edition® novels and my free surprise gift. After receiving them, if I don't wish to receive anymore, I can return the shipping statement marked cancel. If I don't cancel, I will receive 6 brand-new novels every month, before they're available in stores! In the U.S.A., bill me at the bargain price of $3.99 plus 25¢ shipping and handling per book and applicable sales tax, if any*. In Canada, bill me at the bargain price of $4.74 plus 25¢ shipping and handling per book and applicable taxes**. That's the complete price and a savings of at least 10% off the cover prices—what a great deal! I understand that accepting the 2 free books and gift places me under no obligation ever to buy any books. I can always return a shipment and cancel at any time. Even if I never buy another book from Silhouette, the 2 free books and gift are mine to keep forever.

235 SDN DNUR
335 SDN DNUS

Name		(PLEASE PRINT)
Address		Apt.#
City	State/Prov.	Zip/Postal Code

* Terms and prices subject to change without notice. Sales tax applicable in N.Y.
** Canadian residents will be charged applicable provincial taxes and GST.
   All orders subject to approval. Offer limited to one per household and not valid to
   current Silhouette Special Edition® subscribers.
   ® are registered trademarks of Harlequin Books S.A., used under license.

SPED02   ©1998 Harlequin Enterprises Limited

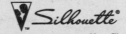

EXPLORE THE POSSIBILITIES OF LIFE—AND LOVE—
IN THIS GROUNDBREAKING ANTHOLOGY!

Turning Point

This is going to be our year.
Love, Your Secret Admirer

It was just a simple note, but for the three women
who received it, it has very different consequences....

For Kristie Samuels, a bouquet of roses on her desk can mean
only that her deadly admirer has gotten too close—and that
she needs to get even closer to protector Scott Wade,
in this provocative tale by **SHARON SALA.**

For Tia Kostas Hunter, her secret admirer seems a lot like the man
she once married—the man she *thought* she was getting a divorce
from!—in this emotional story by **PAULA DETMER RIGGS.**

For secretary Jamie Tyson, the mysterious gift means her romantic
dreams just might come true—and with the man she least
suspects—in this fun, sensuous story by **PEGGY MORELAND.**

Available this December at your favorite retail outlets!

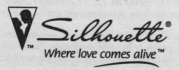

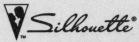

COMING NEXT MONTH

SSECNM1102